"I wo
firm

He believed her. "While you're looking through the mug shots, I'm going to talk to the sergeant."

They rode in silence the rest of the way. Daniel made an effort not to glance at her, but he was aware of everything about Hannah.

Misinterpreting his silence, she looked over at him. "If you're worried that I won't be able to handle this, don't be."

"I like to worry about you." His voice was low and masculine.

Her breath caught and her cheeks tinged pink. Hannah looked away quickly as if trying to hide her reaction. Daniel found himself remembering the last time he'd heard that little hitch in her breath. She'd been beneath him, her warmth open to him.

His body suddenly grew hard. He cursed himself silently. He would never get this woman out of his system. He knew it with a certainty that frightened him. For a man who had never feared anything in his life, this was a new experience....

Dear Reader,

We have a fabulous fall lineup for you this month and throughout the season, starting with a new Navajo miniseries by Aimée Thurlo called SIGN OF THE GRAY WOLF. Two loners are called to action in the Four Corners area of New Mexico to take care of two women in jeopardy. Look for Daniel "Lightning" Eagle's story in *When Lightning Strikes* and Burke Silentman's next month in *Navajo Justice.*

The explosive CHICAGO CONFIDENTIAL continuity series concludes with Adrianne Lee's *Prince Under Cover.* We just know you are going to love this international story of intrigue and the drama of a royal marriage—to a familiar stranger.... Don't forget: a new Confidential branch will be added to the network next year!

Also this month—another compelling book from newcomer Delores Fossen. In *A Man Worth Remembering,* she reunites an estranged couple after amnesia strikes. Together, can they find the strength to face their enduring love—and find their kidnapped secret child? And can a woman on the edge recover the life and child she lost when she was framed for murder, in Harper Allen's *The Night in Quesiton?* She can if she has the help of the man who put her away.

Pulse pounding, mind-blowing and always breathtaking—that's Harlequin Intrigue.

Enjoy,

Denise O'Sullivan
Associate Senior Editor
Harlequin Intrigue

When Lightning Strikes

Aimée Thurlo

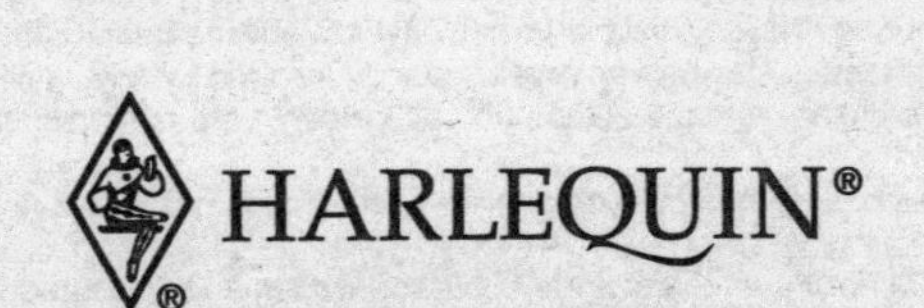

TORONTO • NEW YORK • LONDON
AMSTERDAM • PARIS • SYDNEY • HAMBURG
STOCKHOLM • ATHENS • TOKYO • MILAN • MADRID
PRAGUE • WARSAW • BUDAPEST • AUCKLAND

ISBN 0-373-22677-2

WHEN LIGHTNING STRIKES

This edition published by arrangement with Harlequin Books S.A.

Visit us at www.eHarlequin.com

Printed in U.S.A.

ABOUT THE AUTHOR

Aimée Thurlo is a nationally known bestselling author. She's written forty-one novels and is published in at least twenty countries worldwide. She has been nominated for the Reviewer's Choice Award and the Career Achievement Award by *Romantic Times*.

She also cowrites the Ella Clah mainstream mystery series, which debuted with a starred review in *Publishers Weekly* and has been optioned by CBS.

Aimée was born in Havana, Cuba, and lives with her husband of thirty years in Corrales, New Mexico. Her husband, David, was raised on the Navajo Indian Reservation.

Books by Aimée Thurlo

HARLEQUIN INTRIGUE

109—EXPIRATION DATE
131—BLACK MESA
141—SUITABLE FOR FRAMING
162—STRANGERS WHO LINGER
175—NIGHT WIND
200—BREACH OF FAITH
217—SHADOW OF THE WOLF
246—SPIRIT WARRIOR
275—TIMEWALKER
304—BEARING GIFTS
377—CISCO'S WOMAN
427—HER DESTINY*
441—HER HERO*
457—HER SHADOW*
506—REDHAWK'S HEART**
510—REDHAWK'S RETURN**
544—CHRISTMAS WITNESS
572—BLACK RAVEN'S PRIDE
677—WHEN LIGHTNING STRIKES†

*Four Winds
**The Brothers of Rock Ridge
†Sign of the Gray Wolf

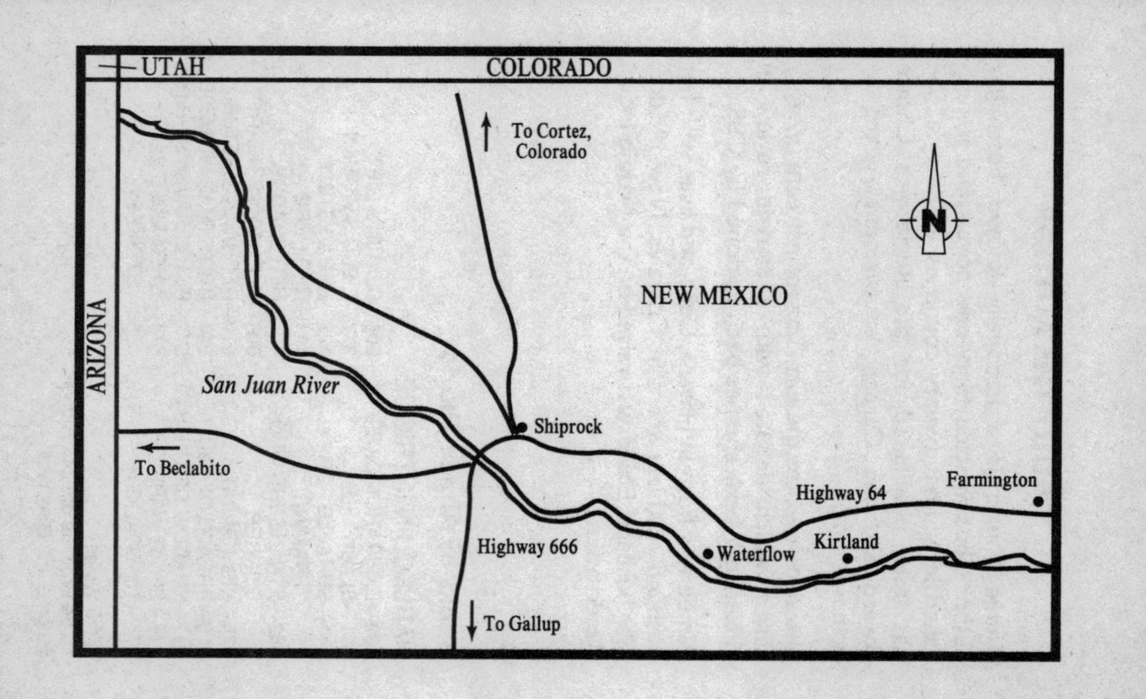
UTAH
COLORADO
To Cortez,
Colorado
N
NEW MEXICO
ARIZONA
San Juan River
Shiprock
To Beclabito
Farmington
Highway 64
Kirtland
Highway 666
Waterflow
To Gallup

CAST OF CHARACTERS

Handler—Just who was the faceless owner of Gray Wolf Investigations and why did he have so many friends in high places?

Hannah Jones—Would the truth keep her out of jail, or destroy her future?

Daniel Eagle—He was the only Gray Wolf operative who didn't carry a weapon. An expert in martial arts, he'd vowed to protect Hannah. But he'd never dreamed it would cost him his heart.

Deacon Robert Jones—He was Hannah's uncle, but what was his real reason for hiring Gray Wolf Investigations to track her down?

Pablo Jackson—All the church's money went through his capable hands. So where were the missing funds now?

Reverend Brown—He loved his church, and trusted everyone—perhaps too much.

To the three editors who helped us on this project:
Angela Catalano, Patricia Smith and Priscilla Berthiaume

Prologue

Hannah Jones opened her eyes and looked around in confusion, fear squeezing her heart. She was alone in the passenger seat of a car, but it was one that was totally unfamiliar to her and, worst of all, she couldn't remember how she'd gotten there.

A faint ray of sunlight stabbed at her eyes and she shut them, trying to will away the merciless pounding in her head. Gathering her courage, she drew in a deep breath, but regretted it instantly. The smell of cheap cigars that permeated the worn upholstery made her gag and start coughing.

She tried to sit up, but something yanked her arm back hard, pinning her down on the right side. Pain swept across her skull in waves that left her feeling weak and shaky.

Moving more carefully this time, she leaned forward slightly and looked down. Her right wrist was handcuffed to the seat belt bracket that was bolted to the floor of the car beside the door.

Her heart began drumming frantically, one thought paramount in her mind. She had to find a way to get out of the car and escape. Every instinct she possessed screamed that she was in mortal danger.

As she tugged at the handcuff, Hannah became aware of a man's voice nearby. She raised up slightly in her seat and looked out the driver's side window. A tall, disheveled man was standing a dozen or so feet away beside a juniper tree, speaking into a cell phone. Shadows crossed his face, distorting his features, but even without that she knew he was bad news. His beefy hand was wrapped around a can of the area's most popular beer, and he was pacing as he spoke, his steps slightly unsteady.

"Isn't there some other way? You never said I had to kill her."

Terror seized her like a cold, clammy hand squeezing her throat. Desperate to escape, she tugged and twisted the handcuff looking for a weak spot. The bracket was rusted and worn, and the more she tugged, the looser it became.

Putting everything she had into it, Hannah yanked once more and the bracket broke loose, freeing her hand. Though she still had the handcuff on her right wrist, she was now able to move.

Hannah looked over at the driver's side and saw that the key was in the ignition. She had her chance now. She started to slide over when the man turned and looked right at her.

"No you don't!" he growled, lunging toward her through the open window.

Ducking back, she grasped the dangling metal cuff in her right hand, and using it as makeshift brass knuckles, turned and punched him. Hannah heard the sickening crunch that signaled she'd broken his nose.

Her attacker groaned and stumbled back, blood flowing down his face.

In a heartbeat, Hannah slipped behind the wheel, switched on the ignition, then pressed down hard on the accelerator. The tires spewed gravel and the rear end fishtailed on the loose road surface as she raced away. One quick look in the rearview mirror revealed her injured attacker running after the car, but losing ground rapidly.

Hannah spotted the highway ahead of her in a gap between the trees and aimed for daylight. Too afraid to slow down, she swung out onto the pavement, tires squealing, leaving the scent of burning rubber in the air. She knew she was in an old car, and it was dangerous to proceed at this speed for long, but the alternative, falling into the hands of a killer, was not an option.

From the road sign, Hannah realized she was south of Shiprock, heading west up the road that led to Narbona Pass. A cop car suddenly raced past her in the other lane, sirens wailing. She hit the horn, but he kept on going. He probably hadn't heard her over the siren and that meant she was out of luck.

She needed a new plan, and she needed it fast. Remembering that her assailant had been speaking to someone else, and afraid that the other person would show up to help him, she turned off the highway and drove down the first dirt road where she could see a roof among the trees. She needed to get to a phone and call for help, and the roof she'd seen was bound to be attached to a house back here somewhere.

Hannah had only gone about a quarter of a mile when she suddenly heard a dull pop and the steering wheel jerked out of her hands, pulling the car toward the piñon and juniper trees that lined her route. As she wrestled with the wheel, she took her foot off the gas pedal and slowly braked to a stop.

Still fearful of pursuit, Hannah looked up and down the road but, for the moment at least, it appeared deserted. She climbed out, guessing she'd blown a tire, and a quick look proved her right. There was no spare in the trunk. From now on she'd have to travel on foot but first she had to hide the car, in case the man came after her.

Hannah climbed back into the sedan, started the engine, and managed to coax the vehicle down to a low spot among the trees before it got stuck. Here, below the road level, it would be hidden somewhat from her attacker if he came down the road.

Hannah climbed back up to the road and, using the soles of her shoes, smoothed out the tire tracks as best she could that showed where she'd left the road. Then she looked around again carefully, trying to spot the roof she'd seen from the highway. Up ahead was a well-constructed fence, a graded road, and a metal gate with a sign that read Private Property. With luck, she'd find a cabin or someone's house up that road.

The fence was strong and tightly constructed, and it was easy to climb over, but the hike became difficult after that since it was mostly uphill. As she pressed on, she searched her mind for answers. She still didn't know how she'd ended up in that man's car. The last thing she remembered was going to the church where she worked as an accountant part-time to search for her uncle, who was a deacon there.

As Hannah concentrated, willing herself to remember, vague images of out-of-focus faces and the sound of angry voices echoed in her mind, filling her with cold terror. She held on to that fragmented vision, trying to make sense of it all, but answers eluded her.

Focusing on the present again, she looked around, unable to suppress the feeling that danger was still close by. There would be time to remember later, after she'd reached safety. Right now she had to concentrate on finding help.

The road was not graded here, and the going was rough. Hannah jumped as a squirrel darted out in her path. The small, frightened animal froze, stared at her, then raced off into the bushes.

Sympathy filled her heart. Fear was the common denominator that bound all of nature in its daily fight for survival. But, in order to stay alive, she'd have to push back her fears and allow instinct and intelligence to guide her. It would be dark soon and she didn't want to be wandering about then. She was alone and no one, except the wolves, ever spared a thought for those lost and seeking shelter in the night.

Chapter One

It was such a great morning to be outside that Daniel Eagle was reluctant to step into the warehouse that housed Gray Wolf Investigations. The sky was a clear blue, and the weather cool though it was late September. It was his kind of day. Even having a flat tire to change on the way here couldn't spoil his mood. He felt energized, and the last place he wanted to be was inside the stark warehouse on the eastern outskirts of Farmington, New Mexico, sitting through a briefing. Unfortunately, it was his job. Using his key, Daniel let himself in through the windowless metal door, then walked over to one of the four overstuffed leather chairs that occupied the small office area.

''Lightning,'' an electronically altered voice coming over a microphone said in greeting. ''You're late.''

''Couldn't be helped,'' he answered curtly, facing the video camera attached on the wall opposite the chairs. If ''Handler'' wanted a long explanation, he'd ask for it.

''You're part of the Gray Wolf Pack. We have an impeccable reputation, and that's partly because I won't tolerate unprofessional behavior like tardiness.''

Daniel said nothing. A warning had been given, and excuses about car trouble wouldn't help. At Gray Wolf Investigations the only thing that mattered was results. The agency specialized in catching thieves, finding missing people, and retrieving lost or stolen property around the Four Corners area, or beyond if required. They were the best. Gray Wolf usually took on cases the police wouldn't or couldn't accept, and their reputation had been built on the nearly one hundred percent success rate they maintained.

The agency also assured secrecy and privacy for both clients and personnel. Cases were kept strictly confidential, and known only to Handler, who was the owner of the agency, Mr. Silentman, his assistant, the operative assigned to the case, and the client. Names were kept to a minimum, once the case was accepted. Each operative had a code name assigned to them by Handler. Daniel's was Lightning, and his cases usually involved a high level of action and/or quick extractions that suited his nature and training perfectly.

The fact that none of them, except possibly Mr. Silentman, ever saw Handler had certainly piqued Daniel's curiosity, especially at first. To make sure everything was legit, he'd done an exhaustive background check on the agency before applying for a job with them, but everything had checked out.

He'd speculated that Handler had chosen to keep his identity a secret because he was a public figure, or maybe Handler and Mr. Silentman were one and the same. Mr. Silentman looked like a man who wanted to be thought of as polished, but knew he didn't quite make the grade. Perhaps inventing "Handler" had been his way of adding a touch of mystique to the agency so that clients were bound to remember. But no matter what the explanation, the bottom line was that Handler continued to be a mystery.

Yet, despite all the open questions, being associated with the best private investigation agency in the southwest had certainly appealed to Daniel. He'd worked hard to get the job though it hadn't been easy. At first Handler had been skeptical about hiring him. Daniel was told that all the operatives were required to carry a firearm, something Daniel refused to do. He'd obeyed that policy during his eight years as a cop, but he'd sworn the day he left that he would never pack a gun again.

Yet, after seeing the full extent of Daniel's skills as a master of several martial arts disciplines, Handler had changed his mind and offered the tough Navajo loner the job. As Lightning had proven, even something as innocent as a straw, in the right hands, could become a deadly weapon.

Now, even after three years with the agency, Daniel only knew two other members of the Gray Wolf Pack—as Handler called them—his cousin, Ben Wanderer, who had recruited him, and Riley Stewart, a former Denver cop they'd both known for many years.

"Lightning, I'm going to turn you over to Mr. Silentman now. As always, he'll be your contact," Handler said.

A tall Navajo man with black hair and brown eyes strode into the room. He was a big, self-confident man who could appear threatening simply by changing his posture and standing ramrod straight. Daniel always got a feeling that Silentman was a street kid who'd spent most of his life trying to forget his roots, and the taint that had left on his soul. Although Daniel knew his first name was Burke, Silentman had made it clear that he preferred to be addressed by his last name.

Daniel wondered if Silentman was a code name or his real name. He'd probably never know. The name wasn't unusual for a Navajo, but he'd never met a family by that name. Then again, the Rez was a very big place.

At the moment, in his Western-cut suit, he looked like a cross between a cowboy and an oilman. Yet something about his eyes and the tension in his rigid shoulders told Daniel that he was a man who'd seen violence up close and personal and was capable of dishing out as good as he got.

Silentman handed Daniel a large, brown envelope. "Examine the contents, please," he said, then sat on the leather chair across from Daniel.

Daniel opened the envelope, and a photo of an attractive dark-haired Anglo woman fell into his lap.

"Meet Miss Hannah Jones. She's the twenty-eight-year-old niece of Robert Jones, a real estate broker and deacon at the Riverside Mission Church in Farmington."

Daniel studied the portrait. Hannah Jones was beautiful in a girl-next-door kind of way. A man would remember Hannah for life once he'd gazed into those hazel eyes. Her black hair fell over her shoulders in soft waves like a dark veil against her alabaster skin. She didn't use much makeup, and that fact only served to heighten the natural innocence mirrored on her face. She was the type of woman who would make a man willingly give up a playoff game to take her grocery shopping.

Hearing a knock, Silentman stood up and opened the door leading to the waiting room reserved for clients.

A tall, balding man wearing a herringbone jacket, conservative brown tie and coordinating slacks came in and greeted Silentman.

He walked stiffly to one of the leather chairs, and as he passed by, Daniel noticed the large bandage that covered an apparent injury on the back of his skull.

"This is Robert Jones. He represents our Riverside Mission clients," Silentman explained, taking the paper sack Jones handed him. "He'll brief you on the rest."

The man never offered to shake hands with Daniel, making him wonder if it was out of respect for the investigator's Navajo ways, or for another reason entirely. Prejudice reared its ugly head everywhere, even here, a stone's throw from the Navajo Nation. Or maybe Deacon Jones just didn't mingle with the hired help.

"I'm very worried about my niece, Mr.…Lightning, is it?"

Daniel nodded once.

"She's been...fragile most of her life."

"You'll have to be more specific," Daniel said.

Robert Jones pressed his lips together and stared at the floor for a long time before answering. "My niece has had severe psychological problems in the past. She's not usually violent...."

"You don't have to mince words with me," Daniel said, addressing the man's obvious reluctance to speak freely. "I'm on your side. But I need to know exactly what I'm up against, and what's expected of me."

"Fair enough." Deacon Jones leaned forward to speak, grimacing from the effort. "Hannah spent time in a psychiatric institution many years ago, and perhaps should be there now. Truthfully, my niece hasn't been right since she came to live with me after her father committed suicide fifteen years ago. But this time, I think she's really gone over the edge."

Daniel thought about the bandage on Jones's head, wondering if someone had coldcocked him. It was clear Jones was in pain.

"There's a bandage at the base of your skull. Did she do that?"

"I was clobbered from behind, so I can't honestly tell you if she's responsible," he said in a heavy voice. "All I can say for sure is that I saw Hannah's purse on a desk when I came into the church office. I heard movement behind the door, then suddenly felt this incredible pain. I went numb and passed out. When I came to, I had the biggest headache in the world, and my hair was wet with blood. Hannah's purse was gone, along with the church's operating funds—about two thousand dollars, give or take. That was yesterday after lunch. Now, nobody can find Hannah. Her car is gone as well."

"What about your niece's mother? Have you spoken to her, and has she heard from Hannah?" Daniel asked.

"Hannah's mother died of cancer sixteen years ago. My niece has had a hard life and, in the past, she's suffered from depression and fugue states. She could turn up just about anywhere without the slightest idea of how she got there, or how to get back. The one thing that surprises me is that she's never been violent before."

"So why is she going sour now? Any ideas?"

"I think it's pressure. She's been trying to run her own business from her home, a small bookkeeping firm, though I advised her against it. In my opinion, she simply took on more than she could handle. A month ago, I learned that she'd been having problems meeting deadlines and that she was losing clients left and right. My guess is that things got too tough for her to handle, just like I feared they might."

"What you've presented to us sounds like a police matter. Why not just go to them and save yourself a private investigator's fee?"

"I don't want to have my niece thrown in jail, or leave her at the mercy of the police, who might end up shooting her if she resists arrest or becomes violent. When I spoke to Mr. Silentman, he assured me you don't carry a weapon. That was one of the reasons I asked the board at the church to let me hire you."

"What about the money she stole. Is that low priority?" Daniel asked.

"It's secondary to getting her back safely, and avoiding unnecessary publicity."

"You didn't mention a husband, so I assume there isn't one. But what about a boyfriend or fiancé? Have you talked to him?" Daniel asked.

"There is no boyfriend at the moment. We haven't asked her clients or anyone else if they know her whereabouts because we're trying not to reveal the fact that she's disappeared. We don't want the police involved and discretion seems the best way to insure that. We're trusting you to be equally discreet,'' Jones answered.

''I'll respect your wishes. Now tell me, do you have any idea where she might have gone?'' Daniel asked.

''No, I really don't. Hannah's probably confused and desperate, and that makes her unpredictable, even more so than normal. I know she hasn't gone home, and hasn't reported in with her clients. I got that much from checking her answering machine. She had several urgent calls waiting there.''

''What are her favorite hangouts?''

''Hannah wasn't raised to be frivolous. She works hard, and when she's not working, she does volunteer work at the church.''

Daniel said nothing. From the look on Deacon Jones's face, it was clear that he didn't approve of leisure time. Daniel had met people like that on occasion, but it wasn't a mind-set he understood. The extreme form of the Anglo work ethic was quite a bit different from that of the Navajos, who believed that work held no virtue in and of itself. It was only a way to live one's life comfortably.

Daniel watched Jones squirm for a few more moments. The man was clearly nervous as well as being physically uncomfortable. Daniel had a gut feeling that there was more to Hannah Jones's story than her uncle was saying.

''Who are her close friends? I need to talk to them and see if they can give me any leads.''

''Hannah has many friends. I've made a list. But most of these people are ones I also know well. I haven't asked them directly, but I know from conversations I've had with them that they don't even know she's missing.'' Robert Jones reached into his pocket, brought out a list, and handed it to Daniel. ''I wish I had more information, but that's all the help I can give you.''

Mr. Silentman, who'd been silent until now, suddenly spoke. ''In that case, we'll take care of things from here,

Mr. Jones. Lightning is your operative and will handle your case exclusively. You *can* expect results, and soon. One more thing. May I assume that this paper sack contains what I asked for—an item of her clothing with her scent on it?''

Jones nodded. ''It's a blouse from her laundry hamper.''

''Thank you for coming to meet with us, Mr. Jones. Lightning will be in touch just as soon as we have something.''

After the client left, Daniel waited for Silentman's final instructions.

''Your usual backup is ready, Lightning. He'll meet you in the garage by the agency's SUV. Your cousin will deliver him to you.''

''I really prefer to handle this on my own.''

''It's not your choice to make,'' Silentman said handing him the paper sack. ''Here. Should the right opportunity arise, your partner will put this to good use.''

Daniel didn't argue further, knowing it would be futile. After parking his pickup in the warehouse's garage, he went to retrieve the SUV. The agency's sport utility vehicle was equipped with a lot of extras. It came with camping gear, a cell phone and pager, flashlights, shovels, special ''run flat'' tires that would allow them to be useable even after being punctured, and a global positioning system that enabled the operative to determine his exact location at any time.

Taking the paper bag containing Hannah Jones's blouse, he walked across the garage. Suddenly, an enormous black-and-gray German shepherd mix came bounding across the covered parking area toward him. Right before he reached Daniel, the dog stopped abruptly as if he'd suddenly hit the brakes. Unable to counter his momentum, the wild-looking dog slid a few inches farther, then came to a rest sitting perfectly, his front paws touching the tips of Daniel's boots.

Daniel stared at the dog, then nodded to his cousin, Ben Wanderer, who followed half a dozen feet behind. Ben's code name was Wind and he specialized in a different type of case—those requiring subtlety, a low profile and a minimum amount of violence. He'd just returned from assignment today.

Daniel glanced back down at the dog. The massive beast's head came up to Daniel's belt, though Daniel was five foot eleven.

"Why the hell did they name him Wolf?" Daniel muttered, glancing over at Ben. "You can tell he's mostly German shepherd."

The animal's eyes seemed to narrow, and Wolf growled low and deeply.

"You could try explaining genetics to him if you feel that strongly about it," Ben said with a shrug.

Daniel stared at the dog, whose eyes remained riveted on him. "Maybe not," he said, wisely recanting. "Time to go to work, Wolf."

The animal trotted off, leading the way back to the SUV and waiting by the passenger side for Daniel to open the door. When Daniel reached for the back door, Wolf barked once.

Daniel muttered a curse. "Yeah, yeah. I forgot. You ride shotgun." He opened the front passenger's door and Wolf leaped up gracefully onto the seat, then turned to look forward, sitting upright.

As he backed out of the parking space, Daniel waved at Ben, then caught a glimpse of Riley Stewart coming to join his cousin. Ben and he had accidentally discovered that the muscular blonde was a member of the Pack a few months ago. They'd been dressing in the locker room at the gym in Farmington and Riley had just returned from the showers. As they'd each seen the very small tattoo of a gray wolf inside their left forearms at their pulse point, a spot normally concealed by their wristwatches, the three had known they were brothers in arms.

That knowledge had strengthened their friendship although they'd never spoken of their affiliation or their assignments. Neither Ben nor he knew Riley's code name, but an awareness of the role they shared had created a formidable bond between them despite the fact that agency policy dictated the investigators remain anonymous, even to each other, except under dire circumstances.

The reasoning for that rule was admittedly sound. As investigators, their ability to go undercover as well as their safety would have been severely compromised if their identities weren't guarded.

As an added precaution for the investigators who lived and worked in the same area, the agency's P.I.s, as a general rule, were prohibited from actively trying to identify the other members of the Pack, or if by chance they already knew another member, from fraternizing in public. This would prevent someone who knew one of them was a Gray Wolf from identifying the others by checking on his associates.

The tattoo itself carried the most risk, of course, but it served a vital function. Special care had been taken to make it small, and easily concealable by a wristwatch, but in case one of the investigators ever needed emergency assistance—when undercover and with a fake ID, for example—the small tattoo would always insure allies had a way to identify each other.

As Daniel pulled out into the street, Wolf moved sideways, panting in Daniel's ear.

"Wolf, give me some room, will ya? Only ladies are allowed to blow in my ear."

The animal gagged as if he'd just eaten grass.

"Can the sarcasm." He'd never wanted to work with a dog, but Handler hadn't given him a choice. Since all the

Gray Wolf operatives were expected to work alone, Handler provided Wolf when backup would be a benefit.

The problem was, Daniel had never been a dog person. As far as he was concerned, having an animal around, especially one the size of Wolf, was just one more complication. Still, he couldn't deny the big beast was smart, and had made himself useful on every job they'd been paired for.

"For your information, our mission this time concerns a lady, so try to keep the dog hair and slime off the seats."

Wolf stared at him a moment, then turned to look out the window.

A BRIEF STOP at the tribal police station in Shiprock gave Daniel his first lead. One of his ex-colleagues had reported passing a car driven by a woman resembling the photo Daniel had showed him, though he'd only had a glimpse of her and couldn't be sure. He'd thought he'd heard her honk as he drove by and glanced back, but she'd turned off the road and had seemed to be all right, so he'd gone on to answer the emergency call he'd been assigned.

On the strength of that information, although the description of the car didn't seem to match Hannah Jones's vehicle, Daniel drove farther into the Reservation until he reached the narrow paved road that led through the foothills and piñon forest. Out of habit he checked his rearview mirror periodically and, before long, spotted a vehicle in the distance.

Heeding the prickle at the base of his neck, he turned off the road at the next dirt path, then looped back. He'd either lose whoever it was, or end up behind them, if he *was* being followed.

He waited, watching in both directions, but the highway appeared empty. Confident now that the vehicle he'd seen hadn't been a tail, he continued on his way.

Daniel kept turning off on side roads, looking for houses

where Hannah Jones might have gone to ground, but he found no sign that anyone had passed that way recently. Eventually, he reached a place that had a new gate locking the access road and a fence that suggested there was a house or dwelling somewhere farther up the hill. The Private Property sign on the gate backed that idea up.

There was only one way to find out if Hannah Jones had come this way. Daniel parked beside the padlocked gate and climbed out of his vehicle. Checking the ground he saw footprints.

Retrieving the paper sack from the back of the SUV, Daniel came around to the passenger side and opened the door. He held up the cotton blouse the deacon had provided in front of the dog's nose, allowing him to catch the scent.

"Wolf, track!"

Daniel opted not to leash the dog, knowing Wolf would work faster in this rough terrain without it, and in the event they met trouble, they'd both need room to maneuver.

The dog walked down the road, sniffing the ground, then suddenly froze, pawing at the dirt. Wolf barked sharply, then dug beneath the fence and shot up the slope on the other side.

Daniel climbed over the wire fence, and followed him. It didn't take long to reach a modern-looking cabin hidden among a stand of tall Ponderosa pines. Wolf was near some waist-high brush, again pawing the ground. The sound of a stream was close by, somewhere to Daniel's right.

Below the cabin was a redwood deck jutting out over a deep pool fed by the stream. A woman was kneeling at the edge of the deck, washing something in the pond. Her glossy black hair cascaded down her back, caressing creamy white skin.

She was wearing only a thin, light pink bra, and bikini

panties with images of a popular cartoon mouse all over them.

Though her whimsical choice of panties amused him, there was nothing funny about the way his body reacted to the sight of her.

She stood up, holding the blouse that she'd just washed, and turned to look around, almost as if she'd sensed his presence. Her bra and panties, dampened from her efforts to clean her clothes, now clung to her like second skin, revealing clearly what lay beneath.

Daniel reminded himself to breathe. Hannah Jones was innocence and raw sensuality all rolled up in one devastating package. The photo of her he had in his jacket pocket didn't even come close to doing her justice. Her perfectly proportioned body cried out for a man's touch.

Miss Jones was a living, breathing temptation but, as tantalizing as she was, he had to push those thoughts aside and focus on the job he'd been sent to do. He wasn't a teenager ruled by his hormones. He was a man, a professional investigator, with a job to do.

As she draped the shirt over a nearby tree branch to dry, Wolf crashed through the brush and leaped onto the deck, landing less than five feet away from her.

She gave a startled cry, and Daniel caught the look of stark terror on her face as Wolf moved closer.

Holding her hands up to ward off the dog, Hannah Jones took a step back, then another. Daniel started to call out a warning, but it was already too late. The woman slipped on the wet deck, and tumbled backwards into the water.

Chapter Two

Normally, the absurdity of the situation might have made Daniel laugh, but the way Hannah Jones was flailing in the water warned Daniel that she didn't know how to swim.

Daniel shot forward, pausing only to yank off his boots as he reached the redwood deck. A heartbeat later, he was in the water.

The pond was as cold as ice, but Daniel had swum all his life in ditches and rivers that were equally as cold. He reached Hannah in seconds but, as he tried to get a grip on her, she struggled wildly against him, gulping water and coughing, completely out of control. Her head went beneath the surface briefly, but he brought her back up, then tightened his hold on her to stop her efforts to escape. Wrapping his arms around her middle just beneath her breasts, he pulled her close, pinning her arms to her sides.

''Don't fight me, not if you want to live,'' Daniel commanded, his voice hard.

She stopped struggling, but he could still feel the tremors that passed through her body.

''You're going to be fine as soon as I get you back onto solid ground,'' he said more gently now, trying to ease her fears.

He could feel the delicate curve of her breasts resting

on his forearm as he moved them both toward the edge of the pond with powerful kicks. Hannah was as soft as velvet in his arms, and she fit against him as if she'd been made to be his.

He disciplined his thoughts, remembering where he was, who she was, and what he was doing there. As he reached shallow water, Daniel stood and carried her to dry land.

Before putting her down, he gave in to temptation, and lowered his mouth over hers, taking a tender kiss from her lips. She didn't fight. She simply melted into him with a sweetness that made his body grow impossibly hard.

It became too hot, too quickly. Surprised by it all, he drew back, then set her down gently. The smoky, dazed look in her eyes, told him she'd felt the same fires coursing through her.

She took a few uncertain steps away from him, then picked up a stout piece of a pine branch, and held it out before her like a sword. "That was your thank-you. And it was nice," she said, her voice husky. "But now I'd like you to go."

Wet, her body glistening in the sun, Hannah Jones was magnificent. The thin cloth of her undergarments did little to shield her from his hungry gaze.

"You have nothing to fear from me," Daniel said, trying to reassure her. He could take the branch away from her in one swift move and pin her to the ground before she ever knew what happened. But he didn't want to hurt or frighten her. As he continued to gaze at her, the thought of her beautiful body beneath his made him tense.

Moving sideways slowly, he reached for her slacks, which were on the deck nearby. The shirt she'd been rinsing out was draped over a low branch a little farther away, and a quick look at the reddish brown stain still marring it suggested she'd tried to wash out somebody's blood.

Wolf crept up silently and took a position behind Hannah, blocking her escape, then barked once. Hearing him, she turned her head and gasped.

"Don't let him frighten you again. He's harmless as long as you behave." Daniel came toward her slowly, holding at arm's length the clothes he'd retrieved for her. "Here. Get dressed. I have a feeling you'll feel better that way."

"Who are you?" she said, glancing back at the dog as she dropped the stick, then slipped her slacks and wet shirt on.

"A friend with a big dog—someone who didn't want you to drown, obviously."

"That's very chivalrous of you, considering it's your fault that I fell in." Watching them both, Hannah walked back onto the deck, picked up her shoes, and slipped them on. Glancing again at Wolf, she added, "Are you sure he's just a dog? He looks like a German shepherd, but I've never seen one that big."

"He's a dog, all right."

Wolf turned his head and curled his lips slightly.

"He's part wolf, I'm told," Daniel added quickly.

Daniel pulled on his boots. The breeze that had come up within the past few minutes made his own wet clothes feel icy.

"You're not in uniform, but are you a cop?" she asked, her voice unsteady.

"I'm one of the good guys," he said, not answering directly. As he looked over at her, he saw she was shivering.

"It's freezing," she said, teeth chattering.

"It's great September weather, but still too cold to be outside, even at noon, when you're wet. Can we go inside? I suppose this is your cabin," he said, deliberately playing dumb. He knew she didn't have a cabin out here, but right now he had other priorities. Bringing her back suffering from hypothermia was not a good idea.

"I'm using it for now," she said, not answering him directly. Hannah headed toward a set of flagstone steps leading up from the pond to the cabin.

He noted Hannah's reluctance to come right out with a lie. The fact struck him as odd. She'd found it okay to steal, but balked at telling a lie? Well, he'd been warned she wasn't in her right mind.

"I hope you have some warm clothes in there," he said.

"There's an old flannel shirt hanging in the closet," she answered. "I'll put that on."

Daniel followed her through the sturdy wooden door that faced the pond, and Wolf padded in behind them as Daniel held it open.

Hannah reached for some towels on a shelf and handed him one. As she patted her long hair dry, Daniel studied her appreciatively.

Hannah Jones was the most beautiful woman he'd ever seen, crazy or not. And those eyes! They were evocative and sensual, the kind that could steal a man's soul. Quickly, he reminded himself that they were also, apparently, the eyes of a woman with a damaged mind. There was no way of telling what would happen if he inadvertently pushed the wrong buttons.

Hannah started to go into the next room to change clothes, but he knew he couldn't risk letting her out of his sight. He motioned to Wolf to follow and guard.

Daniel heard her startled cry as Wolf joined her. "Don't worry. He's a pussycat. Really."

She came back out in seconds wearing an old flannel shirt. It fit snugly around her breasts, reminding him of things he had no business dwelling on.

"Let's get going."

"Where?" she asked, immediately on her guard.

"You *are* Hannah Jones."

"How did you know?" Her eyes widened with fear and she stepped back.

"Wait. You already know I'm not your enemy. Remember, I pulled you from the water? If I'd wanted to harm you, I could have let you drown."

She stared at him for a long moment, then finally nodded. "Okay, that makes sense. But how did you find me, and who are you?"

"I go by the name of Lightning," he said. "Your uncle sent me to find you and bring you back so you can get some medical help. I'm also supposed to bring back the money you took from the church."

"The money I...what?"

"You took around two thousand dollars from the church, then hit your uncle in the back of the head," he said quietly. "But he's okay now, and nobody's pressing charges. The police aren't involved in this at all. Your uncle and the people on the church committee just want to help you. They've even kept your disappearance a secret."

Hannah shook her head. "None of what you've said makes sense. I couldn't have harmed my uncle. He's the only family I've got left. I love him. And I'm *not* a thief," she added flatly.

"Then tell me. What's your version of what happened at the church, and how did you end up here?"

She hesitated, then exhaled softly. "Unfortunately, I don't know *what* happened at the church. I remember walking in there, then the next thing I recall was waking up in a strange car with a man nearby who was planning to kill me. I got away from him as fast as I could," Hannah said, explaining her escape.

Daniel gave her a long, speculative glance. Her story might have been part of her delusion, or simply an attempt to get him to let her go. "Do you have any idea how you ended up in that man's car, or what happened to your own vehicle? It's missing."

Her eyes welled up with tears, but she didn't let them

spill. Instead she met his gaze with a level one of her own. "I don't remember, and I don't understand why I can't. It's not for lack of trying, believe me."

Daniel gazed at the face that was beginning to mesmerize him. There was a slight bump on her forehead, mostly covered by her bangs, which were starting to dry now, but it scarcely looked significant enough to have created a memory loss. "What exactly *do* you remember?"

"I was at the church waiting to see my uncle. I remember going into his office. Then, after that, nothing—that is until I woke up in the car of the man I told you about, handcuffed to a bracket by the seat. I heard him talking to someone else on the phone who, apparently, was telling him to kill me."

"Where are the cuffs? Did you find a key?"

"No. I found some of those little hexagonal L-shaped tools in a drawer. One was small enough to fit into the lock, and I fiddled with it until the lock opened." She walked to the kitchen and held the handcuffs up for him to see. "Here."

He took them and put them in his back pocket. They were definitely not police issue and flimsy enough that her story could be true. But that still didn't prove a word she'd said. She could have had her own pair of handcuffs, depending on what kind of games she liked to play, or maybe she'd had a security guard boyfriend at one time.

"You don't believe me," she said, disappointment evident in her tone.

"Truthfully, I'm just not sure. But it looks like you believe it."

She shook her head. "That's a non-answer. You think I'm a few French fries short of a Happy Meal?"

"I have no idea," he answered. "But you sure look and sound okay to me," he said, in what had to be the understatement of the year.

Hannah laughed, but it was a sad laugh, inspired by

despair—not mirth. He started to say more, but Wolf's whine alerted him.

The dog stood on his hind legs, and stared out the window, sniffing the air as he rested his front paws on the sill.

"What's wrong with him?"

"Company's coming, and I don't think it's the sweepstakes prize patrol."

The off-the-cuff remark reminded him of one of his objectives, and Daniel made a quick visual search of the nearly empty cabin. There was no money to be found there in any readily accessible place. For now, they had to leave. Silentman could send someone to search more thoroughly later.

"Let's get out of here," he said, taking her hand, and letting the dog lead the way as they slipped out the back door.

Wolf stopped suddenly, then, hackles raised and body low to the ground, crept forward. Daniel knew the move. Someone was close and the dog didn't see whoever it was as a friend. More than likely, Wolf had scented alcohol, gun powder, or some other substance he'd been trained to recognize as trouble.

"Hurry," he urged Hannah.

Suddenly two men wearing ski masks and carrying baseball bats stepped out from behind a sandstone boulder. "Hit the trail, Geronimo," the tall, blue-eyed Anglo said, using a worn-out racist label. Their short-sleeved shirts revealed white, but suntanned skin. "We have unfinished business with the lady but none with you. Come with us, Hannah."

Hannah looked startled, and stepped back, away from the men.

Wolf was nowhere to be seen, but Daniel knew the dog would be nearby. He'd probably circled around to wait for Daniel's signal to attack.

"You're out of your league. Take a hike while you can still walk," Daniel warned, bracing himself for a fight.

"You want to dance? It's okay with me. It's your funeral." The big man moved toward Daniel like he was stepping up to the plate but, before he was close enough to take a swing, Daniel whistled sharply.

Wolf erupted like a furry explosion from the bushes to Daniel's right, and hit the big Anglo hard in the side, knocking him to the ground. The bat flew out of the man's hand as Wolf's massive jaws gripped his arm. Screaming, the man hammered at the dog with his fist, but Wolf seemed oblivious to it.

Daniel kicked the second man in the chest at the same time Wolf neutralized the first, then delivered another blow to his target's midsection that knocked him to the ground.

The Anglo fell hard, rolled, then scrambled to his feet, and took off running.

"Out!" Daniel ordered Wolf, who had pinned the taller attacker to the ground. The one-word command caused Wolf to release the man instantly and sit.

The man sprang to his feet and fled, holding his tattered sleeve, now wet with blood. Daniel didn't pursue them. He had other things to worry about. Going after the men would have been satisfying, but not in line with his primary duty.

Expecting Hannah to have fled during the confusion, he glanced behind him. What he saw took him by complete surprise. Hannah had retrieved the tall man's baseball bat, and had it cocked back, ready to swing. Her body was trembling so hard, even the bat was shaking as she held it.

Her gaze remained on his rapidly retreating opponents as he approached her.

"Easy there," he said. "It's over now."

Hannah lowered the bat, then dropped it on the ground.

"Get me out of here," she said, her voice surprisingly firm.

"Two minds with one thought," he said, quickly leading her down the dirt track to where his SUV was parked.

Hannah's show of courage made him look at her with newfound respect. She could have cut and run, but she'd stayed with him, ready to help. That spoke well of her.

Events had also revealed another important fact. He was certain now that Hannah was in real danger, and that put a different slant on things. He couldn't turn her over to anyone else until he was sure it was safe to do so. He'd lived all his life by certain rules, and he wouldn't walk out on a woman who needed his protection…even if that meant risking his job.

AS SOON AS THEY REACHED Daniel's SUV and were safely underway, Hannah breathed a sigh of relief. "They wanted *me.* But why? What have I ever done to them? I don't even know who they are!"

"I don't have the answer to that. But don't worry. No one's going to hurt you while Wolf and I are around."

Hannah wasn't used to anyone defending her, yet this man and his dog had fought to protect her, and had probably saved her life.

"But there's something I want you to tell me." He glanced over at her and she nodded. "You could have run, yet you stayed with us. Why?"

"I couldn't just leave you in the middle of that. You were in that fight because of me. But, by the time I got the baseball bat, it was obvious you two didn't need any more help."

She saw the way he looked at her, his gaze missing nothing. Hannah forced herself to suppress the shiver that ran up her spine. This man exuded power of every kind. He was tall and broad-shouldered, but his strength was more than physical. It came from inside him. He had confidence, the kind that said he wasn't afraid of a challenge because he knew he'd defeat whatever stood in his way.

He was truly a warrior, one whose skills had been honed to the maximum. He'd flattened a much larger attacker with a few effortless moves. Lightning was as quick and powerful as the force of nature he was named for. He was a dangerous man, too, of that she had no doubt, but he was not a danger to her—at least not yet.

Lightning smiled at her with a gentleness that belied all she'd just seen and thought. As their gazes met, Hannah felt a stirring deep inside her and her heart began to hammer in a way that had nothing to do with fear.

She shivered slightly, wondering what it would take—and what it would cost—to win this man's trust. She needed an ally with his extraordinary qualities. But a man like Lightning did nothing halfway, feminine instinct assured her of that.

Hannah's thoughts drifted and she remembered how secure she'd felt in his arms as he'd pulled her out of the water. Raw, carnal emotions had flooded through her as she'd seen the darkness that had smoldered in his eyes and recognized the force of his desire. Most surprising of all, that knowledge had held an eroticism all its own.

"Now it's your turn to answer me. Why did you expect me to abandon you?" she asked, her voice steady.

He blinked, but otherwise gave no indication of what thoughts lay behind his narrowed eyes. "You weren't a match for those men. Running would have been a sensible choice."

"Maybe, but I couldn't abandon someone who was fighting for his life because he chose to protect me. You were in that situation because you stood up for me and that deserved something in return," she answered.

In the quick glance he gave her she saw respect and admiration.

As the SUV reached the main road, she saw the way

her rescuer glanced around, studying the area carefully as if he were expecting more trouble.

Wolf, now in the back seat, gave a low growl, his gaze scanning the wooded section behind them.

"Do you think he sees them coming again?" she asked, her voice shaky.

"No. He'd be reacting differently if he'd sensed approaching danger." He reached for her hand and squeezed it, then gave her a playful smile. "Don't worry. Wolf's just itching for another piece of them. We're on top of things."

Chapter Three

From the moment he'd reached for her hand, cradling it with his own, Daniel hadn't been able to find a good enough reason to relinquish it. He caressed the back of it now with his thumb, making lazy circles he hoped would reassure her, and was satisfied when she made no move to pull away.

"You can't take me back to Farmington," she said, her voice soft. "Now you have to believe that I told you the truth. Someone *is* out to get me. And the fact that they found me here, right after you did, can mean only one of two things—either you're with them, and I know you're not," she added quickly, "or they somehow used you, hoping you'd lead them straight to me."

Daniel considered everything that had happened. Only Handler, Silentman, the deacon, and the church committee who'd hired Gray Wolf had supposedly known about Lightning and his assignment. There was also the police officer he'd shown her photo to, but he seemed a pretty remote possibility.

Yet the fact remained that those two men had called Hannah by name. That meant there was nothing coincidental about the attack. They'd either trailed her on their own, or followed him there.

"If you take me back, you could be throwing me into the lion's den," she warned.

Hannah's gaze was so direct and guileless, he felt the impact of her look all through him. "I have to call someone," he said after they'd traveled a few more miles down the highway.

He pulled off on a side road, took out his cell phone, then stepped out of the SUV. Thinking about the trust he was trying to build with Hannah, Daniel decided to leave the keys in the ignition. "Sit tight. Wolf will guard you."

The animal jumped to the front seat, positioning himself between Hannah and the steering wheel. As Daniel walked a few feet away, so he could speak privately, he saw Hannah reach out to the dog and begin to stroke its massive head. Daniel could see the animal was still focused on his job, but there was something special about the woman that made Wolf treat her like a friend. His tail was wagging, and he actually tried to lick her in the face.

Daniel had seen that dog snarl viciously whenever strangers attempted to touch him. Yet that same beast was now acting like a puppy eager for attention—well, almost. His gaze was clearly focused on the surrounding area, not on the woman scratching him in just the right place behind one ear.

Daniel's call was picked up on the second ring. "I've got a problem," Daniel told Silentman, and proceeded to recount the recent events surrounding his retrieval mission, including the fact that Hannah didn't know the location of her car.

"Handler doesn't like complications, Lightning," Silentman responded. "What's your take on the situation?"

"I can't just turn this lady over to people I'm not sure about—not until I know how those muscle boys found us. I can't take her to the Farmington police either, because the minute they hear about the theft and her supposed attack on her uncle, they'd have to take action. And if they think she's dangerous, she could end up in a psychiatric ward someplace and possibly in more danger from whoever's after her. Besides, our clients specifically wanted to avoid the police. I figure that the best thing I can do is keep her out of sight until I can get to the bottom of this.''

Silentman said nothing for several moments, then finally spoke. ''Okay. It's your call. Just remember, she may be unstable, so her word isn't worth much.''

''Understood,'' Daniel said.

''The hours that she claims not to remember probably hold the key to what's really going on,'' Silentman said. ''Her uncle can't help us fill in any more details on that, other than with his own suppositions, so start with the last thing she remembers doing and try to trace her steps from there. In the meantime, let me do a full background check on Hannah Jones. And get me a description of the man who supposedly abducted her. Maybe we'll get lucky.''

Daniel returned to the car and found Hannah playing tug-of-war with Wolf, using her seat belt. It took him a moment to register what he was seeing. He'd tried to play tug-of-war with the massive animal once, but Wolf had shaken the knotted rope and nearly yanked him off his feet, making it clear that he played to win. Yet, with Hannah it appeared Wolf was going out of his way to be gentle.

''Back seat,'' Daniel ordered Wolf, and the dog jumped through the gap. If Hannah Jones could even get the dog to soften his style for her, the woman was trouble.

''I need to know what you've decided,'' she said, her voice calm, but firm. ''I don't like dragging anyone into my business, or depending on strangers. Unfortunately, I'm in trouble and I could use your help—but only if you're truthful. I'm not interested in lies, no matter what the reason.''

''What are you talking about?'' he asked, his tone guarded.

''I know who you are and Lightning isn't your name.''

Daniel studied her, saying nothing. She had guts, he had to give her that. She confronted things squarely. "Who do you think I am?"

"Your name is Daniel Eagle, you're thirty-two years old, and you're an investigator for Gray Wolf Investigations."

He checked for his wallet. It was still in his hip pocket. "Okay. And how do you know all that?"

She gestured to the glove compartment. "I looked in there while you were talking. This car is registered to the agency, but it's leased to you. The agreement is there on a piece of paper inside the owner's manual." She didn't give him a chance to comment. "I've heard of your firm, and I know it's supposed to be one of the best. But I've also heard that Gray Wolf doesn't always play by the rules."

"I apologize for underestimating you, Hannah. I should have kept the papers in my wallet, I guess."

"I may have a blank in my memory, but I've still got a brain. I know I'm in trouble, and my life is probably hanging by a thread, but I don't know why. I could sure use an ally, but the next move is yours. Are you my friend or my enemy?"

He considered trying to placate her with soothing, comforting words, but decided the truth would be better all the way around. Telling her a lie now would only complicate things if the truth came out later. "I'm not sure yet, but I'll tell you this—I won't turn you over to anyone until I'm certain who the victim really is in all this."

"Fair enough."

Daniel pulled back onto the highway and continued east, still trying to make up his mind about Hannah. The bits and pieces he knew about her refused to fit into one neat package. On one side there was the innocent beauty who wore panties decorated with mice—the woman whose sense of loyalty had kept her from running away in the face of danger while others fought on her behalf.

Then, there was the other side of Hannah. If the reports he'd been given were accurate, he was dealing with a woman who had a history of psychiatric disorders and was capable of bashing her closest relative on the skull, stealing a church's money, then going into hiding.

Daniel glanced over at Hannah again, noting the bump and discoloration just beneath her bangs. He needed to take things one step at a time. "Our next stop is a free clinic I know of in Farmington."

"I can't go there. What if the people after me have places like that staked out?"

"I doubt they have the resources to cover a large area. The two back there weren't high-priced talent. I figure they'll be watching your house, and maybe places where you work. Widening the search beyond that would take a lot of manpower. Besides, we need to check out that bump on your head and see if that's the reason your memory's been impaired. I promise you'll be safe. There's a doctor at the clinic who's on the agency's payroll and who has worked with us before on sensitive cases when we've needed him. He'll keep our visit quiet and check out that bruise to make sure you don't have a concussion or something serious, and then we'll talk."

"I hate doctors and I hate hospitals. This isn't necessary."

"It is to me," he said flatly. "You took a blow to the head, based on that bruise, and you're going to see a doctor. No argument."

"That's what you think. Stop the car."

He glanced over at her.

"Stop the car," she repeated. "I'm not going another mile until you listen to me." When he didn't respond, she started to open the car door, but he reached over to her and grasped her arm. She kept her free hand on the door handle. "Slow down and park, or we're both going to be statistics to the highway department."

He wasn't sure if she was bluffing or not, but he couldn't keep her steady and in the car while he was still at the wheel. Muttering a curse, he pulled over to the shoulder of the road and stopped. "What the hell are you trying to do?"

"You've seen what I'm up against, Daniel. Sure I took a blow to my head, and there are things I don't remember, but fear and my instinct to survive tell me that there are certain things I have to do. I need an ally, but one who's really on my side. From what I can see, you're not certain which side you're on and that scares the daylights out of me. And nobody I'm unsure of is going to order me around."

She started to get out of the car, but he reached for her arm, stopping her.

She jerked free. "I don't care if you can fight like a martial artist, Daniel. No one has the right to manhandle me either."

"I can't let you go, Hannah. It's my job to make sure you remain safe and that's exactly what I intend to do. I'm going to protect you, even from yourself."

"I'm not crazy," she said, her voice trembling. "I won't be treated as if I can't make my own decisions."

"In this case, you can't. I have a lot more experience in these matters than you have. You'll have to play by my rules."

"And your rules are to force whatever you want on me?" Tears filled her eyes.

Seeing it, Daniel groaned. Now he felt like a heel for not having taken the time to treat her with more care. He smoothed his palm across her cheek. "I've been too hard on you. I should have taken more time to explain things. Don't be upset. I really am trying to protect you."

He saw her trying to manage a smile, and pieces of the

armor he'd always kept around his heart broke off, dissolving as if they'd never been. "I'm really sorry."

"Your apology is accepted," she said quietly.

As he looked at her, he felt himself drowning in her gaze. His heart hammered in his chest and he ached with the need to kiss her.

He glanced away. This woman made him feel all soft and crazy inside. What the hell did he think he was doing?

"I really think you need to get that bump checked out, if you expect to make it through the next few days. Concussions are serious, Hannah. What kind of protection would I be giving you if I saved you from those guys back there, then let you get hurt even more seriously because I didn't follow up on an injury."

"All right. At least I know why you're so intent on doing this. But they won't find anything wrong."

"Then that'll be good news we can both live with."

Being with Hannah was like working with nitroglycerine—there was an undeniable excitement about it, but if you got overconfident, or made the wrong move, it could spell disaster. Daniel couldn't be sure of her, and to trust the woman could prove to be a lethal mistake. Yet, despite all that, he liked having her with him.

The plain truth was that he couldn't remember ever being around a woman who fascinated him as much as Hannah did. She was an enigma hidden in beautiful packaging. But he would have been a fool not to realize how dangerous that made her to him. His attraction to her was already undermining the control he always exerted over himself and his emotions. That fact alone made him uneasy and guarded. An investigator needed to know himself and depend on his reactions. Without that, he was headed for trouble.

IT TOOK LESS THAN AN HOUR to reach the free clinic in Farmington. He parked in the small graveled lot, and walked inside with Hannah, guarding her back with his body. He'd left the windows down in the SUV for Wolf, knowing that with him inside the vehicle, there was no danger of a break-in, even in this poor neighborhood.

As they walked inside, Daniel saw the waiting room was nearly empty. As soon as he identified himself to the nurse at the desk, they were shown to an empty examining room.

"Do you plan to stay in here with me?" Hannah asked irately.

Daniel considered it. "I'll give you some privacy once the doctor gets here, but I'll be right outside in the hall."

A short time later, the doctor came into the room. Hannah didn't recognize him, and he apparently had no idea who she was either.

After enduring a thorough examination, and having generous blood samples drawn for tests, Hannah was left alone in the room to dress. Hearing Daniel call out to the doctor in the hall, she went to the door and listened. The doctor was telling Daniel that he'd check for drugs and for any serious injury that might have affected her memory, but that the blood test results wouldn't be available for a few days.

She already knew that they'd find nothing, but understood that Daniel had to make sure. The sad truth was that he couldn't be sure about her, and that uncertainty would undermine their partnership.

Hannah tried to face the situation squarely. Without his trust, she was better off without him and he without her. It made no sense for Daniel to risk his life for someone he didn't truly believe in.

What she needed to do now was catch a ride or walk back to the church. She'd wait until no one was around, then go inside and try to reconstruct the missing pieces of her life. She was convinced that everything she needed to clear herself was there. All she had to do was find some way to trigger her elusive memory.

As Daniel and the doctor's voices moved away from her down the hall, Hannah slipped noiselessly out of the room. A door marked Emergency Exit was only a few steps away.

This was her chance.

She hurried toward it and was nearly there when Daniel stepped around the corner. Hannah ran right into his chest, and before she could take a breath, he clasped her wrist, holding her fast.

She stared at him in mute shock. She wasn't going anywhere and they both knew it.

"I... I was just going to—"

"Save your excuses," he said with barely disguised anger. "I'm here to take you to talk to the doctor."

The young physician looked at them both curiously as they came into his office. The new tension between them was impossible to miss. Hannah sat down in a chair across from the doctor, and Daniel stood behind her.

"The results of your blood test won't be back for three days or so," the doctor began, "but from your pupil reaction and reflexes, Miss Jones, I don't think there are any drugs in your system now. You also don't have a concussion. Your memory lapse, as far as I can tell, isn't being caused by any physical trauma."

"Then that leaves psychological, right?" Daniel pressed.

"That's a fair guess, but you're going outside my area of expertise. All I can say is that I found no sign of an injury that would explain her inability to remember recent events."

Daniel reached down and took Hannah's hand, holding it firmly but without hurting her. "Then we'll be going on our way. You know how to bill the agency for this," Daniel said.

"Good luck," the doctor answered with a nod. "I'll send the test results along when they come in."

As they walked to the door, Hannah felt her stomach sinking. Daniel would never understand why she'd wanted to get away, and why it would have been the best thing for them both. The only thing he'd see in what she'd tried to do was another reason to distrust her. Trying to make things better, she'd succeeded in making them far worse.

She let out a small sigh. For years she'd prided herself on not needing anyone for either her comfort or safety. Depending on a stranger now, and putting him in mortal danger because of it, went against everything she believed in.

"It would have been better for you if I'd managed to get away," she said simply.

Daniel laughed bitterly. "You were doing it all for my sake, right?"

"No, but what I said still stands. It would have been better for you." He walked her to the SUV, and opened the passenger door, waiting until she was in and buckled up before he walked around to his side. Wolf looked at her from the back seat, but sensing something was wrong between her and Daniel, remained still.

They drove away silently, Daniel concentrating on the traffic as they headed west.

She could clearly sense that what disturbed Daniel the most was that she'd tried to trick him. He'd never lower his guard around her again but, unless she could somehow gain his trust, he would be as much her keeper as her ally.

"Where are we going?" she asked.

"To a safe house about halfway to Shiprock. It's the best place I can think of for us right now."

They'd gone a few miles out of town before he spoke again, keeping his attention fixed on the road and not even glancing at her. "Is there someone who has known you for a long time who I can talk to—preferably a person who sees you a lot."

"What do you want, a character reference?" There had

been no sympathy or caring in his tone. Daniel was all business now that she'd shaken his trust.

He glanced at her coldly. "Answer my question, please."

She thought of responding that *he* hadn't answered *her,* but changed her mind. She'd pick her battles carefully from now on. "I wouldn't drag either my friends or clients into this. I'm not sure why those men were after me, but this is a deadly business. I don't want anyone I know getting hurt on account of me."

"We need to find someone trustworthy who might have seen you during that time you can't account for. They might be able to shed some light on what happened during those hours."

"My guess is that only someone who works at the church could do that, but I doubt they'd speak freely to you if you came in asking questions. They don't know you. And I obviously can't vouch for you right now."

"Tell me about your clients and your business."

"I run a small bookkeeping firm out of my home. I don't have employees—so basically, I'm it. My firm is my livelihood and I've worked hard to get it off the ground. Being accused of stealing is about the worst thing that can happen to someone in my profession. Make the victim a church, and you can pretty much write off your career. But ask yourself one thing—what kind of creep would be willing to hunt down a woman and kill her for two thousand dollars—money that, from what you've said, hasn't even been reported missing? There are more blank spaces in that story than there are in my memory."

"I know," Daniel answered quietly. "But no one will hurt you while you stick with me. You can count on that."

Hannah believed him. From everything she'd seen, Daniel Eagle was a man of his word. When he offered his protection, he meant it. To get to her, they'd have to kill him. And from what she'd seen of his fighting skills, it would take a lot to do that.

Like the stereotypical Navajo warrior, Daniel was cool under pressure, quiet and highly dangerous to an enemy. He also possessed a vibrant maleness that only a woman without a pulse could resist. Though at the moment he was a reluctant ally, there was something infinitely seductive about having a man like Daniel protecting her.

Yet that could all change, and she had to remember that. Once he found out the details of her past, would he still believe she was telling him the truth? That was a question she just couldn't answer, and one she had every right to worry about.

"So how much farther is this safe house?" Hannah asked.

"We have less than a half hour of drive time before we get there. The house actually belongs to a buddy of mine. It's near Hogback, just inside the Reservation. No one's living there right now. Mitchell's away for the next two months. He's participating in law enforcement training back east. Nobody will bother us there."

"Is Mitchell part of Gray Wolf?"

"All I can say is that he and I got to be friends when I worked as a cop a lifetime ago."

"But what if the neighbors see us?"

"They know me. We won't have any problems. You'll be safe. It's a tight community with a lot of cops or former cops, and ex-military."

Hannah took a deep breath, then let it out again. "You realize that I don't have a wallet, money, ID, or anything on me except the clothes on my back, and the shirt isn't even mine. Is there any way I can get a few things from my home?"

"No, that's out of the question. It's probably being watched."

She nodded. ''Okay, fair enough. But I'll still need a change of clothes and a few personal items.''

''We can stop at the trading post near where we're going. You stay in the vehicle with Wolf. Give me a list with sizes, and I'll get whatever I can find.''

The stop to buy the things she'd asked for was quick. After that, they continued the drive that took them past harvested cornfields west of Hogback and dry desert above the river valley. Daniel remained silent throughout and, after a while, Hannah decided to do something to break the unsettling quiet that was grating on her nerves.

''I've heard of the brooding hero, but I think I'd rather have a more talkative one,'' she said, a wry smile touching the corners of her mouth.

''I don't brood, and I'm no hero,'' he muttered.

''Well, you handled yourself pretty well against those two men who came after me.''

''It's part of what I do.'' He paused, then added, ''And, to be honest, I don't like to lose.''

Hannah knew that already. Daniel wasn't a man who took second place easily—if ever. ''Then you may have picked the wrong side to be on this time. The odds seem to be stacked against me at the moment.''

''I follow my own judgment about what's right and what's not. Odds are never the issue. And I *never* shy away from a fight I believe in,'' he answered, giving her a crooked smile that made her pulse beat faster. ''Besides, your chances aren't as bad as you think, providing you're as innocent as you say you are.''

Hannah didn't miss the disclaimer. ''So, you still have doubts?''

''Under the circumstances, do you blame me?''

She sighed softly. ''No, I suppose not. What can I do to change that?''

''Work with me. Let's concentrate on what we know

and try to piece the rest together. That's the only way we're going to find the truth."

It was shortly after 3:00 p.m. when Daniel pulled off the main highway, drove a quarter mile south, then parked in front of a wood frame house located in a semirural residential area alongside the river. There were at least five acres between neighbors. "Let's go inside. Mitchell has a computer program designed to make suspect drawings. I helped him install it a while back. If we work together, I think we can come up with a sketch of the man who abducted you."

Hannah went into the house and looked around. It was a simple home with a bare minimum of amenities. A man's house, and a spartan one.

As Daniel sat down at the computer, she tried to keep her spirits up, but it was hard. She couldn't blame Daniel for harboring doubts. And it was going to get worse. Someone was clearly out to frame her and even the apparent kindness of keeping the police out of it was making it easier for her hidden enemy to systematically destroy her. If the missing money wasn't found, she was sure that eventually she'd be arrested.

She'd lose everything but, in the process, she'd also blacken her uncle's reputation as well. He'd vouched for her when she'd taken over the church's accounts and their connection would mean that no one would ever trust him again either. He'd be ruined personally and professionally. A real estate broker needed people's trust.

"I'm not guilty. I'm certain of that, even though I can't remember what happened," Hannah said.

Daniel nodded absently as he switched on the computer.

"And I'm not crazy." She saw the thoughtful look he gave her, and realized that he already knew quite a bit about her history. Just how much, she was afraid to ask, but unless she could make him understand that her illness had only been a result of her parents' death and that it was all in the past, it would shadow everything she said or did.

As she glanced over at him, she noticed the way he was looking at her and forced herself not to react. "I've spent my whole life trying not to let long, thoughtful looks filled with speculation—like the one you just gave me—get to me."

"I'm not sure what you mean," he said, quickly looking down at the computer.

"It's a certain expression that people get that says without words, 'Poor thing. She looks normal, but she's a little touched.'" She paused for a moment. "I hate it, but it's followed me all my life."

"I didn't mean to give you the impression that that's what I was thinking or doing," he hedged, fully aware that she'd hit the mark squarely.

"So you weren't assessing me, wondering what makes me tick?"

He started to deny it, but then decided against it. "Your uncle told me that you're prone to fugue states where you don't remember things, and that you spent time in a hospital for depression."

"I went through six months of therapy after my father committed suicide. I was there when it happened and I went into shock. I was only thirteen at the time, and it was just too much for me to handle." She took a deep, steadying breath then continued. "It took a while for me to find my way back. To this day I still don't remember all the details of that night, but my uncle filled in the gaps and, to be honest, I know all I need. The past can't be changed. I learned back then to accept that and go on with my own life. Mind you, it took a lot of sessions with the doctors before that sank in, but once it did, I never had to go back for treatment."

"And now you can't remember again," he said slowly.

"I'm obviously blocking out something that scared the

daylights out of me. Nothing less could have caused this. I know I had a similar problem when I was thirteen, but I've lived a normal life since that time. I'm not on medication, nor have I had to see a psychiatrist for many years. If you want to know the truth, my biggest problem has been that my history of mental illness has always followed me like a shadow. People see me as flawed, or weak, and no matter how hard I've tried, I've never been able to escape that."

"That's not that unusual. People tend to see the person they knew, not the one you've become."

"And this mess I'm in now will only convince them that they've been right about me all along. To them I'm just Bob Jones's poor, crazy niece," she said, exhaling softly.

"Once we find answers, things will get easier for you."

She shook her head. "No, even if I'm completely cleared, my past will continue to make people feel uncertain about me. It's not fair, but it is the truth." She stuck out her chin. "But I will get through this and clear my name. Nothing can force me to become a helpless victim again. I'm not thirteen anymore."

She knew she was in for the fight of her life but, somehow, she would remember what happened at the church. She owed it to herself, and also to Daniel, who was placing himself in the path of unknown dangers to stand by her now and protect her.

Chapter Four

"Okay, I've got the computer program running. Pull up a chair," Daniel said.

Hannah did as he asked. There wasn't much room and his leg pressed against hers as they sat beside each other. That fluid warmth filled her with awareness.

As Daniel captured her gaze, everything feminine in her came to vibrant life. In his eyes she could see the same fire that was coursing through her. Yet that knowledge did little to stop the crazy kaleidoscope of emotions swirling through her. This man was all male power—raw, immediate and unrelenting.

She tore her gaze from his. Daniel Eagle didn't back away from anything—even this. It went against his nature. But one of them had to put a stop to the sexual tension rising between them. Otherwise things would spiral out of control.

Hannah looked at the computer screen. "Okay. How do we use this program?" she asked, forcing her voice to remain steady.

The work took more than an hour, but after the first fifteen minutes, Wolf trotted over and wedged himself between them, pushing their chairs aside enough to accommodate him. Hannah laughed, and shifted to make more room for him, but Daniel glowered at the animal.

"He's such a nice dog," Hannah said, burying her hand in the thick fur around Wolf's neck.

Jealousy only increased Daniel's irritation. "Yeah. He's swell."

Refocusing on the work at hand, Daniel continued adjusting facial features on the screen according to her directions, manipulating the shape of the face until she was satisfied. "That's the man who was going to kill me," she said at last.

He studied the sketch of the Anglo man, toggling the printer to make a copy. "I don't recognize him. Do you have any idea who he might be?"

Hannah looked up at him and shook her head.

Daniel could see the pain and fear mirrored on her face. She looked fragile—a beautiful flower that had been buffeted by an angry wind. Daniel struggled with the sudden desire to pull her against him. He'd held her once, and her bare skin had felt like velvet and fire. It had left him wanting more.

Fighting himself, he forced his thoughts back to the case. For all he knew, Hannah was an experienced manipulator and he was playing right into her hands. Ignoring the gut instinct that told him he was off base with that, he tried to convince himself that all Hannah could ever be to him was major-league trouble.

Pensively, he dropped his gaze to her hands, which were now resting on the small computer desk. They were delicate and feminine. And memory told him they were impossibly soft. He wanted to feel them on his naked flesh.

Disgusted with himself, he pushed back his chair and walked across the room. What he needed now was a cool head, not a raging sex drive.

"I'll fax this to Silentman. He'll run it through several databases and see what turns up," he said, removing the drawing from the printer output tray and walking over to the fax machine on another desk beside the phone.

As he looked back at her, he saw Hannah wearily rubbing her eyes. "You look really tired. Have you had any sleep at all since this started?"

"I couldn't get much sleep at the cabin the night I was there," she said. "I was afraid someone might just walk in."

"Why don't you go lie down and get some rest now?"

"But there's so much going on...."

"There's nothing either of us can do at the moment. I have to wait for Silentman's call. You might as well take advantage of the opportunity to sleep."

Hannah stood up. "I'm so tired I can't even think straight anymore. You really don't mind if I take a short nap?"

"Go. The bedroom's down the hall and to your left. I won't be far away if you need anything."

"Thanks." Hannah met his gaze and gave him a gentle smile. "There are times when I'm firmly convinced that underneath that tough-guy image is one very nice man."

Daniel watched her walk hesitantly to the room at the end of the hall. Wolf gave him a glance, received a nod, then followed her.

After several minutes, Daniel walked down the hall to the master bedroom to check on the mismatched pair. They were both on the bed, Wolf between her and the door. Wolf was lying on his side next to Hannah. His massive head rested on the pillow beside hers, his body vertical like a person would lie. Her arm was draped across his furry chest. The dog stared at him, but did nothing else, almost as if afraid moving would wake her.

Daniel glanced over at Hannah. The even sound of her breathing assured him that she was fast asleep and he allowed himself a moment more to watch her, studying her face. She looked at peace for the first time since he'd found her. As his gaze drifted down her body, he remembered the feel of those gentle curves against him, and his body hardened instantly.

He glanced away. Hannah Jones was a living, breathing distraction. That was all there was to it. Wolf raised his head as Daniel took a step back out into the hall. "Count your blessings, mutt. That really should be me next to her, not you."

Daniel was back in the den when his cell phone finally rang. Silentman had received the fax and wanted a status report.

"Do you think she's guilty?" Silentman asked immediately.

"I don't know," Daniel replied honestly. "She seems pretty straightforward to me but, then again, that may only mean she's a great little actress."

"I'd give that possibility some serious thought if I were you," Silentman warned. "I've just received a confidential report from one of the nurses who knew her when she was a teen and living in a psychiatric hospital in Albuquerque. The nurse claims that Hannah was a very bright girl, and that was the reason she was released early—too early, the nurse believes. The woman said that Hannah learned to tell the doctors exactly what they wanted to hear. That, coupled with the fact that she was good-looking gave her an edge, one Hannah learned to use to take advantage of young men. But, in all fairness, this woman clearly didn't like her, so the information may be tainted."

Daniel listened, saying nothing. He felt as if someone were holding an ice cube to the small of his back. He couldn't quite disregard the possibility that he may have allowed Hannah's looks and her seemingly desperate situation to sway him too much. Was he being taken for a ride?

"Watch yourself, Lightning."

"Always."

Daniel hung up the phone and went to the kitchen to fix

himself something to eat. The refrigerator was nearly empty. Good thing he'd bought some supplies for them at the trading post. He went out to the SUV, brought back some canned goods, dog food and the loaf of bread he'd bought, then began to prepare some food.

The sound of shattering glass in the bedroom suddenly broke the silence and he ran down the hall, his adrenaline flowing. As he entered the room, he found Hannah with tears rolling down her face, standing on one foot and balancing herself by holding on to Wolf.

"What happened?" he asked.

"I had a nightmare," she managed to say. "I woke up scared and somehow knocked over the lamp and broke it. I'm sorry if I alarmed you."

"It's all right," he said, breathing normally again.

As he looked down he saw that she was barefoot, and one foot was bleeding. "You must have stepped on some glass. Sit back down on the bed and let me get some bandages."

Putting Wolf at stay so he wouldn't cut himself as well, Daniel hurried to the bathroom, then came back with a small first aid kit and a dampened washcloth. Picking up Hannah's injured foot carefully, he saw that the cut wasn't deep and there was no glass in the wound. "You'll be all right. It's not very bad." He cleaned the cut and bandaged it expertly.

As Daniel looked up from his work, he saw her expression soften. The gentleness in that gaze tore at his determination to close himself off from her.

"Thank you," she said.

"Let me get the broken glass picked up, then you can give your bandaged foot a test drive," he said, teasing.

After the glass fragments had been discarded, he released Wolf from the "stay" command and watched Hannah take a few steps around the room.

"Good as new," she said with a grateful smile.

"Thanks." She touched his upper arm and gave it a squeeze.

Desire, sudden and fierce, swept over him again. He nodded absently, and pretended to be only interested in her injured foot.

Her toenails were painted a pale peach color. Somehow that little detail had escaped him until now. The knowledge he'd overlooked something, even if it was insignificant, disturbed him. "Tell me about your nightmare," he said, moving away from her to sit on the easy chair.

Hannah went back to her seat on the edge of the bed, facing him. "It was just a jumble of images and there was this bright red haze that covered everything," she said, suppressing a shudder. "People were there but they were nothing more than bloody shapes." Her voice broke but no more tears fell down her cheeks.

More than anything else, he wanted to wrap his arms around Hannah, but if he touched her now, he'd want to do a lot more than comfort her.

"Did you recognize anyone?" he asked.

"I didn't see the people clearly enough for that."

"Do you think this dream has something to do with what happened at the church?"

"I...don't know."

"Think back. Did anything look familiar?"

She shook her head. "It was an awful nightmare. Those bloody shapes..." She took an unsteady breath. "And there were voices and sounds that seemed to rip through me, like peals of thunder." She held her hands against the sides of her head as if trying to push the memory back inside.

"Did the voices say anything you can recall?" He saw her shake her head, but he continued to press her. "You have to fight to get your memory back, Hannah. Do you understand? When you get dreams like these, hold them, force yourself to look at them squarely,'' he said gruffly. ''They might hold a clue.''

''That's easy for you to say. But that dream was terrifying. I don't want to hold on to it—not for anybody.''

''I'm trying to protect you. If that means forcing you to face your fears, then that's the way it has to be.''

He saw the confusion and the pain in her eyes, and almost regretted his words. Then he remembered his conversation with Silentman. He had to stay focused. Hannah could be a one-way ticket to a hell he'd never even imagined.

She stood up slowly, gingerly putting her weight on her injured foot. ''I'll do my part,'' she said, with that quiet dignity of hers that was either pure class or a great act. ''You don't have to remind me of my situation. I'm very aware of what I have to do.''

He nodded once. ''Come on. It's six-thirty and we haven't eaten. Let's have some food. Afterwards, we'll try to come up with a plan of action.'' Daniel walked with her to the kitchen, nuked a plate of pork and beans in the microwave, then set the dish before her along with two pieces of toast. ''It's not fancy, but it'll have to do,'' he said, getting a plate for himself.

''This is fine,'' she said, munching on the toast.

After seeing her pick at the beans for a while, he realized that they were far from her favorite food.

''What other foods can't you stand?'' he asked with a grin.

She chuckled softly. ''Eggplant, Brussels sprouts, and chile that's too hot. It sets my mouth on fire.''

He laughed. ''Yeah, I know what you mean,'' he said, offering her a can of soup to replace the beans. ''When the chile kills the taste of the food, and you need a fire extinguisher, it's too much.''

Smiling, she looked up at him, and the impact of those guileless eyes slammed through him once more. Swearing that he was going as *loco* as she was rumored to be, he looked down at his plate and took another forkful of beans.

"I have an idea that might give us some answers," Hannah proposed, opening the soup and pouring it into a microwave-safe bowl. "But it's risky."

Daniel shrugged. "At this point, everything we do will entail risk. What's your plan?"

"I want to go to my office at the church. I did some of their bookkeeping, mostly balancing the modest funds in their operating budget, but maybe something there will trigger my memory."

Daniel nodded slowly. "Yeah, that thought occurred to me too, but we can't just walk in there. You'll be recognized. The only way we can go is if I can come up with a really good disguise for both of us. Fortunately, I have some background in that. One of my summer jobs when I was in college was working for a film company that had come to New Mexico to shoot on location. With Silentman's help, we can get the supplies we need together, and then get going."

"What kind of disguise do you have in mind?" she asked, setting the control on the microwave to heat her soup.

He reached past her to set the machine on, then turned her to face him. "Let me surprise you."

IT WAS SHORTLY AFTER TEN the next day when they approached the church on foot, leaving Wolf in the SUV. "Stoop more," he said quietly.

She did as he asked, knowing it would enhance the role they were playing—that of an elderly couple. "You put so much talcum powder in my hair to make it gray that if anyone sneezes, a cloud will lift into the air," she muttered.

"Good. A cloud is good. Think of it as a smoke screen."

Her loose skirt was so baggy it would have fallen to her ankles if it hadn't been for the cloth belt she'd fashioned from the curtain tie-backs. "I feel guilty about having taken this skirt from someone's clothesline."

"Don't. I left a hundred-dollar bill clipped to the line. They'll be thrilled."

"Those baggy pants don't do much for you," she said, "but I've got to say that the way you're walking, in that halting style with the cane, you really do look like an old man."

"Which is why I keep telling you to imitate me. They won't look at our faces, believe me. Even if they do, that dark makeup will convince them. Just look down to the floor, and avoid catching anyone's eye. Two old Navajos just stopping by a church won't be noticed."

They entered through a side door, and she led the way down an empty hallway to her office. No one was usually around this wing of the building in the middle of a week-day. The staff all had day jobs. But, farther down the hall, they could hear a cleaning crew busy inside the chapel, polishing the floors.

"That's just the caretaker and his wife," she whispered. "They clean when no one's around."

Once they were inside her office, Hannah closed the door behind them. There was an open adjoining door to another, similar office, but no one was there and the light was out.

In Hannah's office were two swivel chairs, a multi-function fax and printer, two file cabinets and a supply cabinet. The desk surfaces were relatively clutter free, con-taining only a stapler and tape dispenser. She looked around for several minutes, then just shook her head, dis-couraged. "Nothing. I still can't remember a thing."

"Do what you normally do in here."

She sat down behind the computer. "You better make

sure no one comes in. It'll blow our charade if they see me at my desk."

"I'll listen and keep an eye out. In the meantime, I want you to check and see if there's anything different about the church accounts."

"You mean tampering, like embezzlement? The ones I handle have—at most—a few thousand dollars."

"Check anyway."

It didn't take her long. "Something's very strange. The missing two thousand dollars had to come from one of these accounts if they were part of the operating funds, but there's no indication that a withdrawal in that amount was ever made. Does the agency check the claims of a client? I mean maybe my uncle got things mixed up."

"We assume that no one is going to come to us and pay us the kind of fees we charge to investigate bogus claims. We're not the police department. We're a high-priced private investigations agency. Since Riverside Mission Church is footing the bill and it's their money that's missing, there's no reason to believe your uncle got the figures wrong."

"I just don't know where the cash could have come from then."

He gave her a quick look. "Can you print out what you've got on file?"

"I could, but it would take too long, and the printer makes the lights in the chapel dim for a second when it comes on. It could throw a breaker while the floor polisher is being used. The wiring is very old."

"What about copying to disk? Or e-mailing everything?"

"The files are too large for disks, e-mail would take too long, and I didn't bring a blank CD."

"Forget I asked then." He looked out into the hall as the hum of the floor polisher was drowned out by organ music.

"The organist must have arrived to practice. He'll play for an hour, then leave. It's his regular routine."

"Okay. Let's go to your uncle's office next. I want you to go through his computer records as well."

"My uncle would cut off his arm before he took one dime from this church. You don't know him."

Daniel bit back the response that came naturally—that it was possible she wasn't the only one with secrets. "Let's take a look anyway," he said, closing the door to the hall.

She led the way into the adjacent office. "Going through Uncle Bob's computer will take longer. I don't know his password or whether he encrypts his files."

"Are there accounts that only he handles?"

"No. The Church committees work alongside him. If you're thinking of misappropriated funds, I can tell you that it would be an extremely difficult thing to do. This is not a wealthy church. Every penny matters and has to be accounted for."

Seeing an architect's blueprint on the corner table along with an artist's conception of what the finished church addition would look like, Daniel went to study it. "This is quite an ambitious project."

"It's taken years and years to raise the funds to start construction, and we're still short of the full amount we'll need," Hannah said joining him. "But we're closer now than we've ever been."

Suddenly they heard someone turning the knob and opening the office door leading to the hall. Daniel grabbed Hannah and pressed her to the wall, then covered her mouth with his. Too stunned to resist, she melted against him. With their mouths locked together, he suddenly couldn't think. Her surrender made his body turn to fire, something he hadn't expected. He'd meant to confuse whoever was coming in, not add fuel to his insane desire to make her his.

His body became as hot as a furnace. He deepened the

kiss, greedily taking from her all the sweetness she had to offer him. For a moment he very nearly forgot where they were and why he'd kissed her in the first place.

"What's going on here?" a man's firm voice demanded.

Daniel didn't turn around. Trying to shut out the carnal demands spreading through him, he took a step back from Hannah, careful to block the man's view of her face with his body. "We're hoping to talk to the minister. We want to get married," he said in a creaky voice. "Are you Reverend Brown?"

"No, I'm the organist, but the reverend should be stopping by in about an hour. You're welcome to wait." He paused for a moment. "I know you're not exactly teenagers, but keep the door open, for propriety," he said, then chuckled. "I hope I have half your enthusiasm for life when I'm your age," he said, reaching onto a nearby shelf for a folder of sheet music.

The second the man left, Daniel eased his hold on Hannah. Her lips were moist and partly open, ready for another kiss. Moving away just then was one of the most difficult things he'd ever done.

He heard her sigh, a soft disappointed sound filled with a sweet longing he was man enough to recognize. Had she drawn her hands down the length of his naked body, she couldn't have affected him more.

"Let's get out of here while the going's good," he said, surprised his voice sounded so steady.

"Mr. Jackson, the organist, will wonder where we went," she said, her voice trembling slightly.

"Maybe he'll assume we just couldn't wait any longer," Daniel suggested, then realized how that could be taken two ways.

Fighting to keep his mind on business, he urged her toward the door with a gesture. Under different circumstances, he might have reached for her hand, but right now any contact between them was just too dangerous.

Chapter Five

Daniel kept Hannah next to him as they made their way outside, walking quickly, but not fast enough to attract attention. They'd almost reached the SUV when Hannah stopped in midstride and looked back toward the road.

Every muscle in his body suddenly tensed, ready for action. ''What's wrong?'' he asked, unable to see anything out of place.

''It's the mailbox,'' she said.

It was light blue, shaped like the church, a custom job probably done by a parishioner. But he could see nothing particularly troublesome about it.

''I mailed a package recently and used that box.''

''Do you know what was in the package?''

Her forehead furrowed as she struggled to remember. ''I just don't know. I can't remember.''

''Do you recall who you addressed it to?''

She paused, then shook her head. ''No.''

''When did you mail the package?''

''It had to have been the day before yesterday,'' she said slowly. ''I came out to the street from the church, put the package in the mailbox, and raised the red flag. I remember thinking it was the safest way.''

''To do what?''

She paused. "I don't know. But I know that it was important. I recall being afraid at the time."

"You're making headway. Stay with it."

Hannah stared at the mailbox. "It's like trying to fasten together bits and pieces of a broken videotape, hoping that you can see it again and nothing will be left out." She shook her head. "But it's no use. Whatever flash I was getting is gone."

"For now," Daniel finished for her. "You'll try again another time. Let's go."

Soon they were in the SUV that Daniel had parked a block away from the church. Hannah patted Wolf affectionately and he seemed to enjoy it. "You're just a big old puppy," she said to him.

Daniel expected Wolf to growl, scaring Hannah out of her wits, but the animal did absolutely nothing but groove on the affection. For a dog who was convinced he was part wolf, that was nothing short of a miracle.

"Don't fuss over him too much. He needs to keep his edge," Daniel warned.

She said nothing for a long moment, then shifted in her seat to face him more squarely. "And is that the way it is for you? Do you need to keep an edge?"

"In my job, you tend to live longer if you do."

"You seem to know quite a bit about me, but I know virtually nothing about you, Daniel Eagle. And it's hard to trust a stranger—at least it is for me. Will you tell me a bit about yourself?"

"What would you like to know?" He kept his voice cool, hoping to discourage any truly personal questions.

"How did you get into this business?"

He breathed easier. At least this was something he didn't mind Hannah asking. It was tantamount to wanting to look at the credentials of a bodyguard before entrusting him with your life. "I was a cop for eight years. When I left, I knew I wanted to continue doing something where I could use the skills I'd learned. Being a P.I. seemed the answer because I wouldn't have to follow all the rules cops do. Those usually end up giving the criminals a huge advantage."

"Is that why you stopped being a policeman? You thought the rules were unfair?"

"It was more than that. Sometimes you just know it's time to move on."

"Does that all have something to do with your not carrying a gun?"

Hannah was sharp. He should have known she'd get there. "Yes, but I don't want to get into that now."

"All right." She paused, then continued, taking her questions in a new direction. "You've chosen to get into this mess with me, and there's no telling how long it'll be before we can uncover the truth. Isn't there someone who'll worry about you? As far as I've seen, you've never contacted anyone but the man you call Silentman."

Daniel smiled. "Are you asking if I'm involved with someone, or married?"

"Are you?" she pressed.

"No to both questions. I've never been married, and I haven't been in a serious relationship in years. And that's the way I like it. I enjoy the freedom to come and go as I please."

"Then what you need is the kind of woman who'll give you plenty of personal space."

"In that case, I guess you could say that I've never found the right woman." He shrugged. "With my job, I'm constantly on the go, so the reason I don't have a steady girlfriend is perfectly understandable. But the same isn't true for you. You're a beautiful woman and, even if you've discouraged it, there should be a guy in your life, and a bunch more lined up hoping you'll get bored with the one you have."

"Thanks for the compliment—such as it was," she said, chuckling. "But the truth is I don't find it easy to get that close to people. The men I've met usually want things I can't give them. I don't want to lean on anyone and I *won't* be treated as if I'm defective or damaged because I was ill when I was growing up. All in all, I've found it's a lot easier for me to just keep my dates casual and infrequent."

Hannah sure didn't sound like someone whose elevator didn't reach the top floor. She understood who she was, which was more than a lot of sane people knew about themselves.

"People with troubled pasts like to keep a barrier around themselves. It makes them feel safer," he said, thinking out loud.

"Are you talking about me—or you?" Hannah asked.

"My past isn't troubled," he answered a little too quickly. One look at her told him she'd noticed. "There are things there that changed me forever, but I know what I want."

"And you think I don't?" she countered, suddenly annoyed.

"Do you?"

"Yeah," she snapped. "I want to stay alive. And I want to get to know you because you're my best hope of staying ahead of the people after me."

He said nothing for a long moment, then spoke. "Why are you angry?"

"Because I'm tired of dealing with people who think they know more about what's going on inside me than I do. I'll let you in on something. You can explain feelings six million ways, but what's hurtful will still hurt."

"Do you think that's why you're suppressing the memory of what happened at the church? Are you trying to avoid something that hurt you?"

She stared at him wide-eyed, and he suddenly felt like a heel. "Look, I'm no shrink, and I'm not trying out my own form of psychoanalytical babble on you. It was just a shot in the dark. But think about it, okay? We both know that triggering your memory could provide us with some answers we really need.'' He paused, then added, ''Come to think of it, there's something else we can try. How do you feel about hypnosis?''

She shook her head. ''I don't think I can be hypnotized. Several doctors at the hospital tried it, even with drugs, as part of my therapy.'' She shrugged. ''I think it's wrong to let someone manipulate your thinking that way, so I automatically shut myself off from it. I can't let my guard down enough to let it happen, not even now.''

He decided not to press the matter for now. Besides, from the little he knew, if she was prone to resist, it could harm instead of help her.

''I know you lost your parents when you were young. Was it difficult for you to move in with your uncle, or were you already close?'' he asked, changing the subject slightly.

''To be honest, I was a little afraid of Uncle Bob. My dad and he were always arguing and I didn't like him because of that.'' She took a deep breath and let it out slowly. ''And talk about someone who's hard to get close to. My mom and dad were warm people, but Uncle Bob is very different, and always was.''

''How so?'' Daniel was glad he had Hannah talking about herself.

''It's his whole outlook on life. I'll give you some examples. When I was a kid, I remember wanting to take ballet lessons, but he thought that was a waste of time because it wasn't likely to lead to a career. He said the same thing when I wanted to join the Girl Scouts. Uncle Bob always told me that one could either earn money or spend money, and it was better to occupy one's time doing something productive like earning it. So, as soon as I could, I worked part-time and used the money to pay my own way. I was able to buy most of my own clothes, and whatever else I needed.''

He didn't say anything, disapproving of the way she'd been raised, but admiring Hannah for her loyalty to her uncle. From what he'd seen of the deacon, he wasn't sure that loyalty was reciprocated.

Then again, that was just another element in a case where nothing fit. The woman seated in the SUV next to him didn't fit the profile of the deranged woman he'd been sent to find or the skilled manipulator he'd been worried about.

He'd want to question the deacon again soon. His gut told him that the allegations of theft made against Hannah were false and part of an elaborate frame. Following his training blindly without listening to his instincts had been wrong before—and on one occasion, years back, the situation had turned lethal because of it.

"My poor uncle must really be worried about me. I should call him, if only to assure him I'm fine."

"That's out of the question, Hannah," he said firmly. "Your uncle was authorized by his church to hire Gray Wolf Investigations, and I was given the job of bringing you in. If either of us alert him that you're okay, we'll have to explain what's going on, and we may end up inadvertently giving information to your enemies. I believe we're dealing with a conspiracy, and there are people out there determined to silence you. We'd be gambling with your life."

She seemed to be considering his words, but her thoughtful silence made him uneasy.

"I don't know about you, but I'm beat," he said at last. "Let's go back to the safe house. I'd like to get some shut-eye while I can. Wolf and I will take turns sleeping and guarding tonight like we did last night. But until I get used to that schedule, I'm going to take breaks whenever I can. I need to stay sharp."

"Okay. After you've had a chance to rest, we'll talk."

HANNAH SAT on the living room couch, leafing through a magazine on fishing. It was seven. Daniel was still asleep, and she was restless. Despite everything Daniel had said, she trusted her uncle and it just didn't seem right not to let him know that she was okay. Uncle Bob deserved her trust after taking her in when she'd had no one else to turn to but, for now, she'd respect Daniel's opinion. Still, there were other matters that needed to be handled, calls that had to be made.

She didn't have her appointment calendar, but knew she'd missed important meetings with four of her top clients. They had no way of knowing what was going on either, because the church and her uncle were keeping her disappearance a secret.

Hannah thought of how hard she'd worked to get her firm off the ground. Now, she was letting her clients down in a major way, and some of them depended on her totally. This mess would jeopardize everything she'd struggled to accomplish.

She really needed to talk to the people she was working for. Even if she couldn't tell them the truth, she could at least offer them a plausible explanation for her sudden absence.

Hannah stood, her mind made up. She was doing the right thing. Tiptoeing down the hall, she verified that Daniel was still asleep. She could go and return before he ever woke up. All she had to do was walk to the pay phone at the gas station near the highway at the turnoff. It wasn't much more than a quarter of a mile away and she could be back in a half hour.

Picking up the change that she'd seen on the kitchen counter and in a jelly jar in the cupboard, she headed toward the door. Suddenly Wolf was there, blocking the way.

"Wolf, Daniel's asleep. Guard him."

The dog continued to sit in front of her.

She sighed softly. Maybe she needed to try a different approach. "Want to go for a walk, Wolf?"

The animal wagged his tail once.

She opened the door and, as they walked out, the dog positioned himself on her left side, his shoulder in line with her waist. Twice, she nearly tripped over him.

"You do stick close, don't you?" she said, smiling ruefully down at him.

The dog never looked at her. His gaze was fastened on the area around them. The German shepherd-cross might have looked like someone's very large pet, but there was no mistaking it. The big dog was on guard duty.

Hannah walked quickly down the gravel lane. It was dark now and she wasn't worried about anyone seeing her, let alone recognizing her on this moonless night.

Fifteen minutes later, she reached the pay phone she'd seen earlier. Keeping her back to the building's lights, and her face in the shadows, she made her calls quickly. These were telephone numbers she knew by heart. Wolf sat beside her, warily watching every car that passed by or pulled into the station.

Before long, Hannah headed back. As she'd hoped, Daniel was still asleep when they returned to the house. All in all, she'd been gone only a little over forty minutes. And now she had the peace of mind of knowing that if she ever got out of this mess, she'd still have a business to return to and a way of making a living.

It wasn't long after she'd returned that she heard an alarm clock go off and Daniel emerged from the bedroom.

"You didn't sleep very long," Hannah commented. "It's only about eight."

"I seldom sleep much when I'm on the job. But I like to eat regularly and right now I'm really hungry. What do you say we go get a bucket of fried chicken or something like that for dinner? It'll have to be takeout, but I want something more than a can of beans or a burrito."

"That's fine with me."

Suddenly Wolf ran to the window. His ears were pricked forward as he sniffed the air coming in through the screen. He snarled, a deep, guttural sound that seemed to electrify Daniel.

"Grab your things. We're leaving right now."

Within three minutes they were climbing into the SUV. Wolf's low growl changed to a higher pitch, like someone issuing a warning.

"They're getting close. Hang on!" Daniel started the engine.

Suddenly she heard what sounded like a backfire in the distance. Although it hadn't been particularly loud, Hannah's entire body began to shake and her mouth went dry.

"That was a gunshot. We're out of here."

Hannah had just fastened her seat belt with a shaking hand when Daniel floored the vehicle. Before she could even draw in a breath, they were racing back toward the highway in total darkness.

Chapter Six

It wasn't until they were at least ten miles from the house, and he was certain that no one was on their tail, that Daniel finally slowed down to the speed limit. "How the hell did they find us? I just don't get it!"

Hannah said nothing, but sank into her seat. Wolf lay down in the back.

Daniel glanced at her, then at the dog in the rearview mirror. "You two know something about this, don't you?" he said, his voice ominously soft.

"Look, I'm sure I wasn't followed..."

"What?" The carefully enunciated one word question had been almost a whisper, but there was nothing insignificant about the anger or challenge behind it.

"I took a little walk while you were asleep," she mumbled.

"And the mutt let you go?" His voice rose only slightly, but it held an unmistakable edge.

"Well, no, he went with me. You hadn't taken him out, and it was obvious to me he needed a walk."

"Where exactly did you go? It couldn't have been just around the yard." He paused then added, "Tell me you didn't call your uncle."

"I didn't. But I did make a few calls at the gas station beside the highway."

His hand tightened around the wheel. "To whom?"

"My biggest clients. I had to tell them something, Daniel. They count on me, and I'd just disappeared without warning. One's about to be audited, too. I couldn't just leave him hanging like that."

"We'll figure out how they tracked us later. But, for now, I want your word that you'll never pull a stunt like that again," he said darkly. "No, on second thought, forget it. I've got a better idea. From now on when I go to sleep, you'll be handcuffed to me."

"Now see here—"

"Trouble follows closely whenever I trust you. It's happened twice now, and I have no intention of making it three out of three. We might not be as lucky next time."

"You're talking about when I tried to sneak out of the clinic? But that was entirely different. Don't you see? I wasn't trying to get away this time. I came back on my own."

"All I know, lady, is that from now on I'm not letting you out of my sight."

They rode in silence for another ten minutes and, to his surprise, Hannah didn't attempt to talk to him. Although his mood was decidedly dark, he was still hungry, so he stopped for fried chicken in Shiprock, then pulled into an infrequently traveled side road a few miles northwest of town. Wolf was drooling on the back of the seat by the time Daniel opened the first box of food.

"Wolf, sit!" he ordered. "You'll get your share in a minute."

"I thought dogs couldn't have chicken."

"They can have chicken, just not the bones, and admittedly, a dish full of that dog food in the back would be far better for him—"

Wolf growled.

"But I didn't think he'd take to logic very kindly. He loves this stuff. Besides, I don't want kibble all over the seats.'' Daniel stripped off the meat from two large chicken breasts, then placing it in an empty box along with the crunchy breading and a roll, he set it on the back seat in front of the animal. ''Here, mutt. You saved our skins. Enjoy.''

''On that basis, does that mean I don't get any dinner?'' she joked.

He looked at her consideringly. ''You have a point.''

''Now wait one second—''

''Never mind. You'll need to eat to stay fit. I don't want a fainting female on my hands.''

''You're acting like a macho pig.''

''I've been called worse,'' he said with a shrug. ''But for the record, I'm not cutting you any slack from this point on.''

Hannah closed her eyes, then opened them again. ''If my life gets any worse, I'm going to call hell and see about booking a vacation.''

He handed her one of the two remaining dinners and a plastic wrapped set of utensils. ''Here. Eat.''

''Something's taken away my appetite,'' she said sourly.

''It wasn't a request.'' He opened his own container of chicken, rolls and potato salad.

She didn't argue, mostly because she was hungry.

''Let's bring our thoughts back to business,'' he said after they'd been eating for a while. ''How many clients did you call?''

''Four.''

''Then that means it could be one of them. Either that, or someone bugged one or all of those phones. Or it's possible they had an accomplice in one of your clients' offices, and they just lifted the number and location from a caller ID.''

''It's also possible that someone saw the SUV at your friend's house. Or maybe they spotted me using the phone at the gas station, and followed Wolf and me back.''

"Not likely. What are the odds that they'd find us among hundreds of square miles by just driving around and checking cars and gas stations? I don't buy that. Now tell me about your clients. You said that one of them was being audited."

She nodded. "Norm Gless. He owns a big copy shop. But it's just a routine audit by the franchise owner, not a federal tax audit. And I really doubt he would have told anyone that I'd called him. He's a very private, close-mouthed man."

"What did you tell him?"

"The same thing I told the others. That I'd had a personal emergency and that I'd be back as soon as possible. In the meantime, just in case of a crisis, I gave them each a password they can use to get into my computer and access their account files by modem. Each account file has a different password, so I wasn't worried about confidentiality. I'm the only one with a password that gives me access to anything in the hard drive. But I cautioned them against downloading anything directly, because I've been having some problems with my computer. And if the problem is a software bug, it could act like a virus and mess up their system."

"Anything else?"

"I recommended a bookkeeping firm in town that could take over for me if they needed an accountant right away." Hannah paused, then added, "And that last part hurt. I've worked too hard to just hand over my business to another company."

"I'm really glad you didn't try to call your uncle," he said. "He's one of the people who hired me to find you and once he finds out that I have, he'll demand I bring you in. The problem is that I can't give him any explanations without putting him in danger—not until I know what's going on."

"I told you I wouldn't call my uncle, so I didn't, but it

was really tempting. You see, he's got a direct stake in what's happening. If there's money missing and people believe I took it, he's being victimized as much as I am. Sooner or later people will start wondering if he knew what I was up to. And even if he manages to convince everyone that he didn't, it won't help him for long. They'll soon start blaming him for not knowing."

"Judging from the construction plans in his office, your uncle is a man of some importance. He's in charge of the building fund, right?"

"Yes, along with the finance committee," she reminded him.

"But the records are in *his* computer?"

She nodded. "He does the bookkeeping for that."

"So he *would* be in a position to doctor the books."

"I've already told you, he wouldn't do that."

"What if his back was to the wall? Do you know what his financial situation is?"

This time she didn't answer right away, using the plastic forklike spoon to scoop out a mouthful of coleslaw. Then she took a bite of potato salad.

"I've struck a nerve, haven't I?" Daniel observed. "Is he in financial trouble right now?"

"I think so, but I don't know for sure," she replied hesitantly. "You see, I found out in such a roundabout way..."

"Talk to me. I need to know everything."

She nodded slowly. "It'll stay confidential?"

"As long as it doesn't have anything to do with what's happening to you," Daniel asserted.

Hannah took another bite of potato salad, then at last nodded. "It started about a month ago. I was having horrendous problems with my computer. I'd update a client's cash receipts journal, for example, and everything would look fine on the screen. But when I printed out the work, entries would appear out of nowhere, and nothing would balance. The entire printout would be riddled with incomplete and inaccurate entries I knew I hadn't typed in. It was making me crazy. I tried everything, including consulting computer experts, but no one could figure out what was going on. My reputation started to suffer, as you can imagine, because I was missing deadlines. I was working impossibly long hours, but I was still way behind. Since I donate my services to the church, I gave priority to my paying clients, and the church's accounts fell behind. When my uncle found out, he had a fit."

"Exactly what happened between you two?"

"He suggested I close my firm, farm out my clients and get a job working for an established company. He said that someone with a history of emotional problems should have never taken on something as stressful as starting up their own business."

Hannah stopped and took a deep breath. "That made me very angry. It was a really cheap shot, as far as I was concerned, and I said so. Our argument escalated into a terrible fight. Of course he used that against me, too, and said that my emotional outburst proved what he was saying—that I couldn't handle things."

"Looking back, do you think he may have been right?"

She didn't look directly at him, but Wolf, sensing her frustration, poked his nose between them and rested his chin on the side of her cushion. She stroked him absently. "I was upset, and I shouldn't have lost my temper with him, he was right about that. But everyone gets angry. The only difference is that whenever I get angry, he never stops to think that maybe I had a good reason for it. To him, it's always proof that I'm too emotional and a bit unstable."

"What happens when you get angry?" he asked offhandedly. "Do you throw things, or kick the wall, or something like that?"

The question had been phrased casually, but when he

saw the wariness that suddenly filled her eyes, he knew he wasn't fooling her at all.

"I'm not prone to violence. I've never struck anyone in my life—though believe me, I've been tempted." Hannah scowled, looking him straight in the eyes.

He didn't smile. "That doesn't answer my question."

"When I'm angry, I tend to yell, and that's about it. Not exactly earth-shattering, is it?"

He shrugged. "Not really. So how does the argument you two had tie in to what you found out about his finances?"

"While we were arguing, I noticed an overdraft form sitting on his desk. It was from his personal account. He saw me looking at it, so he stuck it in his pocket. I suggested that maybe he was in no position to judge my ability to run a business since he was obviously having trouble managing his own money. He stormed out, and didn't speak to me for nearly a week."

"About this church building account he handles... Any idea how much money is in there?"

"These days I think it's a little over one hundred thousand dollars. An elderly parishioner passed away recently and left the church some property which we, in turn, sold. That amount came to nearly eighty-five thousand, and I believe we had close to twenty thousand before that."

Daniel put his empty food containers into a paper sack, set it on the floorboards beside Hannah's feet, then switched on the ignition. "Now *that's* the kind of money someone might want to steal and be willing to kill for. I'm beginning to wonder if the church people might have lied to the agency about which fund is missing."

"No one could possibly believe that I'd steal *that* much money. I live a very simple life, and I like it that way. And, besides, I don't have access to that account. That's in the hands of the finance committee and the records are in my uncle's computer."

"But church money *is* missing, you do a lot of work with computers, and you did go on the run," Daniel pointed out. "That's bound to mislead a lot of people."

"Including you?"

"I know only one side of you, and neither one of us has a clue about what happened during those hours you can't recall."

"Then why are you still helping me, Daniel?"

"Because I know that you've got people after you and the thought of that just ticks me off. I want to equalize the odds a bit and give you a chance to find out the truth." He paused, then continued. "Let's assume that it's the building fund that's missing. That means that one of the church people is a thief and the rest of the people looking for the money don't want to let on how much is actually missing for some reason. The thief, I assume, is behind the frame, since having people focused on you buys him time. What we have to do is start getting evidence that will point away from you. Who else knows about that account and has access to it?"

"As I said, the finance committee, which is comprised of the church secretary, Reverend Brown, my uncle and the organist you met at the church. He's actually the head of the committee. And, of course, the bank. But there's something you're not taking into consideration. Those people aren't personal friends, and they're always arguing among themselves. I find it hard to believe that not even one of them reported the missing money to the police."

"It's possible that the extent of the theft was covered up with some creative bookkeeping, or maybe they've decided not to panic everyone by admitting such a large amount is missing," he suggested. "Of course, they may also firmly believe that you have it, or know where it is, and realize that if they call the police and they locate you, you'd be charged with grand larceny based on the evidence. Everything would become public then and that would mean a lot of people would be called to task for not keeping better tabs on that money.''

''It still doesn't sound right, not based on what I know about those people,'' Hannah said, shaking her head.

As they headed down the highway, she looked around, trying to get her bearings in the darkness. ''Now that we can't go back to your friend's home, what are your plans?''

''I'm going to call Silentman and see what he can come up with. It'll save us having to check into a motel that takes wild animals.'' He took a look at Wolf, who had his eyes closed in bliss while Hannah scratched him gently between the ears.

Daniel drove off the highway again onto a dirt road, then pulled over behind a tree and shut off the engine and lights. Flipping open his cell phone, he gestured to the glove compartment. ''Get the map in there,'' he requested.

''This is Lightning,'' he said as Silentman answered. He briefed him quickly on what had happened. ''We need a new safe house, preferably in the area.''

Daniel turned on the dome light and took some notes in a small notebook as he received directions. ''Good thing I have the global positioning device in case I get lost. That sounds like it's going to be hard to find,'' he said at last.

''That's why we keep it as a safe house,'' Silentman answered.

After finding the general area on the map, Daniel headed west. He drove past a bridge built over an arroyo, and turned down a dirt track leading into a canyon. They followed that route until it opened up into a much wider valley. Then, in an unexpected clearing among the stunted junipers and sagebrush, they spotted a small wood frame house. The outside was stuccoed in the scratch coat only, and was gray, with places where the chicken wire showed through. The wood trim around the door and windows was unpainted and weathered, but still intact.

''This must be it,'' he said. ''Silentman said that it

hasn't been used for quite some time, so let Wolf and me check it out first to make sure squatters haven't moved in, or wild animals.'' He grabbed the car keys, then reached into his pocket and brought out a pair of handcuffs. Before she could say a word, he slipped the cuff on her left wrist and locked the other around the steering wheel.

''Just what do you think you're doing?'' she demanded angrily.

''Putting a new habit into place. When I can't be with you, I'm going to make sure you can't wander off. It's my job to keep you safe and this is the best way I can think of doing it. We won't be far.''

''Where is there to wander off? We haven't seen a building or even lights from a house for miles.''

He hesitated then shook his head. ''You were willing to hike before, so this is the only way I can guarantee you'll stay put. I could leave Wolf here, but I need the dog with me. He can sense trouble long before I can.''

Sparks of anger flashed in her eyes and there was a flush in her cheeks. He'd never seen her look more beautiful. For one insane minute, he had to fight the urge to kiss her.

Biting back a curse, Daniel let Wolf out, grabbed a flashlight from behind the back seat, and then handed her a small wool blanket. ''Here. Stay warm. This won't take long.''

Chapter Seven

Time ticked by slowly, and she quickly lost track of the flashlight beam. Both man and dog were apparently inside the house now.

Alone, she tried to make sense out of her attraction to Daniel. The truth was she wasn't sure what was worse—the times when he was her ally, or when he acted as if she were nothing more than an inconvenient part of a job he'd been hired to do. Yet, even now when they were at odds, she couldn't forget the hard feel of his chest or the fire that blazed in his eyes. It called to her—a primitive challenge from man to woman.

All things considered, however, she had a feeling that Daniel was far more dangerous to her during the times when they were getting along. When he'd held and kissed her, it had been as if the entire world had slowly spiraled away. The connection between them had been the only thing that had mattered to her. Although she'd received more than her share of attention from men over the years, she'd never felt anything as powerful as the passionate longings that Daniel brought out in her.

Her eyes filled with tears as she remembered a conversation she'd had with her mother many years ago. Seeing the deep love her mother and father had shared, Hannah had asked her mother if she'd find a relationship like theirs when she grew up. Her mother had smiled and told her that it was said that the women in their family loved only once. She'd warned Hannah to choose carefully and take her time when she finally started dating, because she'd either find heaven or hell the day she fell in love.

Hannah looked at Daniel as he came out of the house holding a lantern. She was attracted to him. Who wouldn't be? He was a fantasy come to life—a man who lived by his own code of honor and rules, tough enough to back up his words. Everything about him excited her. But love? No, surely not. That just wasn't in the cards for her.

Daniel set the lantern down on a rock, then he and Wolf walked around the house, using the flashlight to check the nearby grounds. As they looked around, Hannah considered the situation. Her attraction to him was definitely dangerous and she had to fight it. She decided to focus on the things he did that made her crazy, starting with what was happening between them right now.

She glared at the handcuffs, remembering the last time she'd been trapped this way in a car. Daniel was not her enemy, not like the other man, but he was still an overbearing, arrogant man who was treating her like a common criminal. She'd keep her thoughts centered on that. It was the only safe course.

BY THE TIME Daniel returned to the SUV, Hannah appeared calmer than she'd been when he'd left, but there was a spark in her eyes that told him she was still furious. The blanket was on the seat cushion, unused despite the fact that it was cold. "You certainly took your time coming back," she said.

Her tone was taut, revealing a lot about what was on her mind. He tried to suppress a smile. This was one woman who could never quite hide her emotions, and he liked that about her.

Of course that was precisely why he had to keep his

distance. He liked a lot of things about Hannah, and experience told him that she'd carve out a permanent place for herself in his heart if he didn't watch his step. Her smile, and the feel of her had already been branded in his mind. No matter what the future held, he'd never forget her. Hannah challenged him on every level, but no man would ever win her. Hers was a fire that couldn't be conquered, only surrendered, and that made it all the more precious.

He was getting sidetracked again. The woman was making him crazy. "Let's go. It's all clear." He unlocked the cuffs, grabbed the blanket and guided her inside.

The rustic house consisted of only four rooms, if you counted the tiny bathroom. There was well water pumped by hand, and a large kettle for heating water on the wood and coal stove, but no electricity or telephone. Daniel placed the kerosene lantern in the kitchen and knelt down to light a fire in the fireplace. As he worked, Wolf lay down on a frayed, old rug beside the door, and Hannah took a seat by the small table.

After he finished, Daniel sat across the table from her, but she avoided eye contact and said nothing to him for the next hour. Instead, she stared at the flames as if lost in thought.

"You're too quiet," he said, breaking the silence at last. "Are you still ticked off at me?"

"Yes, but I wasn't thinking about *you*."

"Ouch. So tell me what's occupying your mind? What's my competition?" he teased.

Wolf got up, looked at Daniel, yawned and walked over to her. That made her laugh. "Yes, Wolf, I do like you much better than your companion." She glanced at Daniel. "If you really must know, I was thinking that tonight most of the church members and the board are having dinner at Mrs. Sanchez's. She hosts an annual party for all of us and serves these little empanadas that are just wonderful. Mrs.

Sanchez is really a remarkable person, and I'm always amazed by how well she handles everything. She's completely blind.''

Daniel stared at her, a slow smile spreading across his features. ''You've just given me a great idea.''

''Excuse me?''

''I've been wanting another crack at your uncle's computer, and I think I've found a way to do it.'' He looked at Wolf. ''And you're going to earn your keep again on this one, mutt.''

''You want to go back there with Wolf tonight because of the dinner? It's only nine and the party does go on till late, but just because everyone's been invited, I can't guarantee that no one will be at the church. The doors do stay open until late.''

''If someone is, I'll say that I came to speak with Reverend Brown. No one will be threatened by a blind man and his faithful service dog,'' he said. ''But we both can't go in. If we run into Pablo Jackson again, his seeing a man and a woman together again in uncertain circumstances may raise questions in his mind.''

''Agreed, but I've got to tell you that you may be a good enough actor to pass as a blind man, but no way Wolf's going to pass for a guide dog. He's the size of a small pony, with teeth a mile long.''

''He can act, too.''

The dog barked once as if in assent.

Hannah shook her head. ''You're both crazy. And where will I be while you two are doing all this?''

''In the SUV, parked far enough away from any streetlight so your face will stay in the shadows. You'll be our lookout. And if anyone asks me, I'll say my neighbor, you, gave me a ride. Someone had to drive the blind man over. But we'll have to give you a disguise just in case someone happens to walk by the SUV and sees you.''

''More talcum powder?'' she groaned.

"No, but we are going to concentrate on your face and hair." He looked at her through narrowed eyes. "Would you like to be a redhead or a blonde?"

She cringed. "You want me to dye my hair?"

"No. There should be a variety of wigs inside the upper shelf of the bedroom closet since this is an agency safe house," he explained. "I figure going blond or red is a far enough stretch that no one will recognize you with just a casual glance." He led the way into the bedroom, opened the closet door, and gestured inside. "Take your pick."

She looked the various women's wigs over critically and in silence. Daniel could tell Hannah hated the plan. To her, no one associated with the church could possibly be guilty, least of all her uncle, but facts were facts. And he had a hunch there was something to be found there, if he looked long enough.

"Do you know anything about computers?" she asked as she tried on a chin-length redheaded wig styled in a pageboy with long bangs.

"Some. I'm no hacker, but I can get by."

"What if my uncle's files are encrypted?"

"I'll take it one step at a time," he said with a shrug. "It's worth a shot."

The wig gave her a brand-new look, but even though red wasn't her color, she was still a beauty. He felt a stab of desire but, with a great deal of effort, pushed it back.

"And if someone walks in?" she asked, her hazel eyes contrasting against the garish red of the wig.

"The door will be locked, and Wolf will stand guard. He can give me advance notice. His hearing is really spectacular."

"I've seen." She worked with the wig, brushing it until she was satisfied, then turned around and smiled. "Well, what do you think?"

She was a knockout. Her smile was filled with innocence, and that just made her sensuality all the more powerful. All the muscles in his chest tightened, but he forced his voice to remain neutral. "It'll do. Let me call Silentman now. He'll get me everything else I need."

AN HOUR LATER they were on their way to the church. Hannah rode in silence. No matter how hard she tried, she couldn't quite rid herself of the feeling that disaster was about to strike. She could sense danger with every nerve in her body, but she couldn't think of a logical reason to stop him from carrying out his plan.

"Do you believe in gut feelings?" she asked.

"In my work I take intuition seriously."

"Then don't go in there tonight."

"Sorry. My gut disagrees. Right now it's telling me to go through with this. There are answers hidden in that church somewhere, and I intend to find them."

Her hands began to tremble. Maybe her memory loss was linked to something related to those accounts. "I wish I could remember what happened to me during those few hours. If I could, then I could at least prove my own innocence."

"How can you be so sure?"

"Because I know myself. I'm not guilty of anything, let alone theft. Whatever happened during those hours I can't remember must have really come as a shock to me if I'm reacting like this."

"Maybe your mind can't accept the reality of what happened. Call it a defense mechanism. You may have been forced to do something you can't conceive of doing willingly, and that's why you've suppressed it."

"I'd argue with you—to maintain a good habit if nothing else—but I just don't know." Hannah sighed.

What she did know was that she was suddenly very frightened of the truth, and that wasn't like her at all.

DANIEL WALKED IN through the open front doors. As Hannah had predicted, they were still unlocked and, according to the sign, would remain that way until eleven at night. He looked around the foyer, holding Wolf's harness, a prop Silentman had managed to locate for him and leave at a drop site. A radio mike the size of a shirt button was attached to his collar, and his dark glasses contained a receiver near his ear. "I'm in," he told Hannah. "Let me know if anyone pulls up outside."

"Care to renegotiate your stand on the handcuffs?"

"I should remind you that you have a lot more to lose if I get caught," he said.

"Point taken," Hannah said crisply. "I'll keep watch."

The dog, trained to stay by his side, was reluctant to walk ahead unless tracking someone. "Wolf, forward." The dog took a few steps, then stopped and sat.

"Listen to me, buddy, I know what this is about," he said quietly, crouching down next to him. "I heard you growl when I handcuffed Hannah. You didn't like that one bit. If this is your way of getting even, you're wasting your time. She's staying handcuffed when I'm not around. So knock it off."

The animal yawned, then continued to sit.

Daniel muttered a curse. That was the problem with Wolf's training. The animal had been taught to supersede a command when he sensed it was necessary. It was meant for the protection of the operative, but Wolf sometimes stretched those parameters.

"Okay. I'll tell you what. Shape up now, and you get to sleep on the bed."

The animal didn't move.

"Hey, mutt, what is it with you? You want the bed all to yourself?"

Wolf looked up at him.

"Yeah, right, and I sleep on the floor."

The animal got up, shook and moved forward.

Daniel said nothing, but if the fleabag believed he'd get

the bed while the human slept on the floor, he had another think coming.

Daniel focused on his surroundings, listening for any signs that would indicate he wasn't alone. The hall and adjoining rooms were silent.

Stopping by the door to Hannah's office, he decided to take another look at her computer files himself. He was alone—at least for now—and there was no telling how long it would be before he had an opportunity like this again.

This time the office door was locked, but the lock was easy to pick and seconds later he was inside. "Watch the door," he ordered Wolf.

Daniel deliberately kept the door open a crack so the dog could hear and see out into the hall and alert him before anyone got close.

As Wolf stood guard, he sat at Hannah's desk, and switched on the computer, but the operating system failed to load. When he tried to list the files on the hard drive, all he got was an error message. He repeated the command, but still got nothing. Daniel realized that all her files had been wiped, including her accounting program.

He sat back, surprised. Someone had come in and done this since the last time they'd been here. Unless Hannah herself had deleted them, of course. The thought made him pause. Maybe he should have been watching her more closely all along.

Playing a hunch, he searched her desk from top to bottom. Maybe there was a backup disk around. Finding nothing, he pulled out the drawer and ducked down, looking beneath it. People hid things in the most obvious places sometimes.

Seeing a scrap of paper with faded writing taped there, he removed it carefully. The paper contained two words—"mission" and "drought."

He knew what they were—passwords, but to what? He

tried both words on her computer, but got nowhere. Every file on the hard drive seemed to be gone, including the operating system.

Daniel put everything back the way he'd found it, except for the note that had the passwords written on it, then went to the office door. Wolf hadn't moved.

"Let's go, buddy."

He led Wolf through the adjoining door into the deacon's office, closing the doors behind them. From what he could see, nothing had been moved since the last time they'd been there.

Wolf was placed on guard duty at the outside door, again with it slightly ajar while Daniel sat down by the deacon's computer and switched it on. As he stared at the slip of paper that had been taped to her desk, he remembered Hannah telling him that she didn't have her uncle's password. Following his gut instinct, he typed the first word, "mission." Nothing happened. He then tried the second option, "drought."

The screen flickered and a list of files appeared on the screen. Taking the disk he'd brought from his pocket, he copied a few of the smaller files onto it.

"There's a car coming down the street," Hannah warned through the speaker in a wing of his glasses.

"Just finished," he said.

He slipped the disk back into his shirt pocket, turned off the computer, then left the room with Wolf and walked outside and across the parking lot quickly.

Anger filled him with a blackness of spirit as he forced himself to accept the fact that Hannah had lied to him, perhaps not for the first time. It was clear that she'd had her uncle's password all along. The worn paper and the yellow tape indicated it had been there for a long time. Although he was willing to concede that it was possible someone had blanked out the memory in her computer in order to frame her, that still didn't explain the lie. Now other questions plagued his mind.

Never realizing when or how, he'd lost his objectivity when it came to Hannah. He'd wanted to help her. She'd looked lost and broken somehow—an innocent caught in something she didn't understand.

Feeling like a fool for having lowered his guard like he had, he hurried back to the SUV. Things between them were about to change radically.

Chapter Eight

As Daniel slipped back into the SUV, Hannah noted the change in his expression. She'd expected to see satisfaction or frustration on his face, but the anger that was clearly mirrored there took her by surprise. His black eyes held a spark of barely contained rage. Instinct warned her to let him speak first.

Even Wolf seemed affected by whatever had happened in there. The dog gave her a long, soulful look, then lay down silently in the back, his head between his paws. She could have sworn he was trying to avoid looking at her, though she knew that was clearly her own imagination. Dogs didn't think—did they?

"It's too bad that you don't know your uncle's password. A little piece of information like that could have made my job easier from the start," Daniel said, his voice too hard to pass as normal.

"I never work at my uncle's computer," she said. "Where are we going?"

"Back to the safe house. It's getting late. But, first, as soon as we're a little farther from the church, I'm going to pull over and check in with Silentman."

His words were gruff and spoken without much inflection. Something was terribly wrong.

It was dark outside and only the headlights seemed to

cut through the black gloom that surrounded the SUV. As she waited for him to tell her what had happened, the passing minutes ticked by so slowly, they each made their own version of eternity. Uneasy, she broke the silence.

"Okay, let's have it. What happened in there?" she asked, at last.

"I went to your office first and took a look around." He reached into his shirt pocket. "I found this."

As she took the scrap of paper from him, their hands touched. It was chemistry—or magic—she wasn't sure which. But the warmth of his hand burned into her, wrapping itself around her until she could barely think. When she looked at him, she saw the answering flicker in the darkness of his eyes that told her he'd felt it too.

She looked away and forced herself to focus on business. Hannah read what was on the paper, and drew in a breath, recognition and understanding slowly dawning over her. "I totally forgot about this," she said, her stomach sinking.

There was an odd twist to his smile. "Oh, come on! I'm sure you can think of something better."

His eyes were all coldness and shadows. Sadness filled her as she realized what had been troubling him. Like many others in her life, Daniel was quick to condemn her. "You found this and now you think I've been lying to you all along," she said.

His gaze was unwavering. Though she was sure he'd meant it to be icy and unfeeling, she could feel the hurt that lay just beyond his hooded eyes and it tore at her heart.

He pulled off the road and parked beneath the glow of a street lamp just outside a filling station. "I'm going to call Silentman."

"Wait. Before you do, we need to get this settled. I haven't lied to you," she said softly. "I truly had forgotten this was there." She held the paper out in the palm of her hand. "Look at it. Don't you see how faded the writing is? And look at the traces of yellowed tape around the edges. That tells you that it has been there for a long time. That piece of paper has been stuck there for years and that's the reason I'd totally forgotten about it."

"How long would you say you've had these passwords?" he asked.

A trick question? She wasn't sure, but she desperately needed him to be on her side. As she looked him straight in the eyes, she realized that she wanted him to believe her—but the reason for that went beyond the demands of the case. His opinion of her mattered to her on a much deeper and disturbing level.

"I can't say exactly," she said slowly, "but I think it's been about two years. I remember that my uncle gave me his password right before he went away on a business trip. He wanted me to have access to the reports he'd made out for the finance committee. I wrote it down in the same place I kept the password I used to access the church's monthly accounts payable. But, honestly, I'm not sure how valid my uncle's password is now. For all I know he's changed it several times since then."

"He hasn't." Daniel watched her, questions alive in his eyes.

Hannah knew he was still trying to make up his mind about her. "I don't know how else to reassure you that I haven't lied and I'm not guilty of anything." Soon, if he hadn't already done so, he would remember and misconstrue her earlier reluctance to have him go inside alone to search. She cursed herself silently. It was not only that the evidence was stacked against her, her own mistakes were now helping her enemies.

More frightened than ever, and struggling to make him understand, Hannah continued. "I take pride in my work, just like you do in yours. If just making money had been my priority, I would have tried to get a job with a large corporation or moved out of state where I would have had more opportunities because no one would have known about my past.''

Daniel nodded slowly. ''That makes sense. But you realize that if I was able to find the passwords so easily, anyone else could have, too.''

''But who else would have looked?'' she responded. ''Daniel, I trust the people who work there. They're my friends and in a lot of ways they're as much a part of my family as my uncle.''

''You're too quick to dismiss them as suspects. Look at things squarely and consider the possibilities. For example, if one of them searched your office and found your password, it could easily explain the computer problems you've been having. Someone with access to your office at the church could have messed with your computer at home via modem. With your password, they could have done almost anything to your records. Do you leave your home office computer on all the time?''

''Yes, but no one at the church would do that to me. Only a person intent on destroying me would do something that nasty, and the truth is, I don't have any enemies.''

''You *do* have enemies, Hannah. Remember the pair who came after you? And what about whoever it was that sent them?''

''You're right.'' Despair and sadness settled over her like an oppressive mantle. She couldn't hide from this. She did have an enemy—one who would apparently stop at nothing to destroy her. They didn't get any worse than that. ''My life is unraveling, and I don't know how to stop it,'' she said, her voice a mere whisper.

''Fight with everything in you. That's your only choice.''

''I don't know how to win this kind of battle.'' Bewilderment and sorrow made a tremor race up her spine. ''These people want me in jail, or dead.''

''Which is why you can't afford to give anyone, no

matter who they are, the benefit of the doubt. Everything is at stake and your enemy could be the person you least expect.''

He was right, but it wouldn't be easy for her to start looking for the worst in her friends—to expect it, in fact. But as he'd pointed out, she had no other choice. She was fighting for her own survival now.

''I have more bad news, Hannah. Someone erased the hard drive in your computer. Not even the operating system remains.''

She pursed her lips for a long moment. ''Finally something I'm prepared for. It's a nuisance, but I can deal with it. I have tape backups that I make after each work session. They're in a safe in my home. I can retrieve everything, though it'll take some time.''

''Who do *you* think did that to your computer?''

There was something in his voice that made Wolf sit up in the back seat and look at her as if he, too, were expecting an answer.

Hannah knew without a doubt that Daniel was wondering if she'd done that somehow, probably when they were in there together. ''It wasn't me. It would have been pointless, and too much of a risk with you there next to me. Besides, I have those backups I just told you about, and they're all dated. They'll bear me out.''

''Unfortunately, we can't go there right now. Your home is probably being watched by whoever's looking for you.''

''Then we'll have to wait until we can,'' she said.

''Is the safe in your home easily accessible? In other words, if the ones after you break in, are they bound to spot it? And who else knows it's there?''

''No one except you and me. It's built into a wall in the laundry room and not very visible because there are shelves in front of it filled with laundry supplies.''

''I'd sure love to know what happened to your computer

at the church. No way that was an accident,'' he said thoughtfully.

''Before you jump to conclusions, I should tell you that it's happened before. One of the organist's teenage sons sneaked into my office last year while I was talking to Reverend Brown. He was showing off to a friend, and ended up reformatting the hard drive by accident which, of course, erased everything. That's when I learned to make backups.''

With the matter settled, at least for now, Daniel dialed Silentman's number but when he got voice mail, hung up. ''I'll call again in a minute. I hate electronic voice mail. I prefer to speak to something with a pulse.''

As they waited, she considered what he'd said. ''I guess you also checked my uncle's computer while you were there,'' she said hesitantly. ''Was his hard drive erased, too?''

''No, and that's the reason I'm trying to reach Silentman. I copied a few small files from the directory your uncle kept on the church's building fund. I want Burke to have an accountant check them out for discrepancies and the like.''

Daniel dialed again. This time he got through. As usual, his conversation with Silentman was quick and to the point, taking only a few minutes.

Daniel closed up the cell phone. ''We'll leave this disk in a storage compartment the agency uses as a secure drop. But, after that, we'll have to wait for it to be processed. I was hoping to take you straight to the safe house next and call it a night, but we have to make one more stop. Silentman says Reverend Brown wants to speak to me, and tonight would be a good time for him because the reverend will be up until late.''

''What's he want to see you about?''

''You, mostly. He's concerned and wants to do whatever he can to help. With a little luck and some careful questioning, I may be able to get some answers he doesn't even know he has. It often works that way in my line of work."

Daniel stopped at the drop site, a storage facility close to an apartment complex, on the way to Reverend Brown's. It was nearly eleven by the time they arrived at the pastor's home. Daniel parked down the block, then got ready to use the same mike and receiver setup he'd used before.

"I want you to listen in carefully," he said. "You know all the people at the church and you may be able to catch an inconsistency or an outright lie, if he goes that route."

"Reverend Brown would never do that," she said flatly.

"You'd be surprised how far people go when they're protecting something they care about."

Hannah started to argue, but decided against it. The only thing they needed to concentrate on now was finding whoever was framing her.

Daniel reached up and moved the switch on the dome light so the interior wouldn't be illuminated when he opened the door. "It's dark and that will shield you from any busybodies, but Wolf will stay with you in case of problems." He stopped, glancing at the handcuffs on the seat beside him. "There's a lot of danger in surveillance work, Hannah. I'm not going to cuff you any more. Sooner or later I'm going to have to trust you and it might as well be now. If someone recognizes you, take off. I'll leave the keys in the ignition. If you're not being followed, go to the safe house and I'll meet you there. Otherwise go to Gray Wolf Investigations. Mr. Silentman will take care of you." He gave her directions.

Daniel left the SUV and walked to the reverend's home. He was glad to have dispensed with the handcuffs. The simple fact was that it hurt his pride to resort to them. Women generally liked him, and gaining people's trust had never been a problem for him. But nothing seemed to work the way he was used to around Hannah.

To make matters worse, Hannah had managed to get him to shred a hard-and-fast rule he'd made for himself a long time ago—when working a case, never make it personal. He expelled his breath in a rush. That was a great rule, and one that was all shot to hell now.

THE PASTOR WAS a small-boned man with a longish face and a salt-and-pepper beard that had been trimmed close. His brown eyes peered across at Daniel from behind wire-rimmed glasses. He looked like he belonged in a library guarding one-of-a-kind books and rare editions.

As they took a seat in Reverend Brown's small home office, Daniel declined his offer of tea.

"I understand that you wanted to see me," Daniel began.

"We've all been very worried about Hannah. That young woman has had a very difficult life. I want to do something to help her before things get worse for her. To be honest, people have been talking a lot about her lately and that always leads to trouble."

"What have you heard?" Daniel asked, glancing around casually and noting the pastor didn't seem to have a computer.

"People have begun to notice that she hasn't been around. So far, her uncle has told everyone who's asked that she's fine, and that she's just taking a much-needed break, but that's being regarded with skepticism, I'm afraid. Gossip is starting up and that's bound to hurt everyone."

"What kind of gossip are we talking about here?"

"We have good people at our church, but they're human. When they think I'm not listening, they speak their minds about Hannah. The simple truth is that her behavior these past few weeks has been erratic, to say the least, and everyone has noticed. It seems she's been very distracted, and continually making mistakes with her clients' accounts. Most of her business comes from the members of our church, and several of them are getting pretty fed up with her service. I'm afraid that if news leaks out about our missing funds, the membership will demand that we go to the police."

"Do you believe that her erratic behavior may have contributed to her taking the funds?"

"Yes, I do, but frankly I'm more worried about what might happen to her than I am about the money. Living in our community among people who know and love her, Hannah's been protected in a way, but I'm not at all sure what will happen to her if she's on the run and ends up someplace where she has no one to help her. I've known Hannah for many years, and I don't want to see anything bad happen to her."

"Is there any chance you've misjudged her? Maybe she's missing or hiding out for another reason entirely."

The pastor hesitated. "There's nothing I'd want to believe more than that, but based on her history and her recent actions, I can't see what other conclusion I can reach."

Daniel stood up. "I'll stay in touch. Meanwhile, if you hear of anything that might help me on this case, call the agency office. They'll know how to get in touch with me."

Hearing a door open and shut, Reverend Brown smiled. "That's my daughter now. Would you like to speak to her? She's a little younger than Hannah, but they've known each other for many years. She may be able to give you another perspective on her."

Daniel nodded, aware that Hannah had already been convicted in the court of popular opinion, but unwilling to pass up a chance to question someone else who might know something useful. "That sounds like a good idea. Thanks for your cooperation."

HANNAH LISTENED to the exchange with a heavy heart. Everyone was convinced she was guilty of something. Although she understood that they were simply going on the circumstantial evidence and that the board was really trying to give her a break by not going to the police, it still hurt to think that they'd condemned her so quickly.

Trying to make herself understand, she looked at the facts dispassionately. The truth was that she *had* been having software problems that had turned her bookkeeping into one major disaster. The stress had been monumental.

On top of it all, these were people who knew all about her background, and although her days at the hospital seemed like a lifetime ago to her, they'd never quite forgotten it. They'd been willing to give her a chance to earn her living managing some accounts, a task she'd been proficient at, but their trust had been fragile and was now completely shattered.

A past was a difficult thing to outrun. Maybe that was why Daniel, a man who only knew the woman she was now, was willing to give her a chance. When Daniel looked at her, there was no pity in his eyes. He didn't see the frightened, mixed-up girl she'd been. He only saw a woman fighting for her life—a woman who needed him desperately to even out the odds against her.

She took a deep breath, and the scent of him filled her nostrils. That mixture of pine and the outdoors was earthy and masculine and called to her on a primitive level.

Everything about Daniel spoke to her in ways she'd never even imagined possible. His strength, his code of honor, that intense masculinity, all beckoned to her, drawing her no matter how hard she tried to fight it. She pushed the thought away. This was no time for distractions.

Twin headlight beams illuminated the street as a car drove by, and she saw inside the van parked half a block ahead of her. She sucked in her breath, her blood turning to ice. Two men were in the vehicle, and the one with long hair and beefy arms was holding what appeared to be binoculars.

The pair was staking out Reverend Brown's home and she seriously doubted that they were cops. Pushing back her fear, she considered her options. She could see this as trouble, or as an opportunity. Hoping for the latter, she opened the SUV's door.

"Wolf, we're going for a walk." With the dog close beside her, Hannah stepped onto the sidewalk, remaining in the shadows and moving quietly past a line of trees. As long as she didn't go near a porch or street light, she'd be well hidden. The communications device that kept her in touch with Daniel looked like ordinary earphones, so even in the unlikely event someone saw her, it would appear that a woman listening to her tape player or radio was taking a stroll with her pooch. Confident that she would be safe, she made her way toward the van, approaching from behind.

As she drew near, Wolf's attitude changed drastically. His gait slowed, his face became alert, his body tense and ready for trouble. He held his head high, sniffing the air, ears pricked forward.

"Wolf, we're just going in for a closer look. Take it easy, boy," she whispered.

She was about five car lengths away when one of the two men stepped out of the van. As he flicked open a lighter and lit a cigarette, she saw his face. It was no one she recognized.

Realizing she was very visible in the glow of house lights here, Hannah edged back into the deeper shadows, ready to return to the SUV. But the man caught sight of her movement out of the corner of his eye and turned his head. From the way he sprang forward, she knew he'd recognized either her or the dog.

She ran, Wolf easily keeping pace beside her, but as she glanced back, peering through the half-light reaching the street, she saw the clear outline of a gun in his hand. Hannah tried to keep running, but her legs were suddenly rubbery and weak. She tried to focus on the SUV ahead, but a red veil descended over her eyes. Images from her past came flooding back into her mind. For a terror-filled moment the past and the present merged into a heart-stopping reality.

Unaware of the path before her, Hannah caught her toe on a raised joint of a section of sidewalk and stumbled. She fell down hard, barely able to put out her hands to keep from hitting the rough surface face first.

Scrambling to her knees, she turned to look at her pursuer. He was advancing rapidly toward her, but Wolf stood between her and the man, hackles raised, a low, menacing growl coming from his throat. The man stopped a short distance away from her, suddenly hesitant to come any closer.

Hannah saw him slowly moving his gun hand around toward the dog. At that moment, she caught a glimpse of a flash of light somewhere to her left and heard the sound of a door closing. Every instinct she possessed assured her it was Daniel leaving the pastor's house.

Breaking through her fear, Hannah got up and spoke as loudly as she could. "If you shoot, people will come out. This is New Mexico and a lot of people own guns besides you. Walk away now."

Hearing the sound of running footsteps, she looked to her side, her enemy doing the same. Daniel was heading toward them on an intercept course.

Before Hannah could think of what to say or do next, the armed man whirled, racing back toward the van. He reached the slow-moving vehicle in seconds and jumped in. His partner gunned the engine, and the van sped away, tires squealing.

Daniel reached the SUV at the same time Hannah and Wolf did. "We're going after them. Buckle up," he said.

Daniel floored the accelerator. The van had the advantage of distance, but the SUV's engine was equipped for speed, and he was a skilled driver.

"You're going sixty on a city street," Hannah managed to say in a thin voice.

"The street's clear. We're going to catch them," Daniel responded sharply, the excitement of the challenge coiling in his gut.

In a few minutes they left the residential area and reached the main highway. Daniel's speedometer climbed up to ninety and the white dashes in the center of the road seemed to merge into a solid line. The red taillights of the van quickly grew in size, and it was clear the vehicle was no match for theirs. Daniel had narrowed the gap between them when one of the men leaned out the passenger's side window with a shotgun and fired two rounds in rapid succession, the muzzle flash like flashbulbs going off.

Daniel swerved as much as he dared at high speed, and the tires screamed in protest. He took his foot off the gas pedal, and the gap between the two vehicles widened another three car lengths.

Hannah moaned, and her fear sliced through him like a knife to his heart. "It's okay, they missed us by a mile. Just duck down below the windshield," he said, reaching for her hand. Violent tremors shook her body, and she curled up in a fetal position on the seat.

"Hannah, it's all right," he murmured cursing himself for not having anticipated something like this. She wasn't a policewoman accustomed to high-speed pursuits. She was an emotionally fragile woman fighting for her life, and quickly reaching the limits of her courage.

Though he hated to give up the chase when he knew he had a good chance of catching the men and getting some answers, Hannah was more important, and her safety was his priority. He slowed down, trying just to keep the vehicle in sight, but it wasn't long before they lost the van completely.

Daniel called Silentman, making a report he knew would be relayed to the authorities after a few facts were omitted, then pulled over.

As he glanced at Hannah, his gut tightened. Her eyes were tightly closed, and she was trembling.

"Honey, it's all right. I'm sorry. I just wanted to catch them so badly I never stopped to think of anything else."

He reached over and pulled Hannah against his chest, holding her. She didn't cry, but was shaking as if she'd just been pulled from an icy lake. He brushed a kiss on her forehead, and tried to reassure her.

More than anything, he wanted to tilt her head back and kiss her like she'd never been kissed before, erasing her fear with the passion he felt. Yet a code he couldn't break held him back just at the edge of his control. He wouldn't take advantage of her when she was at her most vulnerable.

An eternity later, Hannah pushed away from him and sat up straight in her seat. "I'm sorry. That shouldn't have happened. I became a liability to you. I won't do that again, not if I can help it."

Her voice wasn't steady yet, but he had to give her credit for trying. As he watched her regain her composure, he tried to ignore the fire coursing through his veins. He had to focus completely on business now.

"I told you to stay in the SUV, Hannah. Why in the world did you get out and go after those guys?"

"I just wanted to get a closer look at them," she explained quietly. "Do you really expect me to just sit back and do nothing while you put your life on the line for me?"

"It's my job," he said gruffly.

"Why are you angry? Do you think I was trying to do *your* job for you, or are you upset because I was willing to take the same kind of risk you've been taking all along?'' she challenged.

''I'm angry because you scared the hell out of me.'' Wrapping his hand around the back of her neck, he wrenched her toward him and sealed her mouth in a desperate, soul-searing kiss.

Hannah felt the shudder that traveled through him as he held her. His kiss was rough, hot and so demanding it sparked fires all through her. Surrendering to the passion he'd kindled in her, she held on to him tightly, parting her lips and drawing him into her.

He ravaged her, his tongue dancing and mating with hers, coaxing even as he mastered all her senses.

She'd never been kissed like that before and was unprepared for the blinding heat and the desire that grew stronger with every beat of her heart.

A lifetime later, he eased his hold and moved away, leaving her body hot and tingling as if she'd lingered dangerously close to an open flame. Then again, maybe she had.

He swore darkly, then focused his attention back on the wheel. Switching on the ignition, he pulled back onto the road.

''Where are we headed now?'' She ran the tip of her tongue over her lips, tasting him there.

Seeing it, he suppressed a groan. ''To hell and beyond,'' he muttered, his voice barely audible over the roar of the engine.

Chapter Nine

By the time they arrived at the safe house, Daniel felt that familiar deep-bone weariness that always followed an adrenaline high. He would need some rest soon, but right now other matters demanded his attention.

As he built a fire to warm up the interior of the house, he noted that Hannah was unusually quiet. He suspected that the terror that had gripped her had finally given way to exhaustion.

"I know you're tired and you probably want to rest, but we have to talk," he said.

She stared at the crackling piñon burning in the fireplace, and nodded, taking off the wig and shaking her hair loose again.

He felt like a bully for pushing her now, but he had no choice. He had some tough questions to ask her and her exhaustion would give him an advantage he couldn't pass up.

"Tell me exactly what happened after you spotted the guy back at Reverend Brown's," he said. "When I came out of the pastor's house, you were on the ground, and that guy was practically in front of you."

"I went for a closer look, realized I didn't know him and started back, but he saw me and came after me. I ran, then, when I turned my head to check where he was, I saw the gun in his hands. Crazy images suddenly flashed in my mind and I ended up falling down. Before I could get back up, he was there. Thankfully, so was Wolf.'' She looked down at the dog, lost in thought.

''What did the guy look like?''

''Long brown hair, muscular, Anglo-looking definitely. But I didn't see him clearly enough to be able to positively identify him,'' she said. ''I wish I had, but things happened too fast.''

His gaze strayed over Hannah, taking in everything about her from the silky black curtain of her hair, to the way her full breasts rose and fell.

Seeing her begin to tremble again, it was all he could do not to take her into his arms. But physical contact between them now was out of the question.

He forced himself to look away, and focus back on his job. Unless he found a way to control his feelings for her, they would both end up dead.

''Talk to me, Hannah,'' he said softly. ''I want to know about the images you saw. I need to find out exactly what went through your mind.''

''Why?'' she demanded, a lifetime of pent-up emotions and hurt feelings behind her words. ''Do you want to try and psychoanalyze me so you can figure out if I'm sane or not?''

''No,'' he said, recognizing the outburst for what it was. ''But I need to know you as well as I know myself. We're in this together now and that means your strengths, and your weaknesses, are also my own. Whatever happened back there made you vulnerable and I've got to know exactly what that was.''

''All right.'' She took a deep, steadying breath, then continued. ''It was seeing the gun in that man's hands that threw me. Guns, to me, mean only death. Since the day my father shot himself I haven't been able to look at a weapon without panicking. Can you understand?''

"I'm starting to," Daniel answered gently, wanting her to continue. When he'd asked her to confide in him, he'd made it sound like it was all part of his job. But it was far more than that. He *wanted* to know Hannah. Maybe then he'd understand the woman who drew him so much she was never out of his thoughts.

"I only caught a glimpse of that gun but, at that moment, I felt as if I'd suddenly been propelled backwards in time to the day my father killed himself. Everything in front of me became covered in a blood-red haze. Yet a part of my mind remained clear. I knew the guy chasing me was real and that I was in mortal danger. I kept running, but I wasn't watching where I was going and I fell. Thankfully, Wolf bought me enough time to get myself together."

"Do you now remember more about the day your father died?"

"No, not really. What came back to me most strongly were the feelings I'd had back then—that somehow I'd failed him." Hannah stood and began to pace in front of the fireplace. "That's the real reason I spent so much time in a psychiatric hospital. Dealing with that loss and all the guilt I felt because I hadn't found a way to stop him nearly destroyed me."

Daniel started to go to her, but she shook her head, and returned to the couch.

"But why on earth did you blame yourself? How could you have prevented what happened?"

"It wasn't a logical response. It was an emotional one. I was thirteen at the time. I'd known my father was having an even tougher time than I was coping with my mother's death. After his suicide, I blamed myself for not having seen or sensed trouble long before anything happened."

"Your father made his own decision, Hannah. You can't take responsibility for another's actions. That's one very hard lesson I've had to learn over the years.'' There was no condemnation in his words.

''From a logical standpoint, I know that, but what's in the heart and what's in the head are two very different things,'' she said with a sad smile. ''No doctor will ever erase that shadow from my heart. I let my father down—not willingly, of course, but the fact remains I wasn't really there for him when he needed me most.''

Hannah's pain touched him deeply. Feeling responsible for the death of someone you cared for could destroy you inside, locking you up in a prison of guilt forever. He knew that from personal experience.

''Maybe it's a blessing that you don't remember every detail of that night,'' he said quietly.

''Yes, I agree,'' she admitted. ''To be honest, my uncle gave me more details and background than I wanted to hear. It seems that after my mom died, the hardware store was barely doing enough business to run our household and make small payments on the enormous medical bills my mother's illness had run up. Then one night my uncle came over and discovered my dad holding a gun to his head. It was over in seconds.''

''And you saw it happen?''

''Apparently. I came in when I heard them arguing, and saw the gun go off. I do remember the sound, but nothing after that. It's like a dark curtain goes down after that, blocking the rest. And you know what? I'm glad. It's the only mercy fate has ever shown me.''

''And now there's something else you're blocking out....''

''That's what scares me so much, Daniel,'' she whispered. ''Whatever I'm blocking must be pretty awful, otherwise I wouldn't be doing this to myself. The only reason I've ever blocked a memory is to help myself survive.''

''Is it possible that instead of images from the day your dad died, what you were actually remembering back at

Reverend Brown's was something that happened at the church?''

''But no one died at the church and everything in front of my eyes was shrouded in blood. It was horrible. It had to be a flashback from my distant past.''

''Your uncle *was* hurt at the church. He was struck from behind. There was probably blood associated with that injury.''

''What I saw was more than that.'' She shook her head. ''But that's based on a feeling, nothing else. The truth is that I can't tell you anything for sure.''

Seeing the raw pain in her eyes brought his own memories to the surface. He knew what it was like to live with a heart weighed down by darkness and shadows.

''I know you better than you realize,'' he said, surprising himself by revealing even that much.

''You can't know what my life's been like, Daniel. No one can. The hurt never goes away. The best you can do is put it in a place inside you where you can deal with it on your own terms.'' She brought her legs up and hugged her knees to her chest to keep from trembling.

''And, after a while, the pain begins to feel like a cruel companion that won't leave you alone,'' he said, letting her know that he did understand because he'd been there himself.

She looked at him then, compassion mirrored in her eyes. ''You've known loss, too,'' she observed quietly.

''Yes.'' Daniel sat beside Hannah and pulled her to him, needing her warmth and softness. To his own amazement, he found himself wanting to tell her about something he'd kept locked inside him for years. He'd never spoken about it to anyone, except once to another cop during a debriefing.

''I know exactly what it's like to lose someone and feel responsible, Hannah.'' Daniel's voice was soft, but held the heaviness of someone who'd lived with sorrow for a very long time. "My partner was shot and killed because of me."

Hannah held on to him even more tightly, empathizing with his pain and trying to soothe the storm raging inside him.

"I'm a martial artist—that's always been my greatest strength. But that day I went by the book. I trusted that more than my instincts. When my pistol jammed at a critical time, I wasn't in a position to use my fighting skills. My partner was shot in the back. She died in my arms before help arrived." His voice shook but he paused for a moment, then continued in a firm voice. "Had I depended more on my skills—on myself—I think she would have been alive today."

"That's why you left the force?"

He nodded. "I make my own rules now. No one else will die on my account—not while I'm still alive." He held her gaze. "As I said, we're a lot more alike than you realized."

Hannah nodded and rested securely against his hard chest. The comfort of having found, at long last, another person who understood the darkness in her soul drew her to him more than ever. They'd both known intense pain and had survived in their own fashion. That bond—one forged from an intimate knowledge of hell—brought an unexpected gift—a gentle, healing light that warmed her heart.

With his arms wrapped tightly around her, Hannah felt safe and cherished. "We've both lived with pain, the kind that doesn't go away," she said softly. "But you've helped me see that there's another side to life, one I didn't know existed. I now know how tenderness can soothe those scars that never heal."

He gazed down at her and the need to love her, to bind her broken heart even as he soothed his own, became too great to resist. "We need each other, love," he murmured, his mouth closing over hers. He tasted her yearnings, and in the sweetness she offered him was a respite from the pain and the emptiness that had haunted him for far too long.

Hannah drew back slightly, catching her breath, then looked up at him. "I know you can feel what's in my heart when you touch me and when you hold me. But, without trust, we have nothing. I need to know that you believe in me…that you know I'm as sane as you are."

Daniel saw himself reflected in her gaze. "When I look at you, I see the other half of my broken heart."

Hannah let her fingers glide down his cheek, then traced the curve of his mouth. He needed tenderness in his life and that was just what her feminine heart longed to give him.

"Show me everything you feel," she whispered, her breath hot against his mouth.

"If we go on, there won't be any turning back," he warned.

"I know," she said, her lips brushing his.

Her gentleness was his undoing. "We've both known death, sweet Hannah, but tonight we'll share life." Daniel took her mouth in a kiss that was raw fire and aching needs.

Heat spiraled around her, passion guided her. Hannah followed her heart. Fate had once again stepped into her life, but this time it had come bearing a gift she couldn't turn away.

Daniel kissed the sensitive skin at her throat. As he moved his hand to her breast, gently caressing it, pleasure made her blood sizzle. "Tonight I'm going to teach you about flames that are never too hot to bear."

She tugged at the buttons of his shirt, needing to touch him, to feel him, skin to skin, heat to heat. There was something wildly exciting about the hardness of Daniel's chest. She smoothed her palms over his skin, loving the feel of him and heard the rasp of his breath. Feeling a surety that came from knowing she was giving him pleasure, she rained soft, wet kisses down the center of his chest, then moved lower, drawing a line with the tip of her tongue over the waistband of his jeans.

A groan was ripped from the depths of his being. Bringing her back up toward him, he pulled her into his lap and pushed her blouse away from her shoulders, then her bra.

Her skin was flushed and as he gazed at her, her breasts tightened. He took one into his mouth, suckling gently.

His body was hard and as hot as the noonday sun, but he wouldn't take her fast. What was happening between them sang with a magic of its own and begged for an eternity of care and prolonged pleasures.

As she shifted, her buttocks pressed against his hardness. Blinding pain and pleasure tore the air from his lungs. He stood and lifted her up, guiding her legs around him. As her feminine center pressed against him, he shuddered. He had to slow down, or everything would end far too soon.

Hannah kissed him then, and for a moment the world ceased to exist. As her tongue darted into his mouth, coaxing and teasing him with its aggressiveness, fires danced in his blood.

He started to carry her to the bed, but suddenly stopped.

"Will you trust me?" he whispered.

"My life is in your hands. What more can I give you?"

Giving Wolf the command to remain on guard, he carried her outside to a clearing inside a circle of pines.

He set her down gently on the soft earth, then lay beside her. "I want you out here where life is primitive and simple. Just a man and his woman," he breathed.

He kissed her slowly, then rained kisses down her neck and lower. Her cries as he used his tongue to tease her nipples into hardness tore through him. The soft sounds ripped from her soul spoke of needs yet to be discovered, and the promise of nourishment that only two who were meant to be together could give each other.

Moonlight danced on her skin as he finished undressing her. He touched her intimately, invading her softness and feeling her yield to the pleasure he was giving her. Her surrender was sweet and knowing he was the man who had brought her to the edge made him feel more powerfully male than anything he'd ever experienced.

Lost in passion, she pushed his unbuttoned shirt away from his shoulders, but her trembling hands hampered her efforts to loosen his belt. "I want to feel your skin next to mine."

"You'll have that—and more," he said in a raw voice. Taking both her hands in his, he kissed them, then moved back and stripped the clothes from his body, his gaze never leaving hers.

He stood proudly before her, his body fiercely aroused. As he saw her eyes hot with passion, wanting him, he struggled to hold back and his muscles trembled with the effort it was taking.

She took a deep unsteady breath as he lowered himself over her, straddling her but not attempting to join their bodies. His hands played over her hot skin and she writhed in a storm of emotions. Hannah shifted, her hips moving upwards, searching for completion, but he remained out of her reach.

She whimpered, unable to stand the pressure that was building to fever pitch inside her. "Please," she begged, her voice thick with desire.

"Easy, my love." He shifted to one side and distracted her with slow, burning kisses as his fingers eased inside her. She was so hot and so tight.

She cried out helplessly as he continued to stroke and penetrate her. Desire, raw and unbridled, made every sensation as mind rending as a wave of pure fire.

She closed her eyes, burning, wanting, unable to think

of anything except the world of passion she'd found in his arms. The emptiness in her soul slowly vanished. This was the love she'd waited for, and Daniel was the man who'd claim her heart. Liquid heat flowed from her center as he whispered dark words encouraging her to surrender.

Flames consumed her and formed her anew. Daniel held her, letting her know she was his and safe with him. When the storm that had rocked her began to subside, he slipped gently inside her, renewing the fires.

Her body stretched around him, all fire and velvet. Suddenly he felt a barrier and froze. It took every bit of control he possessed, but he forced himself to remain perfectly still. He should have known by the tightness of her body, but he hadn't thought—he'd been past the ability to do much except feel.

"This...is your first time."

"Yes." Her eyes were dazed, and heavy-lidded. She blinked as if trying to focus. "Is my body too tight? Will I hurt you?"

Her innocent question filled him with tenderness. "No, but for a moment you may feel pain," he said, his voice thick with restraint.

"You'll take it away," she managed, her body shifting restlessly as hunger filled her.

Determined to be gentle, he moved slowly at first, not thrusting deep, letting her body open wider naturally to fit his.

"More."

The whispered plea slammed into him with incredible force.

"Please," she cried, her fingers biting into his back.

He groaned, knowing that any attempt to hold back was beyond him now. Cupping her bottom, he drove into her with enough force to make her arch. Her body melted around him, all heat and wetness and she began to move with him in the rhythm of love. It was the greatest moment of triumph he'd ever known. He guided her hips, and each thrust made her come alive beneath him. The hot, wet heat that gloved him drove him to the edge of sanity. "You've opened your body to me, now open your soul."

She tried to answer, but no words came. Passion rocked her as their bodies moved in perfect counterpoise.

Daniel's gaze never left her face. He wanted to remember her like this—lost in love, embracing surrender.

At long last he felt her tremors and knew it was time. With a cry that was ripped from the core of his being, he followed her into that dark edge knowing that they'd both find peace and light on the other side.

Their hearts eventually slowed and their breathing evened, but he remained inside her. Then, rolling onto his back, he positioned her on top of him. Refusing to think of anything past that moment, he held her, whispering sweet words of love until she fell asleep in his arms.

AN HOUR LATER, Daniel carried her back inside the house and placed her gently on the bed, covering her with the blankets.

She opened her sleepy eyes and smiled up at him.

"Go back to sleep," he murmured.

He settled beside her until her breathing evened again then, reluctantly, he moved away, careful not to wake her. As he looked down at her, guilt gnawed at him. Hannah had deserved better from him. He'd compromised his own effectiveness on the case by giving his feelings for her free rein and becoming even more involved with her than he already was.

With a soft groan, he left the room, gesturing for Wolf to guard her. It wouldn't happen again. He cared deeply for Hannah and he wanted her feelings for him to be more than just a reaction to the danger they faced, or because she'd been searching for healing. And that was precisely why pursuing this was so dangerous. This wasn't their time. Survival would demand everything from them now and left no room for love.

SUNLIGHT WAS COMING THROUGH the windows when Hannah opened her eyes. She was alone in the bed and the house was quiet. Jackknifing to a sitting position, she looked around, trying to get her bearings. "Daniel?" Fear, sudden and fierce, chilled her blood.

He appeared in less than a second. "I'm here. Are you okay?"

"I didn't know where you were... I was afraid I'd dreamed everything... I didn't, did I?"

"It wasn't a dream," he said, his voice low.

She'd expected him to come to her, but he held his ground. There was a new barrier between them. She could see it in his eyes. The warmth and love he'd shown her the night before had been replaced by new caution and wariness.

"Get dressed. We have a lot to do today," he said brusquely.

As he walked out of the room, Hannah felt a piece of her heart break. As it always had been in her life, love was once again being followed by pain and loss. She'd been a fool to think that last night could have meant as much to him as it had to her. He was a man of experience. Though to her it had been a union of souls, to him it had clearly been only a few hours of pleasure.

She stood up, pulled on a sweater and jeans, and wiped away her tears. She wouldn't mourn for what she'd never had. Feelings of love couldn't be trusted under the best of circumstances. Life had taught her that. But it was even more so now that she was fighting for her life. She couldn't afford to give in to a myriad of gentle emotions that would leave her vulnerable at a time when she could least afford it.

Clinging desperately to that sound reasoning, she prepared herself to face him on his own terms.

Chapter Ten

They had a quick breakfast consisting of bread, canned lunch meat and instant coffee, then cleaned up, heating wash water from the big kettle on the stove. Their silence stretched out, heightening the awkwardness between them, but neither was willing to speak of the night before.

As they got ready to leave, Daniel packed up his clothes. "You can leave a few things behind, but for the most part take everything you'll need with you. The way things are going on this case, nothing is certain. Depending on what happens today, it may not be practical to return here again."

Hannah placed her clothes into a paper sack and looked around, making sure she hadn't left anything else behind. "Do you have a plan for today?" she asked, matching his crisp, businesslike tone.

He nodded. "I want you to put on one of the wigs. The redheaded one will do. I'm going to pay Norm Gless a visit. I want a closer look at him and his business."

"My client? How come?"

"You said he was being audited?" Seeing her nod, Daniel continued. "I want to go in for a closer look. While you were dressing I asked Silentman to give me the address of his copy shop."

"Norm will probably be there in the back. He has a

profitable business, but he puts in long hours. That's where I reached him the other night.''

''We'll stop by and get a feel for the place. If we keep our eyes and ears open around the employees, they'll let us know in their own way if there's anything irregular going on. What I want to find out is whether the guy appears to be stable, financially and personally. Criminals aren't always motivated by greed, but it never takes me long to discover if they're trying to keep a secret.''

''We can't just stand around his copy shop and take notes, like in a psychology lab. How do you plan to do this?''

''We're going to take the sketch of the man who kidnapped you and say we want several copies made. We'll tell the employees that he was a good Samaritan who helped you when you were having car trouble and explain we're offering a reward to anyone who can tell us who he is so we can thank him properly. If nothing else, that should start the ball rolling. If Norm and he are connected, his staff may have seen them together.''

Daniel picked up a small leather pouch from the table next to the couch, and placed it in his athletic bag.

''What's that?''

He held it out for her to see. ''It's what my people call a medicine bundle.''

''What's it used for?''

''It's to ward off evil and attract good. In it, there's soil from the four sacred mountains that surround the Navajo Nation, corn pollen, turquoise, white shell and other things.'' He looked at it pensively. ''I'm not a traditionalist, but my father gave it to me the day I joined the police department. I've always kept it with me.''

''Does your dad live on the Reservation?''

Daniel shook his head. ''Both my dad and mom died many years ago. They had chronic lung problems, a common ailment on the Rez. They might have done better had they moved to Shiprock, closer to the hospital, but for most of their lives, they chose to live in one of the least populated areas. We burned wood for heating and had no electricity. It was how they were raised, so they felt more comfortable with the old ways. But my dad decided that he wanted me to choose my own future and have more options, so he sent me off to boarding school as soon as I turned thirteen.''

''What about your mother? How did she feel about that?''

''The same. She knew I'd demand more from life than what their lifestyle offered. She was a traditionalist who wouldn't move into Shiprock, even when the Navajo doctors at the hospital told her she needed special medication and therapy. To her, hospitals were a place where people died and, as a Navajo, she wouldn't go near any place that had been contaminated by death.''

''She was afraid she'd catch something?''

''No, it's not that simple. You see, my people believe in the *chindi,* the evil in a man that stays earthbound after death. The *chindi* is said to be able to cause the living great harm and she would no more have gone near a place where a death had occurred than an Anglo would have stepped inside a lion's cage at the zoo.''

''I never realized how different your culture is,'' Hannah said slowly.

''The old ways are a part of me, but I live my own life. I value our traditions, but I have my own path to follow.'' He glanced around the cabin, his mind on business again. ''I've got to give Wolf a chance to walk around.''

''No problem. I'll follow you out in a minute.''

As he opened the door and nodded to the dog, Wolf rushed out. Daniel watched him for a moment as he dashed among the trees, scattering birds and barking at a piñon jay who cackled right back at him.

"Are you ready?" Daniel said, turning to look inside minutes later.

Hannah came out of the house wearing the red wig. "Whenever you are," she answered.

AS THEY DROVE down the highway, Daniel remained thoughtful and quiet. He'd have to keep his guard up. It was too easy to talk to Hannah, to reveal things that drew them closer, and that was the last thing either of them needed. She needed a cold professional to guard her, not a man who was falling in love with her.

He gripped the steering wheel hard enough to make his knuckles turn white. He would stay focused. There was too much at stake for both of them now.

Nearly an hour later, Daniel finally turned onto the street that would lead them to the copy shop. "Remember that this'll be a fact-finding expedition only. I want you to avoid Norm if possible. If you see him at the front with the employees, go back to the SUV and wait. If you find you can't avoid him, then make sure you don't volunteer any information."

"I think I can remember that," she muttered sarcastically.

"I just don't want you taking unnecessary risks. I would have liked to go to the copy shop alone, but I don't want to leave you to your own devices for any length of time."

"Are you afraid that trouble will find me, or that I'll find it?"

He glared at her. "Both. So play it my way at the copy shop and don't argue." He glanced over at her. She was staring out the window, a thoughtful look on her face. "Are you really *listening* to me?"

"Of course. I always listen—then I do whatever seems right to me."

Daniel expelled his breath with a hiss. The woman was going to drive him crazy.

Glancing in the rearview mirror, Daniel saw Wolf sitting up, looking at him. He appeared to be grinning.

THE COPY SHOP, in a strip mall with several other small businesses, didn't seem overly busy at the moment, probably because of the early morning hour. Hannah glanced around when they entered, but Norm wasn't in the room. She shook her head, assuring Daniel that they had nothing to worry about for now.

Looking over the shop casually, Daniel saw a caller ID box next to the telephone. That could explain how Hannah's call had been traced and how their enemies had found the first safe house.

Daniel walked to the counter, and placed the sketch of the man who had kidnapped Hannah down in front of an employee.

The young clerk looked at the sketch, then at Daniel. "You a cop?"

"Me? Nah. But I've got this great computer program that helped us make this sketch. The guy on this printout helped my lady when her car broke down in the middle of nowhere south of Bloomfield. He stopped and managed to get the car running again so she could make it into Farmington. But he left in a rush and forgot some of his tools. They're expensive and I thought I'd try to get them back to him."

Hannah stared at Daniel, hoping that the burning she felt in her cheeks hadn't really been a noticeable blush. When he'd called her his lady, she'd felt the most wonderful rush coursing through her. Of course it meant nothing. Daniel had made it clear that he wasn't interested in permanent relationships. She disciplined her thoughts quickly. They had work to do.

Daniel suddenly glanced back at her and gave her a devilish grin, making her wonder if he'd seen her reaction to his words. "The guy in this drawing really came through for her,'' he said, looking back at the clerk, ''and I'd like to return the favor. I'm offering a twenty-five-dollar reward to anyone who can tell me who he is so I can square things with him. You don't happen to recognize him, do you?''

The young man, probably no older than eighteen, studied the sketch for a moment, then finally shook his head. ''Wish I did. But let me ask around.''

There were two other employees, one a college-age girl, and the manager, who looked like retired military.

While the young man was showing the sketch to his co-workers, Daniel reached over and pressed the review arrow on the caller ID box. He quickly found one indicating a call from the convenience store location at the time Hannah had called Gless. Either Norm had tracked her down, or one of his ''customers'' had.

Hannah, noting what he was doing, looked at him questioningly. Daniel nodded.

The clerk came back and handed the sketch to Daniel. ''Sorry, man. None of us can recall having seen him before.''

''Can you make me several copies of this sketch? Ten ought to do it. We'll put them up in different places and see if anyone can help.''

The manager came over while the clerk was making the copies. ''Good thing the lady got help. It's dangerous on those roads. You don't know who you can trust nowadays.''

Out of the corner of his eyes, Daniel saw another man enter the room from the back office. Daniel looked back at Hannah casually and saw that she'd already started walking back toward the entrance, keeping her back to them.

The manager, probably anxious to look busy now that his boss was in the room, nodded to Daniel and moved away to a stack of bound copies on a table.

Daniel smiled at the new guy, certain he was Norm. ''This sure looks like the kind of business I've been looking to set up. How hard is it to get a franchise?''

''They've got a lot of rules about where and how you can get set up, but once you get past the first few months, the place practically runs itself, if you get good help,'' he said.

''Then you must be the owner?''

''Norm Gless,'' he said with a nod, but didn't offer to shake hands.

Norm apparently knew Navajos rarely shook hands with strangers, Daniel observed. Gless was a short man in his midfifties with glasses as thick as headlights. He didn't seem rushed, however, or harried, qualities he'd often associated with Anglo businessmen.

''You look like you really enjoy your work,'' Daniel said casually, finding it hard to imagine from the man's appearance and unassuming bearing that he'd sent killers after them.

''I do. There are few intangibles here. The print jobs either come out good or they don't, and the equipment is pretty reliable. The only hassle is dealing with the franchise paperwork, but I don't have to do that very often.''

Daniel received his copies, and paid the clerk. A few minutes later they were driving away in the SUV.

''You saw the call I made to him listed on the caller ID box, right?''

''It was there, and it identified the address because the pay phone was at the convenience store. Still, it's hard to believe Gless wants you dead. Can you tell me anything else you remember about your conversation with him that night?''

''He was waiting on a customer, I think, and whoever it was must have overheard Norm's side of the conversation. If it was one of those men who was trying to find me through my clients, it would have been pretty easy for him to get a look at the location. You didn't have any trouble doing it,'' Hannah said. ''What do you think?''

''It's a possibility, but we may never know for sure how they tracked us down.'' Daniel stared at the road, trying to figure out their next move. ''We're going to stop at the Farmington police station next,'' he said. ''Make sure your wig's firmly in place. I don't think we'll meet any of the people after you there, but I have a job I want you to do.''

''What do you have in mind?''

''I did a lot of interdepartmental investigations with the Farmington cops, and I have a buddy who works in Records. I'm going to leave you downstairs with him so you can look through some mug books. I want you to see if you can recognize the man who kidnapped you.''

''That's a good idea. Who do I say I am, if your friend asks?''

''He won't ask, and you're not to engage in a conversation with him. Clear?''

''I thought you said he was a friend of yours.''

''He'll assume you're a client of mine, and leave it at that.'' He thought about Ken and how he had a tendency to flirt with the ladies. ''If he doesn't, just ignore him. But whatever you do, don't volunteer any information. I'm counting on you, Hannah. If this goes wrong, we'll both be in a heap of trouble.''

''I won't let you down,'' she said firmly.

He believed her. He knew that when the chips were down, he could always count on her. ''While you're looking through mug shots, I'm going to talk to a sergeant I know and do a little fishing. I'd like to find out if the police have any ongoing investigations that could be linked to the men after you or our case.''

They rode in silence the rest of the way through the city of Farmington. Daniel made an effort not to glance at her, but he was aware of everything about Hannah.

Misinterpreting his silence, she looked over at him. ''If

you're worried that I won't be able to handle this, don't be. I'll be fine."

"I know, but I like to worry about you," he said, his voice low and masculine.

Her breath caught and her cheeks tinged pink. Hannah looked away quickly as if trying to hide her reaction, but it was too late. Daniel found himself remembering the last time he'd seen her face flushed and heard the little hitch in her breath. She'd been beneath him, her warmth open to him.

His body suddenly grew hot and hard. He cursed himself silently. He would never get this woman out of his system. He knew it with a certainty that frightened him. For a man who had never feared anything in his life, this was a new experience, and one he wasn't at all sure how to deal with.

DANIEL LEFT HANNAH downstairs in an interview room looking at mug shots. No one except his old buddy knew she was there, so she'd be safe. Still, a sixth sense warned him not to leave her alone for long.

He pushed back the thought. He was acting like a lovesick kid who couldn't stand to be away from his girl for more than five minutes.

Daniel walked into a small office and greeted Sergeant John Yazzie, who was sitting behind a desk. "So what's been going on lately?" Daniel asked, sitting back in one of the chairs and trying to project an image of cool indifference.

Yazzie gave him a speculative look. "You take on that P.I. attitude every time you want something. What are you after? If you'll tell me that, we can save time."

"Relax. I just came to visit with an old buddy," Daniel said.

Yazzie didn't answer, but his searching look never wavered. "You don't really expect me to buy that, do you?"

"It's true." And it was, at least partly.

"You're on a case, right?" Yazzie pressed. "You want to know what we've been doing to see if we're investigating anything that may tie in with your job. Maybe save you some legwork, huh?"

Daniel considered denying it, but Yazzie and he went back too many years, and their minds ran along the same lines. "Something like that. But let me assure you that the case I'm on isn't a police matter."

"But the events surrounding it might be?"

Daniel said nothing. Yazzie was too close.

Yazzie leaned back in his chair. "You should have stayed a cop, Daniel. We could have used you in our department. Private sectors are great, and they may pay more, but there's a lot of community value in what we do here."

"I'm not arguing that point, and for the record, the reason I left had nothing to do with money."

Yazzie nodded pensively. "I know. I heard."

Daniel lapsed into a momentary silence as memories came flooding back. Pushing away the pain that still haunted his nightmares, Daniel finally answered. "I'm where I need to be now."

Yazzie rubbed the back of his neck with one hand. "Well, for old times' sake, I'll tell you what's going on. The only current felony investigation we know about is an Anglo John Doe the Navajo Police found dead beside the highway near Narbona Pass. He had a phony ID with a blurred image on it that could have been him, or not. We're helping the Rez cops check into it. He also had a woman's photo in his pocket, a Farmington local, and we're trying to follow up on that in a cooperative effort with your old PD."

"Hmm. Was the photo of a Navajo woman?"

"Nope. Anglo. A real beauty, too."

"How did the guy die? Gunshot?"

"No. It's believed he was the victim of a hit-and-run. Or murder by vehicle."

"Do you have a description? I know a lot of people in this area and may be able to ID him for you." As Daniel listened, he silently acknowledged that it sounded like the description Hannah had given him of her kidnapper.

"Sound familiar?"

"I can't ID him for you, not just based on that. It's too general."

Yazzie brought out a file, then slid it across the desk. "That's the photo of what's left of the guy's face."

Only years of discipline and training helped him keep his expression neutral. "The collision must have damaged the car too, if it did that to him."

"Yeah. That's our guess." Yazzie reached for a small photo at the bottom of the file. "This is the woman we're searching for now. We hope she isn't in some shallow grave somewhere. She's the only lead. Her name is Hannah Jones, and she's the niece of one of the deacons at the Riverside Mission. Do you know her?"

Daniel glanced casually at the photo of Hannah wearing shorts and a halter top. From the redwood table in the background, he guessed it had been taken at a picnic. "That's the type of babe I normally avoid," Daniel said, not answering directly. "Attractive, but probably the marrying kind."

"Does that mean that you do know her?" Yazzie's gaze studied him with razor sharpness. "What aren't you telling me?"

"Only my lustful thoughts after seeing that photo," Daniel joked.

Yazzie laughed. "Yeah, well, you're not the only one around here who's said that after seeing this picture."

He found Yazzie's response unbearably irritating. "What's her connection to the dead guy? Any theories?"

"There's no link—at least none that we can find," Yazzie answered, "unless she's his victim. Or vice versa. When we went looking for her, we discovered that she's disappeared, which brought up a possible kidnapping angle. He might have kidnapped and killed her, then died, or she may have killed him trying to escape. We just don't have enough to even take a halfway decent guess. What we know for sure is that her uncle doesn't know where she is and what we've learned about her indicates that the dead guy was no friend of hers. We questioned a lot of other people, too, including her neighbors, but no one had answers. In checking her home, there was no sign of foul play, but her car is gone. So far, no one's been able to shed much light on this. How about you?''

Daniel shrugged. ''She hit the guy with the car and then took off for Arizona? Who knows? But hit-and-run is serious business. Have you checked the lady for priors?''

''Yeah. She's clean as a whistle.'' Yazzie leaned forward. ''We're going to be running an artist's sketch of the John Doe in the afternoon newspaper. Maybe we'll get some answers then.''

''Will you run the missing woman's photo, too?'' Daniel asked, forcing his voice to remain casual.

''No, not at this time, not unless we or the Navajo cops find her car abandoned or uncover actual evidence that she might have been taken by force. She's wanted for questioning, nothing more, and we don't want to spook her or someone who might be able to give us a tip on her. It's a touchy situation. Apparently, she does some financial work for the mission and the people there are adamant about not having us do anything to damage her reputation even through inference.''

''Since when did that stop the PD?''

''It may not—at least not for long,'' Yazzie said with a shrug. ''But for now, we'd rather keep things on a friendly level. I have a feeling that the hit-and-run victim is bad news. The bad ID stuff reeks, you know? My guess is that once we find out who he really was, we'll have a reason to pull out all the stops, find the woman and get her in here for questioning—if she's still alive. For now, we're just distributing her photo to all our patrol officers. The Navajo cops are doing the same.'' He gestured out into the area known as the bull pen. ''That's the picture the secretary is handing out now.''

''Sounds like you have it under control.'' Daniel stood. ''It was good seeing you.'' He had to get Hannah out of the station fast. ''If I hear anything that might help you, I'll let you know. In the meantime, I'd be interested in knowing when you find the car used in the hit-and-run. I suppose you're checking all the body shops for vehicles with suspicious damage.''

Yazzie nodded. ''We'll find it. You can count on that. It's just a matter of time. Officers from both PDs are still searching the general area where they found the John Doe for evidence.'' Yazzie stopped Daniel before he reached the door. ''One more thing. We go back a long ways, but don't ever let me catch you working at cross purposes with this department. I won't cut you any slack and obstruction of justice is a serious charge.''

''I hear you,'' Daniel said with a nod. The warning had been given. He'd expected it, of course. Sooner or later, his old friend had to set some limits. Professional courtesies would be shown to a former officer, but crossing certain lines would not be tolerated.

Daniel walked downstairs quickly, but not so fast as to attract attention. Crossing the long hall, he entered one of the conference rooms and found her alone. ''Where's Ken?''

''He went upstairs to get me a cola.''

Daniel muttered a curse. ''We've got to leave now.''

She stood and walked to the door.

''Wait, let me take a look first.'' He opened the door slightly and peered out. Ken was talking to one of the secretaries, balancing two cans of pop in one hand and holding a copy of the photo they were handing out upstairs in the other. Ken, who was as nearsighted as they came, probably hadn't noticed the similarity. But once he studied the photo and saw Hannah again up close, it would be all over.

"The window," he said, gesturing to the far wall. "We can make it through that."

"Are you crazy? That's up at ceiling level. I can't climb up there."

"Don't argue. There's no time." He hoisted her up, she undid the latch and scrambled out. He followed her immediately. As he closed the basement window from the outside, he heard the door to the interview room open.

"Let's go. He'll check in the halls, then come outside next," Daniel said, rushing with her to the SUV. Wolf was waiting in the shade of an old cottonwood next to the vehicle.

They all climbed into the vehicle and within seconds they were pulling out into the street. As Daniel glanced in the rearview mirror, he saw Ken at the side door looking around curiously, still holding two cans of soda.

"Well, that's one place we won't be coming back to visit," Daniel said.

"What happened back there? I thought everything was going fine."

He shook his head slowly. "I didn't think things could get much worse but, believe it or not, they have."

Chapter Eleven

Daniel told her what he'd learned at the station and, to her credit, she took it with the same courage she'd shown since the first day he'd met her.

"I looked through several books filled with mug shots, but I never found the guy," she said. "Well, it doesn't matter. We'll just have to use another approach."

She was trying to be tough, but he could sense her fear. There was little she could hide from him now. Mistake or not, something that went beyond the physical had happened between them last night. He'd seen her soul, as she'd seen his. He could feel the connection between them now as tangibly as he could the cool breeze coming through the window.

He swore softly under his breath. Since when had he become such a romantic jackass? He was as hard-nosed a P.I. as they came, one who only believed the cold hard facts and his own hunting instincts. And he *liked* himself that way. How could he have allowed any woman to screw up his thinking like this?

If he wanted to get out of this alive, he'd have to draw back into himself. Retreat had never come easy to him, but this time it was the only option.

As Hannah reached back to pet Wolf, her hand was shaking slightly. Seeing it tore at his gut.

"If the man they found dead had my photo in his pocket, he must have been either my kidnapper or one of the others after me," she said somberly. "But I didn't kill anyone. I did punch the guy who kidnapped me right in the face using the handcuffs as brass knuckles, but he was running after the car when I drove off."

"Think hard. When you were racing away, is it possible that you may have struck him with the car?"

"No way. I remember looking in the rearview mirror and seeing him chasing the car. The only way I could have hit him was if I'd stopped, put the car in reverse and gone back. And, trust me, that's the last thing I would have done. I wanted out of there as fast as possible. I'd never been so scared in my life."

"You were fighting for your life, Hannah. Things get blurry in situations like that. But think really hard now. Is it possible that someone else was also there—that there were two men, not just one?"

She considered it carefully. "Maybe, but I didn't see anyone else. What seems more likely is that he was dazed and maybe dizzy from being punched so hard. He might have wandered out into the highway looking for me, and got hit by a passing car. If that's the case, then I'm still responsible for his death, though I didn't kill him."

"If the guy wandered out into the road and got hit, it wasn't your fault. You acted in self-defense," he said. "But until we can make that abundantly clear to the police, you're going to have to lay low. They only want you for questioning now, but they won't back off. They'll keep turning up the pressure until they get results."

"My life was so simple once... I wonder if it will ever be that way again," she said in a shaky voice.

Hatred for the men who were terrorizing her filled him. He'd always held special contempt for any man who harmed a woman, but it was even more so now. They were going after *his* woman. Although he realized he didn't have any right to think of her as his, after what they'd shared, he couldn't see it any other way.

He wouldn't lose this fight. She needed him to come through for her, and that's exactly what he intended to do.

"Facing this much danger has one benefit. You're going to learn a lot about yourself as we get through this, Hannah, and it'll make you stronger than you ever dreamed you could be."

"If we survive," she answered.

"We'll make it through this in one piece. And we'll beat these people, because we'll fight until we do."

Hannah said nothing for several minutes. Worried, he glanced over at her. Their eyes met for an instant and he felt the gentle feminine power of the woman behind those hazel eyes.

"I have an idea I'd like us to try," Hannah said, taking a deep, steadying breath. "I've been thinking a lot about this and I believe that the men staking out Reverend Brown's home were there hoping I'd show up asking for help. It's the only logical reason I can think of for them to have been there. If I'm right, then it's also likely that they're watching other places, like where my clients work, my uncle's home and maybe even my own home, hoping to catch me. Let's go by those last two places and see if I'm right. If we're lucky, we might be able to get a closer look at these men and maybe follow them and figure out who they're working for."

"The police are looking for your car, and they'll also be keeping an eye on your place now that you're wanted for questioning. I could drive by, but taking you with me is just asking for trouble."

"I'm not hiding away while you do the work. I'll duck down and stay out of sight, but this is my mess, and I'm going."

He wouldn't be able to talk her out of this. He could feel it in his bones. "All right. We'll go, but we need to take a few precautions first.'' He took the cell phone out of his pocket, and dialed Silentman's number.

WITH HANNAH'S HELP, Daniel gave the SUV a face-lift. Thanks to the removal of the back seat, a stick-on sign and big sealed boxes in the back, it now could pass for a delivery vehicle. The rear windows were blocked now, too, giving Hannah additional cover.

Daniel entered Hannah's neighborhood, keeping a close watch on parked cars and anyone who seemed to be hanging around.

''Stay low back there,'' he said. ''There's an unmarked police car on stakeout. I recognize the detective from the Farmington PD. We've worked together before.''

''Which also means he's sure to recognize you,'' Hannah warned him.

''True, but if I speed up now, it'll just raise questions in his mind, and he'll come after us. Hang tight and stay hidden behind the boxes.''

As Daniel drove past the parked sedan, the towheaded detective behind the wheel glanced over and waved at him. ''I'm going to pull up beside him and keep it friendly,'' Daniel told Hannah in a soft voice. ''Stay out of sight,'' he repeated, stopping the SUV.

Daniel backed up even with the unmarked police unit, rolled the driver's side window down, and leaned out to talk. ''How's it going, Ryan?''

''It's one of those days, Daniel. You know the ones that bounce back and forth from boring to really boring. How about you?'' He gestured to the van's sign that read You Pack It, We Ship It. ''Are you moonlighting? I thought you were a hotshot P.I. these days.''

Daniel laughed. ''Your definition, not mine.''

''Let me take a wild guess. You're doing surveillance work in this neighborhood.''

''No, not really. I've been following someone around

all day trying to establish his routines and patterns for a case, but the guy's home now doing yard work, so it's time for me to call it quits and go buy myself a beer."

"So you just happened to be passing by, huh?" Ryan got out of the sedan and walked to the back of the SUV. Huge boxes covered his view of the interior. "What the heck are you carrying back there?"

"Mostly empty boxes. They provide my cover as a delivery guy."

Daniel saw the slight narrowing in the detective's eyes and knew that he wasn't going to let it go.

"Satisfy my curiosity. Open up the back and let me take a look," Ryan said.

"You think I'm smuggling cardboard, or maybe boxing up city air and moving it to the Reservation?"

"Let's just say I find it hard to believe anyone needs that many boxes to establish a cover," he answered. "But why are you sweating it? You've got nothing to hide, right?"

It was said with a smile, but Daniel recognized the challenge. He knew that Ryan's cop instincts had gone into hyperdrive. He was clearly one detective who didn't believe in coincidences.

Daniel quickly considered his options. If he insisted on him getting a search warrant first, Ryan would only detain him on one excuse or another until he got what he wanted. But there was another way.

"Okay. I'll open up the back for you, but I better warn you. I've got my cousin's idiot dog lying back there. I picked him up at the vet's earlier, and the beast's surly as hell."

Ryan laughed. "Hey, you've always been a wuss around dogs. You didn't even like the beagle the Department of Agriculture guys brought in once."

"This is no beagle, trust me. But okay. Have it your way. It's your funeral."

Daniel climbed out of the SUV, flipped Ryan the keys, then stood to one side as the detective went to the back and opened the hatch.

Ryan had the hatch halfway up when suddenly Wolf pushed his way between two empty boxes and came muzzle to nose with the cop, blocking his way. The oversize shepherd growled, a deep menacing tone that was made even more effective when he bared his teeth, saliva dripping from his mouth.

Ryan didn't move a muscle. ''Holy crud,'' he managed. ''Good boy, good boy!''

''Just step back slowly. He probably won't attack unless he smells fear.'' Daniel came forward and closed the hatch back down. ''Like I said. He's a little upset right now.''

''Upset? What's he like when he's really ticked off?'' Ryan stepped away from the SUV. ''You'd better get him home before he gets hungry and starts eyeing your leg.''

''Good advice. I'll be seeing you, Ryan.''

Daniel slipped behind the wheel and started the engine. As soon as they were a half block away, he turned around for a quick glance. ''You okay, Hannah?''

She started laughing, shifting the boxes enough so she and Wolf could look out from her hiding place. ''His voice went from bass to soprano when Wolf started growling. I wish I'd have seen his face.''

''One good thing came out of this,'' Daniel said chuckling. ''He'll never tell anyone that he saw me here today. That whole episode did some serious erosion to his ego.''

''If it hadn't been for you, that might have turned into a complete disaster,'' Hannah said, petting the dog.

''Good job, Wolf,'' Daniel said. ''But don't let it go to your head, furball. The job's not done.''

Wolf yawned, wiped his muzzle with an enormous paw, then sneezed, spraying Daniel.

Hannah laughed.

Daniel scowled at the dog. Sometimes he had the feeling

that Wolf did things like that on purpose, just to be annoying. He stared at the dog, but Wolf stared back blankly.

Daniel gathered his thoughts. "Things are closing in, Hannah. We've got to do something and I've got an idea," he said, growing serious. He glanced over at her, a worried expression on his face. "But it may be tough on you."

"What do you have in mind?"

"I'd like to go find the car you used to get away from your kidnapper. Admittedly, the police may still be in the area searching for evidence, but we'll have two advantages. First, you know where you left the car and they don't, and, in a wooded area, it'll be easy for us to stay out of sight."

"Let's go then."

He gave her an approving nod. "I was hoping you'd say that."

As soon as they were out of the city, he pulled over and she climbed back into the front seat. She sat there stiffly, not speaking.

"Are you still okay with this? Going back to a place where you were forced to fight for your life won't be easy."

"I'll have you with me this time. That'll help," she said with a shaky smile.

The way she looked at him touched his soul. Tossing caution aside, he pulled Hannah to him and held her against his chest for a moment. She fit in his arms as if she'd been made for him. Daniel fought the urge to tell her how he felt about her, that he would protect her with his life, not because it was his job to do so, but because he cared deeply for her.

Yet, as long as there was the possibility that he could get killed, there was no way he could speak freely to her. She'd suffered too many losses in her life already. Certain admissions would draw them even closer as man and woman and should something happen to him then, she'd be left feeling more alone than ever. He'd do far more for her by remaining silent and just doing his job.

Hannah gently pulled away from him, then buckled her seat belt. "I'm all right," she said softly. "Let's go on with your plan. It's a good one."

His cell phone rang, and he flipped it open. It was Silentman.

"I just got a call from the doctor at the clinic. Hannah's blood tests came out clean and her CBC is normal."

"I expected that," Daniel said.

When Silentman said nothing for a long moment, Daniel knew that it wasn't a good sign.

"Something wrong?" he prodded, growing impatient.

"Lightning, this woman's history is littered with gaps. From what I've been able to piece together, I know she's also savvy enough to manipulate people. Be careful with her. I have no way of knowing how far she's willing to go to get what she wants from you."

"Understood." He saw no point in arguing with Silentman. He knew in his gut that Hannah hadn't tried to manipulate him. He would have seen through it, if that's what had happened. But Silentman had stumbled on one thing that really did worry him. Hannah needed him now, and ties made during a time of crisis seldom lasted. Emotionally, she'd pulled back, just as he'd done, to focus on the case, but he was man enough to know when a woman cared for him, and he could sense that her feelings for him ran deep.

Yet, despite that, the chances were good that once the case was over and she was free to go, Hannah would walk away. He'd be part of a dark time in her life, and memories she'd rather forget. So she'd reluctantly move on, putting him behind her. And the better he was at his job, the sooner that moment would come.

The worst part of it was that he had no one to blame

but himself. He'd walked into this one, eyes wide open. Now all he could do was try not to think about the hole she'd leave inside him when she walked away with his heart.

Chapter Twelve

After approaching Narbona Pass on the Navajo Nation southwest of Shiprock and seeing police cars still there, they'd decided to return to the safe house and wait until the following morning.

Shortly after seven, as the sun rose in the clear blue sky, they set out again. Daniel was dressed in jeans and a brown leather jacket. Hannah glanced at him and felt her pulse quicken. He was tough and all male and everything about him resonated with masculine power.

He gave her an infuriating grin that told her he'd sensed her reaction and she looked away quickly. She had to close the door to thoughts like those. Daniel would never be hers. Lightning never stayed in one place for long. She had to accept that and concentrate on the present. They had work to do together before she could go back to her own life.

The drive took about an hour and, as they drew near Narbona Pass, small rivulets of perspiration began to run down her spine, chilling her to the bone. Almost simultaneously, her mouth went as dry as the desert and she wished she had some chewing gum to relieve the discomfort in her throat.

Determined not to let Daniel see how badly this place

frightened her, she forced herself to sit still and kept her expression as neutral as she could manage.

"There's no sign of the police today, and we didn't see any officers along the way," Daniel said. "My guess is that they've finished their search of the vicinity. Let's go see if the car you left behind is still in the area." He glanced over at her. "I'll need you to guide me from here," he said. "Where did you leave it?"

"It's quite a ways ahead." She directed him around a curve in the road. "Why is it so important to you that we try to find it now?"

"I need to go over the car myself—preferably before anyone else does. I want to see if there's any evidence we can use."

Hannah took a deep breath and steeled herself. "Are you trying to verify that it wasn't the car used in the hit-and-run?" She rubbed her palms on her jeans, wiping the perspiration away.

"I'll check it over for that, sure, but this has nothing to do with trust, Hannah. All my years as a cop and as an investigator have shown me how people's perceptions can become muddled when they're in the middle of a life-and-death crisis." He paused, then continued. "But just so you know, what I'm really hoping to find is some evidence that will point to the people who are after you. The car's probably stolen—ones used for a crime often are, but it's worth a shot. We need all the breaks we can get."

She indicated that he should drive several miles farther up the road. Somewhere ahead was the spot where the tire had blown and she'd been forced to abandon the vehicle. Memories came crowding back. She tried to push back the fear and retain the rest, searching her mind for more clues, but a cold dread filled her.

"Are you okay?" Daniel asked as he drove slowly up the graveled road.

"I can handle it." Aware she'd been trembling, she tried to will her body to grow still, but it was a losing battle.

It took a few more minutes for them to find where she'd left the vehicle. It was hard to pinpoint the location because there were no markers and all the piñon trees and rocks seemed to look pretty much the same.

"Okay, stop. It's over there," she said, pointing to a spot ahead. He pulled to the side, and they got out of the SUV.

"It's down in that low spot in the middle of all that scrub brush. If you look hard, you can just about see it from here," Hannah said.

"I can understand why the cops didn't spot it. Their search area was a little over ten miles back and the car was well hidden. It appears that our John Doe made it quite a ways before he was killed."

Daniel walked ahead of her and Wolf, cautioning her and guiding the dog over hard ground so they wouldn't leave their own footprints behind and mislead the police once he called it in and they came out to investigate. Choosing a suitable spot for Wolf, he ordered the dog to stay before they actually reached the car.

Daniel walked around the vehicle once, then, taking a pair of latex gloves from his pocket, he slipped them on so he wouldn't contaminate the scene with fingerprints. "The car certainly doesn't look like it's in very good shape. I'm surprised it carried you at all in this terrain. But one thing's clear. It wasn't used in a hit-and-run. There are no new dents, and no traces of blood anywhere," he said, going over the exterior carefully. "The flat tire is here just as you described and, from what I can see, this car hasn't moved an inch since you left it here."

"Which means someone else hit the guy who was going to kill me." She wondered again if she'd caused the man's death, even indirectly. The possibility made her blood go cold. If she had, his blood would be on her hands for the rest of her days.

Almost as if reading her mind, he added, "Remember, his death is probably not connected to what you had to do to get away. My guess is that his boss doesn't like failure, and he was run down by his own people."

Daniel opened the door, then began searching the interior. "I can see on the passenger side the spot where you pulled out the seat belt bracket that was used to fasten the handcuffs." Extracting the car registration from the glove compartment, he called Silentman. Their conversation took a few minutes, but Daniel finally turned to Hannah as he hung up.

"The registration is for the real owner, but the vehicle was stolen a few days ago in Arizona, and the tags were taken from yet another hot car. There's nothing more for us here. The rest is up to the police department. They can dust the car for prints and try to match them to the John Doe they found. Hopefully, they'll be able to ID the man who kidnapped you in no time at all."

"My fingerprints will also be in the car," she said in a flat voice. It was easier not to allow herself to feel anything right now. She had to think clearly and that meant pushing back her fear and keeping it locked away inside her.

"I know, but there's nothing we can do about that. We can't wipe prints—not without destroying other evidence that might lead to the suspects." He captured her gaze with his own. "Don't worry. We'll see this through, too. We're going to win this."

"But once the police find this car, my enemies will score another victory." She saw the flicker of emotions in his eyes and knew he'd reasoned it out, too. "There are traces of the man's blood on the driver's door, and that'll indicate that there was a struggle. Once they have that information, I'll become their prime suspect. It's inevitable."

"They can't prove that struggle was with you—only that you were in the car sometime," he pointed out.

"It'll still look pretty bad for me, particularly because I'm on the run," she said in a heavy voice. "I wish there was some way I could force myself to remember those missing hours at the church. I've been thinking a lot about it, Daniel. I can't help but wonder if what happened that day is linked somehow to my father's suicide."

"Your uncle was present both times and that supports the possibility that there might be a connection. Maybe the link to your past is something that was left unsettled and has now resurfaced because of something that you saw or heard."

"I know you think that my uncle is a crook and behind all this somehow. But that's not the kind of man he is, believe me. After my father died, I desperately needed him and he was there for me. He takes his responsibilities very seriously."

"But, because you did need him so much at the time, is it possible that you blocked out something that he did—or didn't do—the night your father died?"

"Even if I had, how would that tie in with recent events? It just doesn't make sense!" She shook her head, exasperated. "No one died at the church."

"We don't really know that for a fact," Daniel said thoughtfully. "But I admit it does seem unlikely. Nobody else has been reported missing that we know about, and your kidnapper sure didn't die at the church. Is it possible you misconstrued something you heard or saw?"

"I'm not someone who falls apart at the slightest thing. You've seen that. We've been on the run and having confrontations with people who clearly want me dead, and they haven't broken me yet. Whatever happened was far more than a misunderstanding on my part."

"But when something happens that reminds you of the past—like seeing the gun in one of the men's hands—

you're certainly not yourself. Remember how you locked up before?''

Hannah nodded. ''Images get jumbled in my mind, that's true. But I didn't forget that incident.''

''Good point.'' He paused then continued in a slow somber tone. ''But you're more fragile than you realize, Hannah. I have a gut feeling that the memories you're suppressing are like a time bomb of major proportions.''

His voice was gentle, but guarded, as if he were working hard to hold something back and Hannah noticed it immediately. She realized then that, despite everything, her past stood between them because it made him uncertain of her. Her heart breaking, she pressed him to speak his mind. ''Talk to me. Tell me what's bothering you.''

''There *is* something I've been meaning to talk to you about.'' He paused, then continued, his unwavering gaze now on hers. ''I owe you an apology, Hannah. What happened between us the other night—well, it shouldn't have happened. I took advantage of you—''

She held up a hand, interrupting him. ''I wanted the same thing you did. But you're right. It shouldn't have happened.'' Hannah saw the surprised look on his face, and suddenly wondered if he'd thought she would try to hold him and exact promises from him he couldn't make because of what happened.

She shook free of the thought. It didn't matter, not anymore. The important thing was that she had to stop thinking with her heart once and for all. The truth was that she had no future, not until she faced all the demons in her past. The only thing she could offer Daniel now were feelings that were as fragmented as she was. And that just wasn't good enough—not for her and not for him.

She moved away silently and Daniel let her go without pressing her for more answers. That fact alone hurt her far more deeply than she'd imagined possible.

Daniel waited several long moments before finally

breaking the silence. "I'm going to make an anonymous call to the PD," he said in a businesslike tone. "Don't say anything until I hang up." As she nodded, Daniel flipped open the cell phone. He spoke to the officer on duty in a low, barely audible voice, reported the abandoned car and its location, then quickly hung up.

"What if they trace that call back to you?"

"They don't have the sophisticated equipment it would take to trace a cell phone. We're okay for now as long as we don't hang around here any longer."

Once they returned to the SUV, Hannah leaned back into the seat and closed her eyes, fighting back tears. "You know, even if I win this fight, I wonder how much of the life I left behind will still be there for me when I return? I may have to move far away, someplace where no one has ever heard of me, and rebuild my life."

Wolf, sensing she was upset, stuck his nose between the seat backs and tried to lick her hand. Absently Hannah scratched the big dog on the muzzle.

When Daniel remained uncharacteristically silent, she glanced over at him. There was a quiet acceptance on his face. She suddenly understood that he'd known all along what the price of survival might be.

DANIEL STEPPED OUT of the SUV to talk to Silentman while Hannah took Wolf on a brief walk. Getting good reception on a cell phone out on the Rez was a tricky thing sometimes, with relay towers few and far between. He ended up climbing to the top of a hillside before he got a signal strong enough to dial out. Even then, the transmission was weak, though he managed to hear enough to know that the situation continued to be bleak.

Minutes later, he walked back to the SUV, noting that Hannah and the hairy beast had already returned, and were back inside. Although he'd hoped that Silentman would uncover something useful from the files he'd copied from

Robert Jones's computer, no discrepancies had been found. The deacon looked to be as pure as the driven snow. The news would please Hannah, but he wasn't in the mood to celebrate. His gut was telling him that they were missing something important. This case had more twists and turns than he'd ever expected. It had been that way from day one. Maybe the flat tire on the way to Handler's office that morning had been an omen.

Hannah's story still had more holes in it than Swiss cheese, but he believed in her innocence, and the scanty evidence he'd obtained from the car had backed her up. Hannah lived with more shadows than light. There was no denying that. Yet, at the core of her was a strong spirit that called to him.

He ran an exasperated hand through his hair wondering when he'd become such an emotional sap. Maybe he'd been inhaling too much car exhaust lately and that had scrambled his thinking.

The sad truth was that these days he didn't even recognize himself. Though he normally avoided relationships, he'd dived headlong into this one. Now his life was hopelessly entangled with Hannah's, proving what he'd known all along. Love was a lot like a trick knee. You could beat back the pain by gritting your teeth, but from the moment you first got hurt, things were never the same again.

As he climbed back into the SUV, she looked up at him with those hazel eyes that did strange things to his mind. He looked away and started the engine.

''Your uncle's files, the ones I managed to copy, were clean,'' he said.

''I told you they would be,'' Hannah smiled briefly. ''But what now?'' she added in a serious tone. ''Is there anything else we can follow up on?''

''Silentman suggested I go talk to Pablo Jackson.''

''Our church organist? Why?''

''He's the chairman of several church committees as

well as being a prominent businessman. He may know something useful.''

''You're forgetting something...''

''You mean that he's seen us together at the church?'' He shook his head. ''No, I haven't forgotten. But what he saw was an old Navajo man and woman.''

''What if he recognizes something about you and puts it together?''

''Not likely. Remember he only saw us briefly and neither of us looked directly at him. I think it's an acceptable risk considering we're pretty much out of leads.''

She nodded. ''I wish you'd never gotten involved in this mess. You can't be sure of me, Daniel, not under the circumstances, yet you're risking your life nearly every moment of the day. That's just not right.''

''I wouldn't walk out on anyone who was in a situation like yours—least of all, you.''

''And that's precisely why you *should* walk away,'' she said quietly.

''I know. I've let it get personal between you and me and that's not a good thing for you. But I *am* the best man for this job. You don't need a P.I. who's packing or goes by the book. So you're stuck with me, lady. I'm not turning this case over to anyone else.''

Wolf sat up in the back seat, barked and put a paw upon the seat back. ''And that goes for him, too,'' Daniel added.

She reached back and patted the animal on his head, and he sighed contentedly. ''You're both too stubborn for your own good.''

''The mutt and I are in this with you for the count, Hannah. Get used to it.'' He turned all his attention back to driving for a while before speaking again. ''Now tell me, how much do you know about Jackson?''

''I run into him now and then, and we exchange greetings, but that's as far as it goes. We're not friends, just acquaintances. Are you going over to talk to him right now?"

"Yeah. Silentman arranged for me to meet him over at the church office."

"I'd really like to go inside while you do that and just sit quietly in one of the pews. I know that the key to everything is remembering what happened at the church, and I can't help but feel that if I sit there alone with my thoughts, I'll somehow remember. I've always felt secure in that setting."

"Then by all means go for it. But Wolf will have to stay in the vehicle, and you'll have to wear your wig. We need to figure out a way to hide your face somehow, too. Otherwise it's just too risky. Maybe a veil?"

"How about if I wear a scarf? It's really windy outside today, so if I'm wearing one loosely around my hair no one's going to think much of it."

They stopped at the trading post and Daniel went inside. Instead of doing his usual, simply picking whatever was right in front of him, he took his time. For some crazy reason it was important to him that she like what he selected for her.

He came out several minutes later and handed her a small paper sack. He watched her as she took it out, knowing that she couldn't hide her thoughts from him easily.

Her expression as she admired the vivid turquoise and deep sunrise gold silk scarf made him smile.

"It's really beautiful. Thank you."

Her smile warmed him. He'd wanted to cheer her up a little, if only for a few moments, and it made him feel good to know she'd liked what he'd bought for her. Had things been different, he would have romanced her, bringing flowers and wine and little gifts for no reason at all. But as it was, this was the best he could do.

Anger at the sleazy thugs who had put her in this position coiled in his gut like a rattlesnake. Her enemies were his now, and he would equalize the odds against her. That was something else he could do for her, and do well.

Chapter Thirteen

When they arrived at the church, Daniel took a careful look around the parking lot. It was empty except for the pickup Hannah identified as belonging to Pablo Jackson.

"I'm going in through the side door, Hannah. Give me a few minutes to get him occupied, then come in quietly. Just remember to stay out of sight."

Hannah looked back at Wolf. "Will he be okay alone in the SUV?"

Wolf barked once as if in assent.

"Sure he will. I'll leave the back open, and he can climb out over the gate if he gets too hot, but with the low temperature and the breeze, he'll be okay. I'm more concerned about you."

"Don't be, Daniel. The front doors are always open this time of day, and I'll go right in. All I intend to do is sit there and let my thoughts drift."

She paused, looking thoughtfully at the church. "For years I protected myself from memories I couldn't handle. But not having the knowledge I need is now more of a threat than anything I could possibly remember. I'm not a little girl anymore. I know who I am and that I can depend on my own strength to help me cope with anything."

She smiled hesitantly. "Sounds great, huh? Now if only my memory would cooperate."

"It will," he said encouragingly. She was in a fight against herself, and those were the toughest battles of all. "See you in a bit then. And be careful."

"I will."

Daniel entered the church and walked down the corridor. Hearing footsteps ahead, he headed for the deacon's office. Jackson was inside sitting on a small sofa, studying building plans he'd placed on the cushion beside him.

Jackson gave him a nod. "Come in and make yourself comfortable. I'm glad your boss called me. All he wanted was more background information, but it made me realize that it was time we spoke. There's more to what happened here than you were told and you need to hear the whole story."

"So you *have* been holding back on me. I always suspected that there was more to this case than I was told." Daniel sat down on the chair opposite him.

Jackson rolled up the blueprints and placed them back inside a cardboard tube. "There's something we should have told you right from the start, but we'd made an agreement..." He shook his head. "Let me start again. This is complicated, and you need to understand."

"Take your time, and start at the beginning. I'm listening." At least Jackson hadn't recognized him as the old man from the other day. Maybe their luck was finally turning. But as much as he wanted to believe that, he couldn't ignore the instincts that were warning him to remain on his guard.

"I'm afraid that none of us have been really up-front with Gray Wolf Investigations. Bob Jones made the contact on our behalf, but we all decided as a group how much you were to be told. We share the responsibility—and the guilt—equally."

Get to it, Daniel urged silently. He didn't like leaving Hannah alone in this place. A survival instinct he couldn't explain warned him that the danger to her was greater here than anywhere else—but so was the chance of finding the answers.

"You see, we like to protect those close to us," Jackson continued. "This is a relatively small church, but it means a great deal to all of us. We raised the money to build it, and we've kept it going through the years despite our shoestring budget. It hasn't been easy, but we're proud of what we've done for the community. We have an open door policy and anyone who needs us can always come here and get help. That's the reason we've found it so hard to cope with the fact that one of our own felt it necessary to steal from us."

There was something about Jackson that was making Daniel's skin crawl. He was trying too hard to justify himself and his friends, and his words sounded rehearsed. "What exactly did you keep back?"

"The amount of money that's missing from church accounts is far more than a few thousand. It's closer to one hundred thousand. Every dime that had been allocated to the construction fund is gone, and we don't know how it disappeared."

Daniel remained still. This was something he'd already suspected. "Why did you decide to cover that up?"

"It was out of respect to Bob Jones, Hannah's uncle. He's one of the most trusted and dedicated members of the congregation, and we were afraid that if the real story got out, Hannah would be facing grand larceny charges. Our church's image in the community would be hard hit if the news got out, too. Let's face it, the cops would have been all over us, turning everything upside down, and the newspaper reporters would have put it on the front page," Jackson said, shaking his head. "We really thought that it was just a matter of finding Hannah, and by hiring you, we felt our problems would be solved. But we didn't expect it to be such a big deal, or that it would take so long to track down a disturbed young woman. No one here believes she acted out of malice.''

It irritated him to hear this man discuss Hannah as if she were a child, and at the same time essentially accuse the agency of incompetence. ''Why have you decided to tell me all this now?''

''The board had a meeting yesterday and we all feel that things are getting out of hand. There's still no sign of Hannah or the missing funds and, now, to top it all, Bob Jones is at home, bedridden. He's been ill for the last few days and it doesn't look like he's getting any better. He claims it's just the flu, but I honestly think it's just overwhelming stress. I believe this whole thing with his niece is just too much for him. Do you know that the police came around asking about Hannah? She's wanted in connection with a hit-and-run. A man was *killed.*''

''Did you tell the police about the theft?''

''Yes, I did. I'm not covering up for her anymore and I've advised Bob to do the same.''

''You went to see him?''

Jackson shook his head. ''No, I spoke to him on the phone.'' He paused, then added, ''The other reason I wanted to speak with you is that we've all decided to ask Gray Wolf Investigations to bring in more people to work on this case. We have to have the money back, and Hannah too. There are just too many open questions about her activities now and we have to protect our reputations. It was never our intent to shield a criminal. We were only trying to protect someone we believed was mentally ill and posed no danger to herself or others. We still don't want to press charges if she returns the money, but we can't protect her from a hit-and-run.''

''Our agency has its own way of working. It's not a matter of increasing manpower, but of getting some leads,'' Daniel said, studying Jackson.

Sudden honesty always made him uneasy, especially

when the man's eyes didn't match the words coming out of his mouth. He needed to press Jackson for more answers, and study his mannerisms for inconsistencies. Fortunately, that was one of the things he did very well.

HANNAH SAT in one of the pews in the empty church. The answers to all her questions were close, like a name at the tip of her tongue. She could feel the memories pushing in from the edges of her mind. A brief flash here, then a feeling, but the second she tried to hold on to them, they drifted away again like wisps of smoke.

She looked around the church, wishing Daniel was with her now. Daniel exuded a calmness that always bolstered her own confidence. She closed her mind to that thought as instantly as it had appeared. She wouldn't allow her feelings for Daniel to come to the surface. There was no place for them in what she had to do. They both had their own demons to fight. Passion drew them closer, but logic demanded that they keep their distance. Survival had to take priority now.

Hearing voices just outside the chapel, Hannah was jolted back to the present. People were drawing close and would undoubtedly try to introduce themselves once they saw her.

She tugged at the sides of her scarf, trying to shield her face even more. As she looked around, searching for the nearest safe exit, she caught a glimpse of Reverend Brown by the main chapel entrance speaking to the caretaker. They'd apparently just arrived. For a brief moment, as his gaze swept over her, she bowed her head as if in prayer. A second later, Revered Brown moved away from the doorway back into the foyer. Seeing it as an opportunity, Hannah quickly walked to the back door and left the church.

Hannah was walking in the direction of the SUV when she saw that Reverend Brown had also stepped outside and now stood between her and the vehicle. He was looking at the condition of the lawn and speaking to the caretaker, and hadn't seen her yet but, if she went past him, he was bound to recognize her.

Hannah angled toward a cluster of young pines in the empty lot next to the church. She'd have cover there in the shade, and still be able to watch for Daniel.

A few minutes later, Daniel came out. He studied the area around him carefully, an ingrained habit of his, and spotted her. Realizing her problem immediately, he said something to Reverend Brown that made him go back inside the church. Then, moving fast, Daniel went to the SUV and drove up to where she was waiting.

"Thanks," she said as she jumped into the vehicle and they got underway. "What did Mr. Jackson have to say?"

"Nothing we can use," he answered, filling her in.

"Poor Uncle Bob! I had no idea he was sick," she said. "I wish I could be there to help him out."

"Don't even think of it. There's no way you can go see him," he said, then quickly changed the subject. "What about you? Did you remember anything?"

"No," she said, frustration evident in her voice. "The memories are still there, but whenever I get too close, a wall goes up and I can't get through."

"Do you have any idea what it is that scares you so much?"

She nodded slowly. "I wish I could say no, but the truth is that I'm afraid of the answers. They may be very different from what I want them to be," she said and paused, trying to gather her thoughts. "Have you ever had to face yourself squarely, Daniel? To see yourself not for the person you might have liked to think you were, but for who you really are?"

"Yeah," he said, his voice taut. "I had to come to terms with myself after my partner was shot. And you're right. It isn't easy. We often fall short of our own expectations."

"But at least you knew that you weren't guilty of anything. Someone else pulled the trigger. I have no way of knowing what, if anything, I'm guilty of doing. Finding out may not free me at all. In fact, it may do the opposite."

"I wasn't blame-free in my partner's death. I could have made different choices and if I had done that, she might have been alive today. But I decided to play it safe and by the book and that mistake will haunt me until the day I die." He wrapped his hands so tightly around the wheel that his knuckles turned white. "Nicki left a two-year-old boy behind, and her sister, Mary, took custody of him. I tried to help financially, but Mary didn't want anything to do with me."

"Why?"

"Because I was her sister's partner and I lived and her sister didn't. I tried to drown my guilt and the pain in a bottle, but it didn't work. It was tough finding my way out of that pit. I had to learn to redefine who and what I was and that took a long time." He took a deep breath and let it out slowly. "But if I could do it, so can you."

"I wish I had half your strength."

"You have all of it," he said, then reached for her hand. "My strength is yours. I'll stand by you and help you through this."

The intensity of his gaze, so full of passion and gentle caring, took her breath away. But, in a heartbeat, that feeling turned into hot awareness, making it hard for her to keep her thinking clear.

Hannah looked away, trying to gather herself. "I *will* find the answers I'm keeping locked in my mind, Daniel," she whispered, "but there's no telling what's on the other side. You're betting on a long shot."

"People saw me as a long shot and a poor risk after my partner died. No one except my cousin Ben ever really believed I'd make it back. But I did. And so will you."

"I don't even know where to begin. How did you do it?"

"I focused on the side of me that I understood and liked—being a martial artist. I'd practice ten hours a day and think about things as I worked."

"More violence? After what you'd been through? How could you stand it?"

"The martial arts don't just teach you how to fight. What you learn is more about control—not over an opponent, but over yourself. It takes dedication and patience to master the techniques, and what that teaches you is that you can accomplish anything, if you're persistent enough. I needed to reconnect with all of that—the disciplines and the hard work—to find myself."

"I don't have anything like that in my life. I wish I did now. What I do have is the knowledge that no matter what life throws at me, I can survive. I may not be a fighter in the same sense you are, but I know I can endure almost anything."

"And from that comes your strength. Focus on it. It'll help you face things squarely and defeat your own fears."

Daniel picked up the cell phone as soon as it rang. Flipping it open with one hand, he listened for a moment, then spoke into it softly in clipped sentences.

"What's wrong?" Hannah asked, seeing the somber expression on his face as he hung up.

"It was Silentman," Daniel said. "Your photo's on the front page of the evening newspaper. We need to pick up a copy and see how good a snapshot it is. The article says that you've disappeared and both police departments are looking for you now. They want to question you about the hit-and-run death of an unemployed ex-con out on parole. Apparently they only found three sets of prints in the car—the original owner's, yours and those of the dead man, a career criminal named Calvin Beck. Beck usually worked as a wheel man during armed robberies but most of his old gang members are in jail. The cops believe he may have been killed by some old enemies, but they're still trying to come up with a suspect. That's why they're looking for you.''

''So, it's like I feared. I've become their prime suspect.'' Black despair settled over her. Everything was falling apart around her, and she was hurting the people she loved most. Her uncle was in disgrace because of her and, as it had been with her father, she couldn't do a thing to help him. To make things even worse, the police were involved in this now, and by protecting her, Daniel was risking his own future.

''Daniel, we have to change our tactics. I can't let you and my uncle suffer because of me. This stops now. I think the moment has come to use me as bait to draw my enemies out of the shadows.''

Daniel gave her a startled look. ''Absolutely not. We're not that desperate.''

She saw the stony look on his face and knew she wouldn't be able to sway him. ''Keep in mind that if we don't find answers soon, we may not have a choice.''

She'd made a good point, but risking her life that way went against everything he'd tried to do from day one. ''If it comes to that, then you can count on one thing—I'll be right there beside you, and you can pity anyone who tries to harm you.''

Chapter Fourteen

Daniel bought a copy of the afternoon paper at a machine in front of a convenience store, then drove away quickly, giving the paper to Hannah without even taking time to glance at it.

Hannah looked at the headlines. "The reporter found out about the missing funds, and is breaking the story as his exclusive."

Daniel found a deserted trail with plenty of ground cover, then continued down the bumpy road. Once he was sure they couldn't be seen from the main road, he stopped and parked.

"I assumed that the police would run the photo of you the kidnapper had, but that's not the same shot," he said as they studied the front page together. "Where do you think he got that one? Have you seen it before?"

Hannah looked away. "It's not important. The only thing that matters is what we do now. This photo is a close-up of my face and a clear one."

"You'll have to wear the red wig full-time. Your most striking features are your light hazel eyes, and that shows up really well in the paper's photo, despite the grainy quality."

"And when I'm inside?"

"Don't make eye contact. I'd tell you to wear the sunglasses then, too, but it'll attract even more attention."

He shifted in his seat, his back to the door, and regarded her squarely. "But I'd still like to know where that photo came from. I have a feeling you know."

"Yes, I do," she answered, her voice taut. "My uncle took that picture a few months ago. It used to be on his desk at the church."

A muscle tightened in his jaw. "I think it's time I had another talk with the deacon. And I think you'd do yourself a world of good by listening in carefully."

"You're right. He may mention something that'll give me an idea. He knows everyone I do, but his perspective is different from mine."

Daniel could sense a change in her. Hannah was still afraid, but she'd turned that fear into an asset like a seasoned cop or a veteran investigator. He looked at her with new admiration.

As a kid, Hannah had done what she'd needed to in order to survive. Now as a woman she was using the same iron will that had helped her cope back then to shatter the very doors her mind had closed.

"You're one hell of a woman, Hannah."

"That's a nice thing to say," she said, astonished.

"Why do you act so surprised?" he asked.

"You may not have noticed, but you're not exactly big on compliments," she said with a laugh.

"I've told you how beautiful you are."

She laughed softly. "Yes, but once it was matter-of-fact and it didn't sound like a compliment, and the next time…well, because of what was happening between us at the time, I don't think it counts."

"Of course it does. It matters even more," he said with a purely masculine grin. "I was in a position to see exactly how beautiful you are."

Seeing her blush, he smiled. He remembered every second of that night, the way her body had opened to him, how he'd fit inside her warmth. Quickly his memories became vivid images that were impossible to brush aside. Desire grew inside him hard and fast, making his body impossibly hard.

Control. He had to stay focused now. He kept his eyes on the road, but he was aware of everything about her—from the gentle curve of her breasts pressing against her shirt, to the wild strand of dark hair that curled and brushed against her cheek.

The observation had a positive result, however, and he reminded her to put on the wig. There could be no slipups now.

A half hour later, they drove down the long residential street that led to Bob Jones's home.

"Give me a chance to get into the back and duck down so I'm not easily seen. I don't want my uncle to spot me and this red wig isn't going to fool him for more than a few seconds."

The words had come out slowly and heavily and he realized that despite everything she'd said, a part of her was afraid that the protector she'd counted on throughout her life would turn out to be a traitor.

He felt her pain as keenly as if it had been his own, but there was nothing he could do to protect her from the truth.

He pulled off to the side of the road. "Okay, it's time. Get in the back and stay behind those boxes."

"Let Wolf and me change places and have him sit in the passenger's seat. No one will get close to the SUV."

"Good thought."

Once they were ready, Daniel continued toward Bob Jones's home. Daniel slowed down, looking for the house number Hannah had given him, but as he drew near he saw two officers he recognized standing on the front porch of a large home on the next block. "Let me guess. Your uncle's home is blue and has a large elm in the front."

''Yeah, that's the one. Can't you see the house number?''

''Not from here, but the other signs tipped me off.'' He filled her in as he parked across the street in the shade. ''I recognize both those cops. They moonlight when they're off duty.''

''Why are cops keeping an eye on my uncle?''

''I don't know, but I'm going to find out.'' He picked up the small microphone he'd used before and stuck it in his shirt pocket.

''I'm glad we still have our delivery truck disguise. At least the cops won't be able to see me back here from across the street.''

''It's some protection, true, but those guys are good. I don't like to take anything for granted around them. Take care.'' He tested the mike assuring himself it was working properly. ''I'm going to talk to the cops first. Listen carefully to everything that's said. Something's going on and, with luck, it may turn out to be something we can use to our advantage.''

''Maybe the same people who came after me went after my uncle and that's why he's being protected. Will those guys tell you honestly what's going on?''

''They trust me, and they're friends of mine—well, at least one of them is. But whether or not they'll confide in me depends on how delicate the situation there is. I'll give it my best shot and see what happens.''

Daniel left the SUV with Wolf watching out the front driver's side window. As he approached the porch, Frank, a tall, blond-haired, broad-shouldered bodybuilder with no neck gave him a casual lopsided grin.

''What brings you here, Eagle? I haven't seen you in months. I heard that you're freelancing cases these days. Is that true?''

''Sure is, and right now I'm handling a little business for the deacon,'' Daniel answered.

"Jeez, how many of us has this man hired?" Gary, a short, athletic-looking black man asked as he came up to greet Daniel.

"I'm not part of his protection, guys. I'm just settling a business matter for him. And, as far as I know, there's nothing dangerous about it. I'm surprised to see the two of you here."

Frank shrugged. "The money's good, even if the guy's a bit paranoid."

"How so?"

"He hired us to protect him, and you know we know our business," Gary replied. "But he gets really squirrelly if we so much as take a break. He actually times us. And it's not as if we both leave together, or anything like that. It's almost as if he wants a show of force for whoever drives by."

"What's the threat?"

Frank shrugged. "You'll have to ask him about that."

"What's the deal when you two have to leave to do the cop thing?"

"Another team comes in," Gary answered.

"More cops?"

"One of them is, Billy Skinner. Remember him? The other guy is ex-military, the son of a member of his church. Bigger than Frank, with goalposts for shoulders." Gary smiled.

"What's the deacon do when he has to leave the residence? The team on duty provides an escort?"

"That's just it. He never steps foot out of his home," Gary continued. "He hasn't gone to work or even to the store since he hired us the day after his niece took off. He has everything delivered, and he has us check it all before it enters the house."

Frank cocked his head toward the front door. "If you want to see him, I've got to go talk to him first. Otherwise, I can't even let you get as far as the front porch."

"Go ask then. I have no intention of leaving here without talking to him."

"If he says no, you'll either leave, or I'll have to toss your butt back to the curb." Frank crossed his arms on his chest.

"Easy to say, hard to do," Daniel said, his voice calm.

"I've heard about your martial arts skills, and I've always wanted to see just how good you are," Frank said with a smile that challenged. "I just love a good scuffle."

"Anytime you want to play, just square off. I won't take long."

Gary laughed. "Boys, boys, that's enough." He glanced at his partner, who was a head taller than himself. "Frank, go talk to the deacon and see if he's accepting any visitors."

"Don't take my partner too seriously," Gary told Daniel as soon as Frank walked off. "He's been training in martial arts and pumping iron, and now he's itching to show what he's learned. That's all there is to that."

"He hasn't learned much if he still needs to prove himself."

"He's young. He'll learn after he gets bounced around a few times."

A moment later Frank returned, scowling. "Jones said for you to come right in."

Gary laughed. "And that probably was the biggest favor fate ever did for you, Frank."

Daniel gave Frank a nod, then strode past him. As he did, Frank tried to trip him up by sweeping with his right leg.

In the blink of an eye, Daniel pivoted around the sweep, simultaneously driving his clenched fist into Frank's midsection, knocking the wind out of him. Frank, gasping for breath, tried a jab of his own, but Daniel slipped inside the punch, blocked his arm as it flew past, then grabbed it and pulled back his index finger with a minimum of force.

Daniel bent it backwards, forcing Frank to his knees. "Stop now, and I'll let you go."

"Yeah, man. I was only going to tempt you to go a few rounds at the gym."

"You're not ready," Daniel said quietly. "You still need to learn about judgment and self-discipline."

As he stepped forward and knocked on the door, Daniel heard Gary light into the younger cop. "You're lucky he wasn't interested in a little exercise. I've seen him pile four drunken bikers into a silent heap before the bar owner could even dial 911."

As the front door opened a few inches, Daniel shifted his attention to the man before him.

"Come in quickly," Bob Jones said, standing inside the door so he couldn't be seen from the street.

Daniel entered the darkened living room. All the curtains were drawn and there was a strong smell of old food and coffee. As he glanced around, he saw leftover pizza and TV dinners.

"I heard you've been ill," Daniel said casually.

"Very. Now tell me. Have you found Hannah, or at least have some very solid leads?"

"You'll be the first to know when I do. Actually, I came on another matter. It seems your niece is now front-page news."

Jones nodded. "I saw it," he said, gesturing to the opened newspaper on the couch. "Do you realize that's the same photo I kept on my desk at the church?"

"Then you gave it to the reporter?"

"No way. This is exactly the kind of situation I was hoping to avoid. Someone must have taken it from my desk," he said, glaring at Daniel. "You're the detective. Find out. Better yet, find my niece."

Daniel looked around slowly. "The security outside and the way you've entrenched yourself in here—this isn't about you being ill. I've been around the block a few times, Deacon. You're scared to death. What's made you afraid to step outside?''

''Had you found my niece, I wouldn't have had to take such drastic measures,'' he shot back. When Daniel didn't answer, he added, ''If you must know, I'm afraid that Hannah might come back and try to kill me. I believe she's lost her mind completely. There's no other explanation. The police came to talk to me. They're looking for her in connection to a hit-and-run. The man is dead, and they think maybe she hit him with her car.'' He ran an unsteady hand through his hair. ''I should have seen this coming. First she bashes me on the head, now this. She's getting progressively worse. Unless we get her back, and put her where she's safe and can't harm anyone else, there's no telling what will happen next.''

''You told me before you couldn't be sure she was the one who'd hit you.''

''Well, yes, but that was *before* I learned about this hit-and-run. Hannah is starting to pop up wherever there's trouble and that's just too coincidental in my book.''

Daniel shook his head. ''There's something that just doesn't add up for me. You told me that Hannah was hospitalized after her father's suicide, but not since that time. Yet you're now willing to believe that she's not only guilty of theft but of hit-and-run as well without even giving her the benefit of the doubt. Why is that?''

''The evidence is there, what else can I do? You have to understand that my niece has always been fragile mentally. I'm no doctor, but my guess is that there's a lot of suppressed anger inside her, and it has finally come to the surface. She has been under a great deal of pressure lately, and I believe she snapped under the strain.''

Jones walked Daniel back to the door. ''I'm scared for myself, but I've got to tell you, I'm just as frightened for her. No matter how it seems to you, I love her very much and I don't want her digging a hole so deep for herself no one will be able to get her out. As it stands, she's already taking people like me and others at the church down with her. You know what I'm talking about, right? I understand that you've already been told that the amount that's missing is far more than I said originally. And now that it's public knowledge, we're going to have to account for our actions to the membership of the church."

"You should have told us the truth right from the beginning. Acting on the basis of bad information is dangerous for everyone involved," Daniel said.

"You know why we held back that information. But you still haven't said if you're any closer to finding my niece and the money."

"I expect to find her very soon," he said reaching for the knob. "I'll stay in touch."

"No details?"

"Not yet. Handling a case like this is a delicate matter. We're all better off if I keep things to myself until I have all the evidence. Once I do, you'll be the first to know about it."

"I don't like your attitude," Jones said firmly. "I'd like to know what's happened and what you're planning to do next. As your client, I have that right."

"Yes, you do. And when I have something concrete, I'll pass it on. Leads and sources have to be protected, and I can't compromise my plans or contacts to you. The church hired the agency because of our expertise. Let us do our job."

Jones scowled. "All right. But try to move things along, will you? Every day there's a new complication, and things just keep getting worse."

As Daniel left the house, Gary came over to meet him. "Jones is a real oddball, isn't he?"

Daniel nodded. "I don't see why he's so afraid. I've heard about his niece..." He shrugged. "But that doesn't jibe. If she's a thief, she's long gone by now. I have a feeling he's holding back on something else,'' Daniel commented, using a technique he'd found effective in the past. People were much less guarded if they assumed you were on their side and knew as much as they did.

''Off the record?'' Seeing Daniel nod, Gary continued. ''I know that the niece he's afraid of is supposed to be a little loony so that's part of it. But she's dropped out of sight, and from what I've heard, she's probably on the run with a chunk of cash. Why he thinks she'll still try to get him is beyond me. He must have done something seriously bad to her if he needs to take all these precautions.''

''Even so,'' Daniel said giving him a skeptical look. ''There's something not right here. He wants us to believe he's holed up like a scared jackrabbit because he's afraid of his niece? What's she got—sniper and demolition training?'' Daniel scoffed. ''There's a big chunk missing from his story, bud. Watch your back.''

''Well, it's a little more than just his niece. Apparently she hired some goons to help her.''

This was exactly the kind of lead he'd been hoping to get. He knew the muscle boys were after Hannah, not working for her. Jones had twisted the story. But to have knowledge of her attackers, he had to be involved. Either he'd been paid a visit by the goons, or he was working with them.

Of course there was a third option. If Jones really didn't know that the muscle boys were after his niece—and he really was afraid that Hannah had hired the same men to kill him—there was a lot he wasn't saying about how he'd treated his niece.

''The deacon's made sure we're all packing,'' Gary added with a shrug. ''The guy's fear is for real. He's spending a lot of money on protection.''

''Yeah, so I see. Take care, Gary.''

Daniel returned to the SUV, deep in thought. He wanted to protect Hannah, but there *was* a conspiracy against her, and half of the campaign was being waged with innuendo. The damage something like that created was far more insidious and harder to fight.

"You heard the conversation?" Daniel asked once they were a few blocks away from the deacon's house. As she sat up, he glanced in the rearview mirror.

"Yes," she said, her voice strained.

Seeing the shock and sorrow mirrored on her face, he cursed himself for having insisted she listen in. "Hannah, I'm really sorry. But there's a lot more going on than we suspected."

She remained silent and he didn't press her. Once he reached the highway, Daniel pulled off the road and Hannah came to the front seat, switching with Wolf again.

"There's something I have to know, Daniel. Do you still believe I'm innocent?"

"I know you are." And he did, with every instinct he possessed. "More than one person is trying very hard to frame you, and stories are being twisted right and left. They wouldn't need to go to all that trouble if you were really guilty."

"I wouldn't have stolen money or tried to hurt anyone, Daniel. True, I still can't remember those few hours, but I really don't believe I'm capable of doing that. I find the whole idea completely revolting." She paused, then continued in a sad voice. "I can't believe my uncle really thinks I pose a threat to him. And how did he conclude that the men after me are people I hired to go after him?"

"You're missing the bigger picture," Daniel said, recounting what he'd deduced.

"Those men must have paid my uncle a visit, and blackmailed him into saying those things. By claiming that he's guarding himself against me, he's keeping the focus on me, not on the real guilty people." She bit her lip, lost in thought, then sighed. "But, even if they pressured him, I expected better from my own uncle."

"I'm sorry, Hannah. If I could do something to shield you from this, I would."

She shook her head. "It's too late for me to be shielded from anything, Daniel, and I really don't want that kind of protection. I've spent too much of my life running away from things that would hurt me, or locking them away in a dark corner of my mind. As a kid, I needed that and I did what I had to do. But, as an adult, I need to prove to myself that I can cope with life, no matter what it throws at me. I'm ready to face all the things I've been blocking out. For the first time in my life, I want to remember everything."

Her courage attracted him as much as her beauty. Life had dealt her some harsh blows, and she'd hidden herself away, trying to heal. But so had he. Maybe that was the reason why he could understand her pain so well. No one ever went through life unscathed, but some paid a higher price than others.

Daniel brushed a strand of hair from her face, and the look she gave him slipped past all his defenses. His heart began to beat double time.

He looked away, bringing his thoughts back into line. He swore he'd help her and the incessant need he felt for her played no part in what he had to do. But fighting the way he felt about Hannah was like battling nature itself. Whenever she fastened her gaze on him trusting him to deliver what he'd promised, a victory over her enemies, she made him feel like a noble knight fighting for some idealistic cause instead of the pragmatic, jaded warrior he'd become over the years.

Daniel watched her absently petting Wolf as the dog stuck his head between the seats. The dog seemed to sense Hannah's heaviness of spirit as much as he did.

"We're going to have to break some rules and push the envelope," Daniel said. "But I don't want to lie to you. There's a big risk involved and your entire world may come crashing down around you. If we go after your enemies with everything we've got, they're going to come right back at us, and they could have a lot more resources and surprises in store for us. They won't play fair, and they're playing to win."

"So am I. I'm tired of running away, Daniel. I want to make a life for myself—a rich one filled with everything that makes it worth living. I've been on the sidelines too long, and I want to be free."

"Then our course is set." Daniel glanced over at Hannah.

"Tell me everything you know, fact or speculation, about your uncle's business."

"He has a real estate firm here in town, and I know he works long hours."

"But you said that he's been having some financial problems. Any idea why?"

She took a deep breath, then let it out again. "I can't be sure, but my guess is that he's hit a slump. Three years ago he bought out his partner, Ed. Unfortunately, Ed was the one who had the right instincts for that kind of business, and was the one who'd kept the company running smoothly for ten years. My uncle spends too much time trying to live up to his image as a deacon for the church. I've heard he's made some very bad deals and I think it's because he doesn't want to appear greedy or materialistic. That's another reason why I know he couldn't have stolen anything. His image is very important to him." She stared at her lap thoughtfully. "Even after what I heard him say about me, it still bothers me to talk about him like this to anyone. I don't like being disloyal."

"Right now your first priority has to be getting to the bottom of things," Daniel said. "When you're fighting for your life, survival takes priority. You can't let anything stand in the way of what we need to do."

"I know, and that's why I'm going to suggest something

that I never would have under different circumstances. I'd like to go to his office in town and take a look at his books for myself. I want to see what he's been up to, and check out the extent of his money troubles."

"I'm glad you suggested that. We need answers right now. There's no telling what'll happen in the next day or two."

"Then let's go."

"Not so fast." Daniel shook his head. "Carrying out an operation like that is tricky. Breaking and entering is illegal, and that alone can get us arrested."

"We won't be breaking—just entering. I know where he keeps a spare key."

"He's bound to have some form of security there, too."

"He does, so we'll have to make sure we don't get caught."

"I'm a private investigator, not a miracle worker. We can't just waltz in there without a definite plan."

"All along you've been telling me and showing me that you're the best at what you do. These details should be right up your alley. I'm sure you have plenty of tricks up your sleeve."

Daniel hesitated. His job was to keep her safe, not take her straight into harm's way.

"Your idea's a sound one, but I'm going there alone," he said at last.

"No chance. My uncle has played a part in what's been happening to me, and I need to understand exactly what's been going on. Besides, I know his accounting codes and understand his method of bookkeeping. You don't. If you go alone, you'll spend half of your time there trying to figure out where to search and what the numbers mean. If I'm with you, we can get in and out fast."

She'd made a valid point, and he knew she deserved to go. But it was hard for him to agree. There was no telling what would happen there.

"You need me there, and I need to go for my own reasons," she added in a soft but firm voice.

He weighed the options, but knew she was right. The truth would bring her heartache, he could feel it in his bones, but she deserved the chance to face things squarely.

"Okay. Where's the key hidden?" he asked.

"Underneath one of the rocks used to landscape the front. I'll show you."

"Slow down. We also need an alternate escape plan in case things go wrong."

"You're making things too complicated," she said. "All we have to do is go in, work fast and take off. That leaves only one rule to remember—don't get caught."

Wolf leaned forward easing between the seats and looked at Daniel with a panting grin. It was impossible, of course, but Daniel could have sworn the dog was laughing at him.

Chapter Fifteen

First, at Daniel's insistence, they stopped at a clothing outlet. Although they'd spent less than five minutes in the store, he'd watched over her carefully as they picked out warm, dark-colored clothes for the operation.

Unwilling to take any unnecessary risks by remaining in public any longer than they had to, he hustled her outside as soon as he'd settled the bill.

"You should have given me time to change clothes inside. Now you'll have to find someplace for me to do that—unless you want me to just get into the back..."

"No." He'd spoken too fast to pass off his answer as casual and the tiny smile on her face told him she'd guessed his thoughts. Damn, what did the woman expect? Did she really think he'd keep his thoughts on the road while she lay down right behind him and stripped? His body and brain would reach meltdown temperature in zero seconds flat.

"There's an outcropping of boulders beside the road up ahead. You can go behind them and change in privacy."

Hannah opened the bag and glanced inside. "These additional clothes will come in handy now that the weather's cooling off even more. I heard over the radio in the store that the temperature is going to drop into the forties tonight."

"That's one of the reasons I knew we needed different clothes. You would not only be cold in that light blue sweater, you would also stand out too easily moving around inside a darkened office if a security guard happened to pass by."

A few minutes later, he pulled to the side of the road and gestured toward the tall boulders beside a cliff. "I'll stay here. It won't take me long to change from this tan sweater into a dark one, and I don't need the privacy. Take Wolf with you." He signaled to the dog, who eagerly followed her.

As she and her furry escort walked toward the rocks, Daniel changed sweaters quickly. The new one fit well, something that was a pleasant surprise considering how much time he'd spent watching over her and how little time he'd spent picking out his own sweater and jacket.

Minutes ticked by. Glancing at his watch, he climbed out of the SUV and called to Hannah, a little concerned. "You okay?" How long could it take for her to put on a sweater and a pair of pants? Maybe he'd hurried her too much and she'd picked out the wrong size.

"One moment," she answered.

As several more minutes passed, Daniel swore to himself repeatedly. He should have known that the word *moment* was only a relative term, compared to an ice age, when uttered by a woman.

An eternity later, Wolf walked into view, and then Hannah finally stepped out from behind cover. As his gaze took her in, he forgot all about the dog.

The jeans conformed to Hannah's body as if they'd been tailor-made for her. Instead of a sweater, she'd picked a black pullover that seemed to have melted over her gentle curves. She had her dark blue jacket thrown over her shoulder and stood casually before him, totally unaware of the effect she was having on him.

"I'm ready," she said. "I wish you would have given

me a little more time at the store. One of the back pockets of my jeans has a small tear at the top.'' She turned around and leaned over slightly, showing him the pocket.

His mouth went completely dry. ''Let's go,'' he said, his voice hoarse. ''Come on, Wolf.'' He opened the door and the animal hopped into the back.

''What's wrong? You told me to pick out dark colors and there wasn't much of a selection. Dark blue jeans were all they had in my size.''

''You're fine,'' he muttered, gesturing toward the SUV.

She gave him a thorough once-over and a slow smile that made it hard for his brain to work, though other parts of his body weren't having the same problem.

''You look great, too—like a warrior, hard and dangerous.''

''You say it as if you don't think I'm either of those things,'' he said, his gaze intent on her.

''You're both, Daniel, but around me, you're a different man—kinder and gentler.''

He gave her a cocky half grin. ''Are you calling me a wuss?''

She laughed. ''Hardly. You're a man who makes his living in a very rough profession and yet, despite everything you've been through, you've never forgotten when and how to be gentle.''

Her soft words penetrated all his defenses. Daniel looked away, getting himself together and didn't say a word as they both climbed into the vehicle. His entire body was throbbing, but he couldn't afford to get distracted now. One mistake was all it would take and they'd both end up dead or dying tonight.

''Once we get to the real estate office, I want you to do whatever I tell you without question, is that understood?'' he said harshly, pushing aside all other concerns except the job ahead. ''Our lives could depend on a split-second decision and I have to know I can count on you not to improvise or go off on a tangent. Agreed?''

She nodded once, seemingly as tense as he was, but the expression on her face told him she was still determined to see it through. Daniel's body was wound tighter than a drum. He remembered another similar operation—the night his partner had died.

Nicki and he had gone to check out the warehouse of a gang of car thieves. An informant had told them they'd have the place to themselves for at least an hour and, at first, everything had gone like clockwork. They'd checked through every window, spotting cars inside and pairing them to a list of stolen vehicles. Then, in a matter of seconds, everything had gone sour. Following procedure, he'd gone back to their unit to call for a search warrant. But while he was gone, Nicki had spotted someone inside the warehouse and taken the offensive.

He'd hurried to catch up, moving in textbook fashion, looking for cover and a clear line of fire, but she'd walked into a trap. To this day, he could still hear the shots and Nicki's voice as she'd called out to him for help.

''Stick close to me. Don't get too far ahead or behind,'' he ordered brusquely. He parked the SUV, and putting her in the middle between Wolf and him, the three of them crossed the parking area and entered the landscaped rock garden. Hannah retrieved the key quickly and hurried to the front door.

Everything was quiet, and there were no outside security cameras, but Daniel couldn't shake the tension that tightened every muscle in his body. Training and instincts were a cop and P.I.'s greatest assets, but right now he wasn't sure if his subconscious was picking up something he should know about or if his tension was simply a result of that other operation that had gone bad years ago.

''Okay, we're in,'' she said, after unlocking the front door.

"I'll go inside first," he said, looking for alarm sensors around the door.

"It's dark inside and no one's here," she protested.

He transfixed her with a cold glare. "Remember our agreement."

She stood back and saw him enter in a crouch.

"Okay, come inside and close the door. But don't go any farther yet."

Wolf worked beside Daniel as the two searched the office methodically and with precision, using only a penlight and acute senses. Finally satisfied, he gave her the all clear.

"Start your search," he said.

Using her own small flashlight, she located her uncle's computer, switched it on, and, keeping the screen at a dim setting, tried the password she knew. It didn't work. "He's changed the password. That's going to make things a little tougher."

"Keep trying," he said, keeping a lookout by the window.

She gave it several more shots then, at last, typed in the word *deacon.* "We're in!"

Hannah accessed his accounting records, then remained quiet, searching each file.

As she worked at the keyboard, Daniel listened for sounds that didn't belong. It was eerie how much all this reminded him of the night Nicki had died. His thoughts drifted back. He remembered the bitter taste of fear when he'd realized that he and Nicki had ended up across the warehouse from each other. Yet, though unable to provide any close mutual support, they still managed to take out three men, but the fourth had flanked Nicki and she'd failed to see him in time. With a clear line of fire, Daniel had tried to make the shot, but his pistol jammed. Though he'd run directly at the shooter then, yelling as loud as he could, he hadn't been able to divert the killer from taking the easy shot.

Nicki was hit four times. Daniel finally reached the killer after being shot twice himself. But he never even noticed being hit until backup finally arrived. They'd found him holding Nicki, her blood mingling with his own. Her killer lay close by in a crumpled heap, his neck broken. He regretted many things about that night, but not that his partner's killer had paid with his life.

He glanced at Hannah, bringing his thoughts back to the present. He'd failed one woman he'd cared about, but it wouldn't happen again. He wouldn't fail Hannah—not tonight, or any other night.

"Hurry it up, will you?" he whispered.

"I'm trying," she answered, "but it isn't easy to sort through this. From what I can see he made two really bad land deals. He wanted to build a strip mall, but there was a problem with groundwater contamination. The contractors pulled out and he had to sell at a big loss. But there are also deposits here that come in on a regular basis. They're for substantial amounts—in the five figures—but I can't tie them to anything. I know his codes for real estate and housing sales, but these entries aren't classified at all. There are also dates showing that electronic withdrawals were made from the church's building fund bank account, but the dollar amounts are missing. All you see are asterisks, like when a password is typed and the characters don't show up on screen. I have no idea whether the amounts were small or in the thousands. But why would he code them with asterisks? He's already implicated himself by withdrawing the money. I don't recognize the bank account number the money was transferred into either. What I suspect is that someone hacked into his system and is trying to make it look like my uncle's the thief."

She switched off the computer and began searching through her uncle's file cabinet using her small penlight. "I'm going to take a look at his written records." She glanced over at Daniel. ''I could use some help,'' she added.

''No can do. I need to stay right here so I can spot anyone coming.''

''Wolf can do that.''

''Not from all four directions at once.''

She continued to search, then suddenly stopped, pulling a sheet of paper out of a red file folder at the back. ''This is a strange letter.''

''To or from your uncle?''

''To,'' she answered. ''It's from a contractor.''

''What's unusual about that?''

''The contractor is Pablo Jackson, and the letter reads funny, like it's in code. 'Your windfall has ended. Vantage points shift and every contract has an expiration date,''' Hannah read aloud.

Daniel came over then, grudgingly leaving his post by the window. He stood close enough to feel the warmth of her body as she held the letter out beneath her flashlight.

''It sounds like a veiled warning,'' she said.

She turned around quickly to look at him and the tip of her breast brushed his chest. Daniel felt the impact of that contact all through him. His hands balled up into fists and he bit back a groan as he took a step back.

''I have a feeling that your uncle's blackmailing someone, Hannah, probably Jackson,'' he said, fighting to keep his thinking clear. ''That would explain the large unspecified deposits that he's getting regularly.'' He paused, then added, ''If Jackson's figured out who his blackmailer is, he'll put a stop to it any way he can. That's probably why your uncle hired off-duty cops.''

''My uncle blackmailing another person—and one who's a member of our church?'' She shook her head. ''If that's true, there's a lot more to that story than appears at first glance.'' She turned back to the file cabinet. ''I'm going to keep looking.''

Daniel felt trouble coming before he ever saw it. When the back of his neck began to prickle, he immediately glanced at Wolf. The dog's ears were up, but otherwise he gave no indication that there was something wrong.

Unwilling to risk it, Daniel kept his voice low. "Move away from the file cabinet and stay out of view of the windows. Turn off the flashlight and don't move a muscle," he ordered.

Hannah did as he asked immediately, without demanding an explanation.

Daniel moved to the front window and, with his back to the wall, peered out. It was quiet, and there was no movement outside. Was the pressure getting to him? Then he noticed a security van rounding the corner of the parking lot, apparently making a routine patrol. It drove past the building slowly, then finally came to a stop. Wolf growled low.

In a crouch, Daniel hurried to her side. "Stay down, don't make a sound, and lock the front door and the side door after I leave."

"Where are you going?" she whispered.

"Haven't got time to explain. Do it."

His tone must have worked, because she didn't argue. "I'll be back." He paused. "If something goes wrong and I'm not, Wolf will come back to the door for you. Wait until the guard is gone, then go to the safe house. I'll meet you there as soon as I can."

"But—"

Daniel didn't give her time to say anything more. He saw her shadowed eyes wide with fear, and followed an instinct as old as time itself. Wrapping his hand behind her neck he pulled Hannah toward him.

He kissed her hard and hungrily, taking everything from her. He wanted to memorize her taste and feel her passion.

When he released her a heartbeat later, the fear he'd

seen in her eyes had vanished. Now her eyes were smoky, filled with desire. And it was time to leave her.

"Why did you—"

He placed one finger over her lips, stilling them. "For luck." And because he couldn't have left her there, afraid, thinking of nothing except the possibility that they'd be arrested.

Handing her the keys to the SUV, Daniel went to the door, signaled for Wolf and, without looking back, stepped outside.

"Time to go to work, furball," he said. "Look sharp."

Daniel pulled the regular flashlight from his belt, and started walking around to the front of the building. The light beam aimed before him would announce his presence before he met the guard on duty. With luck, the guy wouldn't turn out to be a "shoot first, think later" type.

As Daniel turned the corner of the building, a young uniformed security guard intercepted him, his gun trained on Daniel's chest.

"Don't move, man. Don't even breathe," the guard said in TV police-drama style.

The guard took a step back, nervously trying to decide whether to aim his pistol at Daniel or at Wolf. Daniel was sure he could disarm the kid long before he could squeeze the trigger, but that would have long-term consequences and he had a better plan in mind.

"Ease up, Ricketts." Daniel noted the name tag on the kid's uniform shirt. "I saw you pull up in the van. I'm a P.I. hired by Jones to keep an eye on his business and home. Wolf's my patrol dog. Sit, Wolf!" Daniel commanded, and Wolf sat instantly, never taking his eyes off the guard.

"I'm calling this in," the guard said in an unsteady voice.

"Before you do, you'll want to take a look at my ID. It's in my back pocket. Let me pull it out and you can check it over,'' he said, reaching slowly for it. ''Keep in mind that if I'd wanted to neutralize you, we could have done that already. The dog knew you were here long before you ever saw us,'' Daniel said matter-of-factly. ''All you would have seen was fur flying toward your face. You wouldn't have had time to draw your weapon or grab your radio.''

He saw the guard look down. Wolf stared up at him, scarcely moving. With his eyes riveted on the man, he growled low. ''I should also tell you that the gun is making him very nervous,'' Daniel said. ''He's trained to take down threats to his handler. That's me.''

Wolf growled again, baring his teeth for maximum effect.

''You say that Jones hired you?'' the guard said, his voice an octave higher.

''Yeah, the real estate guy. Fifties, losing his hair.'' Daniel flipped his wallet open, giving only a quick glimpse of his P.I. identification before putting it away. ''Jones has been really jumpy ever since someone assaulted him in his office at the church.''

The guard nodded. ''That's not public knowledge, and we've been told to keep the deacon's troubles to ourselves.''

''Jones has some off-duty cops at his home guarding day and night now. And he has me checking his business here and his office at the church twice a day.''

Wolf barked spiritedly, saliva shooting from his mouth as the security guard shifted from side to side. The guard froze.

''Listen, I know you're legit, so I'm going to put my gun away,'' the guard whispered. ''Tell your dog to chill, okay?''

''He won't attack—unless he gets mixed up and thinks you're a threat that needs eliminating.'' He shouldn't have said it, the guard was scared enough, but Daniel hadn't been able to resist messing with his mind a bit.

"Don't you have a leash for him?" The guard moved slowly and carefully as he put his gun in its holster.

"It's okay. He's really well trained," Daniel said, trying not to smile. "In fact, he's the reason why I was able to go through the building so quickly. We've already secured the site. All the doors and windows are closed and locked." He turned the knob and pushed, hoping that Hannah had remembered to lock it. The door wouldn't budge. "As I said, secure."

"I guess I'll move on to the next place on my list," the guard said. "I'm covering over a dozen businesses tonight. My partner is out sick."

"It's time for me to shove off, too. My vehicle's across the parking lot. Stay safe, Ricketts."

Daniel turned and pretended to walk to the SUV as the guard got into his vehicle and pulled out into the street. The moment the security van disappeared from view, Daniel jogged with Wolf back to where they'd left Hannah.

Chapter Sixteen

As Hannah waited, minutes stretched out into eternities. The taste of Daniel was still hot on her mouth. She touched her lips with the tip of her tongue. Maybe that was why he'd kissed her like that—to leave a piece of him behind. Did he plan on simply being a decoy and leading the guard away, or getting himself arrested so she could avoid detection? And what if his plan went wrong and he ended up getting shot? Fear snaked through her and her heart began to pound so hard and fast she could barely catch her breath.

After several more minutes passed, she finally reached a point where she knew she couldn't wait any longer. If he was in trouble, he'd need her help. She had to sneak out and look around. She was moving toward the side door when she heard a knock.

"It's me, open up," Daniel called softly.

His voice filled her with a sense of relief so intense, her knees nearly buckled. She unlocked the door and threw it open. Daniel stood before her with a smug grin on his face. For a heartbeat, she felt torn between the need to kiss him and the urge to sock him in the nose. "How dare you stand there with that self-satisfied look on your face! What took you so long? I've gone through hell wondering what happened to you!"

"You were *that* worried about me?" His eyes twinkled with mischief. "I'm not sure if I should be flattered or not. I mean I'm glad to hear you admit you're just crazy about me, but do you honestly believe I couldn't have taken that guy?"

She fought the urge to shake him until his brains rattled. "You really are insufferable at times. And don't ever kiss me and run off like that again."

"You didn't enjoy my kiss? I was under a different impression."

"You made your move, but you didn't give me time to make mine," she said, a challenge in her voice and a tiny smile on her lips.

"And what would you have done if I'd given you the chance?"

"You'll never know now."

"Then maybe I need to kiss you again."

"After what you just put me through? No chance, buddy." Hannah strode off toward the SUV, leaving Daniel to lock the door. A second later Daniel and Wolf fell into step beside her, Daniel on her right, Wolf to her left. "Why were you so worried? You know I can take care of myself."

"You're overconfident. About everything."

He chuckled and the sound was low and masculine. "Is there a hidden message in there?"

"It's not very hidden. Oh—and for the record—I'm *not* crazy about you. At the moment, I'm not even sure I *like* you."

"Really? Then why don't you let me kiss you again?"

"I haven't had my shots."

Wolf barked once and gave Daniel a doggy grin.

"Shut up, furball."

A few minutes later as they were driving away, Daniel's cell phone rang. He answered it almost instantly.

"Silentman here," the voice informed. "We've had a

serious new development. The police have confiscated Hannah's home computer with the deacon's permission, and they've discovered that she's made a string of electronic withdrawals from the church's building fund and placed the money into a Mexican bank account. Those entries go back about six weeks and date all the way through September seventh. The police are now trying to get the paperwork to find out how much money was actually transferred. All the figures were encrypted." He paused then added. "It was all in a subdirectory with a technical sounding name, so it looked like part of the software program itself. They found it by accident, actually, after checking every file."

"Are you sure about this information?"

"Absolutely. Since this puts everything in a new light, what course of action do you recommend we follow?"

"I'm going to have to get back to you on that."

Daniel turned off the highway and down an alley, then parked. "We have a problem," he said, then watched Hannah as he gave her the news. "How could that have happened?"

"The same way they did it to my uncle's computer though, inadvertently, I made it even easier for them. I leave my computer on all the time. Someone obviously hacked into it, and we already know how my password and my uncle's were compromised. That's probably also why I never could balance anything. There's no telling what else he did to my data files or my software. Did Silentman tell you when the withdrawals were made?"

"He said they went all the way to September seventh."

Her eyes widened. "That date also appeared in my uncle's computer. Remember when I told you that I found withdrawals that had the numbers replaced with asterisks? One of those withdrawals was supposedly made on September seventh. I'll always remember that date because it's the day my father died."

"This is an important lead. It looks like whoever's framing you has been busy doing the same number on your uncle. It's very possible your uncle discovered what was happening, too." He paused. "No, nix that. If he had, your uncle would have deleted those entries."

"My guess is he doesn't know about the entries in my computer or his," Hannah said. "He hates bookkeeping and only balances his accounts every other month. I should have caught what had been done through my computer, but it never occurred to me to search for a hidden directory."

"Pablo Jackson has to be a player in this. I've thought all along that this was a conspiracy, but maybe the truth is even more complicated. We may be dealing with crimes that fed on each other, but were separate—blackmail, and the theft of the church funds."

Hannah's eyebrows knitted together. "I still don't think we've got the whole picture. We're missing something. This just isn't like my uncle. Give me some credit for knowing the man who raised me. To him, accepting responsibility is the measure of a man. That's why he took me on when I was young and, believe me, I was an expensive kid to raise. His insurance didn't cover psychiatric services, so it was all out of pocket for him. It took him years and years to pay it off. That sense of loyalty is still a part of him. He would never betray the church or any of the parishioners. To him, anything connected to the church is part of his religious duty."

"Your uncle's involved in this, Hannah. You know that. Stop defending him. So what if he was short of money when you were growing up. Most parents with kids are."

"You don't understand. To be honest, it wasn't until recently that I realized how many sacrifices he'd had to make. We never had money for luxuries. Do you remember seeing his little sports car in the driveway?" When he nodded, she continued. "It's not a high-priced car, but he told me a few weeks ago that all his life he'd wanted one of those, but he'd never had the money, not even for an old used one. He bought the one he has now from a parishioner and it's certainly no prize, but he was as proud of it as a kid with a new toy. What makes it stick in my mind was that I realized that if it hadn't been for me, he would have probably had the money to buy things like that which give him so much pleasure. I still feel guilty."

"Why? Nothing that happened was your fault."

"But don't you see? While he was trying to dig up enough money to cover my medical expenses, I was working against the doctors every step of the way." She shook her head slowly. "I was really afraid to remember. Something inside me told me that it wasn't the right time yet, and that opening that door would only cause me more harm. But the doctors felt that they should help me come to grips with everything. They believed that it was the only way I'd be free of the past. So it became a war of sorts. The more they pressed, the more I withdrew into myself. My uncle finally stuck up for me and demanded that they help me cope with my present and let the other problem rest. It was thanks to him that I was released and allowed to finally start living a normal life again."

Daniel said nothing for several long moments, then finally spoke. "You told me before that you're prepared to face things squarely now. Are you sure that you're really ready to remember everything you've forgotten—the recent and the distant past?"

"Yes," she said without hesitation. "Everything in my life is different now. My greatest fear as a kid was that I'd find myself suddenly alone again. My mother's and father's deaths were too close together, and that left some heavy-duty emotional scars on me. Whenever my uncle was even an hour late, I'd go into panic attacks. Then, as I grew older, I realized that I didn't like being that vulnerable, so I taught myself not to depend on anyone except myself. Over the years, I've found the confidence to stand on my own and I liked myself for being able to do that. It proved that I'd become the strong woman I'd wanted to be."

Hannah paused to take a deep breath. "That's why losing my memory again has thrown me so much. Everything I believed I am is being tested. I need to face those memories not only because of what's at stake, but because I need to be whole again so I can reclaim my life. I *will* remember. There's no doubt in my mind about that. I just hope it's sooner instead of later."

"There's something we can do to insure that," he said slowly.

"No more psychiatrists," she said. "I've had my fill of them."

"There's another option—something I've mentioned before. Hypnosis didn't work on you before because, as you admitted, you fought it. This time, with you helping, it might."

Hannah considered it. "I've always been against the idea, but after all I've been through, I'm willing to give it a try, but I don't know anyone we could trust."

"I do. Nelson Benally is a good friend of mine. He's also a Navajo resident at the hospital on the Rez, so he does have medical training. But I should warn you, despite his credentials, he learned hypnosis from his uncle, who was a magician. He's really pretty good, don't get me wrong. He put me under one time, and I saw him do it to a friend of mine."

"Let's go see him then." She lapsed into a thoughtful silence, then added, "Do you think Pablo Jackson played a part in whatever happened to me at the church?"

"From the evidence, I'd say yes. The problem is that all we have is a theory with nothing substantial behind it—and that theory still doesn't answer the main question. Who stole the money from the construction fund? And is it all in the account that was set up to frame you and your uncle? Somehow I doubt that.''

Hannah stuck out her chin, determination etched clearly on her features. ''Let's go see if your doctor friend can help us uncover the truth.''

THEY ARRIVED at Nelson Benally's trailer home a short time later. Daniel had called ahead, but he'd only given Nelson sketchy details of what to expect.

As Daniel walked inside his friend's home, he saw the admiring look Nelson gave Hannah. Then slowly, recognition dawned over his features, and it was obvious Nelson had seen her photo in the newspaper.

''You old fox. You've had her all along, haven't you?'' Nelson observed, glancing at Daniel. Before Daniel could say anything, he held up a hand. ''No, never mind. Don't answer. I don't want to know.''

''You know who I am?'' Hannah asked.

Nelson nodded. ''You were hard to miss on the front page of the newspaper,'' he answered.

Daniel saw the way Nelson was looking at Hannah. He was all but salivating. For some reason he didn't want to analyze, Daniel thought about punching Nelson's lights out.

''I was told that you would be able to hypnotize me,'' Hannah said.

Nelson hesitated, then looked at Daniel. ''Hey, on the phone we were talking in abstracts. I had no idea—''

''You did it to me and my cousin just for fun at a party. Now you're a doctor and you'll be even more careful,'' Daniel said.

''What is it that you expect from this?'' he asked Hannah.

''There's a stretch of time I've blocked from my memory and I need to get it back,'' she said simply.

Nelson looked at Daniel who filled him in. Nelson considered everything they'd said, then shook his head. "It sounds too dangerous. If the two memories are linked, I may bring out more than you intended."

"I'll be in far more trouble if I continue to suppress it," Hannah said.

"Her life—and mine—are on the line here, buddy," Daniel said, deliberately not using Nelson's name out of respect. Although Nelson was a modernist, training to be a doctor, his father was a Navajo *hataalii,* a healer. He knew that Nelson walked the road between the two worlds—healing in the Anglo way, but never forgetting his roots.

Nelson looked at Hannah. "All right. I'll try to put you under, but the moment any part of you rallies against it, I'm not going to push any further. Agreed?"

"Okay."

"And if I can get you under, I'm going to restrict my questions to what happened recently. If you appear to be in any distress, I'll bring you right out." Seeing her nod, he picked up an old windup alarm clock from the shelf. "Do you want to get started now?"

"I'm ready."

Her voice sounded confident, but Daniel noted the way her hands were trembling though she'd kept them folded on her lap. She was frightened, and doing precisely the thing that made her the most uncomfortable—putting herself in the hands of a stranger—and that because he'd vouched for Nelson. If Daniel had ever doubted that she trusted him, he didn't now.

Seeing how hard she was trying to hide her fears, he wished he could have found another way to help her. But he knew from bitter experience that some demons had to be faced on a one-to-one basis, or they'd never go away.

"I want you to concentrate on the sound of my voice and the ticking of the clock," Nelson told her. "All I want you to do is relax. Nothing here can harm you. You're among friends.''

Heeding a signal from Nelson, Daniel stepped back into the shadows, and watched his friend work.

HANNAH TRIED TO RELAX and cooperate. She closed her eyes and listened to the soothing ticktock and the calm, sure voice that enticed her to let go. Nelson didn't have the magic of Daniel's rough, deep voice, but he was compelling in his own way.

Then she found herself drifting among soft, peaceful clouds, in a dream where serenity enveloped her.

''I want you to go back a few days, Hannah,'' Nelson urged quietly. ''Do you remember when you woke up in that car?''

Hannah felt herself there, in the seat of that car again, and fear shot through her. She tried to stand up, but soothing, gentle hands guided her back into her chair.

''You're not part of what's going on,'' a faraway voice said. ''You're only a spectator watching from a safe place, like you're viewing a movie. No one can harm you.''

She relaxed again.

''Let's go back one step, before you found yourself in the car. You're in the church getting your work done. Describe what you're doing.''

''I have to go to my uncle's office. I need to get purchase order forms from the bottom drawer of his cabinet.'' Hannah paused, then grimaced. ''The drawer's locked. But I saw him hide the spare key once. I'll just borrow it.'' Hannah remained silent for a moment, then her breathing quickened. ''That money doesn't belong here. And why a gun?'' Hannah began to shake. ''This isn't right. That videotape. Something weird's going on.''

''What are you doing now?'' Nelson intoned.

''I'm going to talk to Uncle Bob. He'll explain.'' Hannah's trembling intensified.

''What do you see?'' Nelson asked.

''My uncle just came in. I've never seen him angrier. He's yelling at me, but I won't let him intimidate me. I want to know what's going on.'' Hannah suddenly looked behind her. ''No!''

She held out her hands to ward someone off, and as Nelson tried to calm her, she jerked free, wildly, glancing around in terror as if surrounded by mortal danger. ''Noooooo...''

''I'm bringing her out of this now!'' Nelson told Daniel. ''Hannah, when I count to three, you'll awaken feeling safe, calm and refreshed. One, two, three!''

Hannah opened her eyes and, disoriented at first, looked until she located Daniel. ''What happened? Did I do all right?''

DANIEL HAD his fists clenched tightly, anger biting at his self-control. Someone had terrorized Hannah, and he wanted them to pay in spades for every second of torment they'd put her through.

''How do you feel?'' Nelson asked her, offering her a tissue so she could wipe her tears. ''Do you remember now?''

Hannah took a deep breath. ''I feel fine, and I do remember more than I did before. But there are still gaps,'' she said, disappointed. ''I recall going into my uncle's file cabinet and finding myself staring at a bunch of cash, a videotape cassette and a pistol. But it was the gun that threw me most. I couldn't believe it. He hates guns! I confronted him about it when he came in, but someone interrupted us. After that, everything goes blank for me again. I have no idea what happened next or even why I can't recall it. All I remember is the fear I felt—the kind that's so overwhelming you can barely catch your breath.''

''It's okay, Hannah. You made progress. Take it one step at a time,'' Daniel said.

"I've learned more about myself and my life in these past few weeks than I ever knew before. But it's just not enough. I've got to keep trying. I'm tired of living with questions and dark shadows."

Her eyes were radiant, full of fire and courage. He would have gladly died for her when she looked at him like that. "You'll clear your name, Hannah. We'll both see to that. And nothing's going to stop us until we do."

Chapter Seventeen

Daniel swore Nelson to secrecy, then said goodbye, promising to come back after the case was solved to answer as many of Nelson's questions as he could.

After taking Wolf for a walk because of his long stay in the SUV, they drove away. Hannah wrapped her wool jacket tightly around her. The weather was cooler now.

"I want to go someplace outdoors where I've never been before. A quiet spot that'll help me free my thinking. I want to piece what I know with our speculations and see what kind of picture emerges. With luck, I may jog the rest of my memories."

He nodded slowly. "All right. It sounds like a good plan. I know just the right place, too. It's private and quiet. I went there a lot after the death of my partner when I needed to spend time alone and get away from my well-meaning friends."

"But it's bound to be filled with bad memories for you then. Maybe we should pick another spot."

"No. It's the perfect place and it's time I went back." The truth was that he wanted her there. He hadn't been able to help his partner, a woman he'd cared about deeply, but he *would* help Hannah. If that sacred place soothed her soul as it had done his, then it would be renewed in his mind as a place of healing instead of one of sorrow.

Hannah's silence stretched out, but when she spoke at last, her words were quiet and filled with understanding. "She was more than just your partner, wasn't she?"

He started to answer her question, then stopped. "You shouldn't let your thoughts get sidetracked right now."

"I thought you and I were way past secrets."

"If I've kept things from you, it's only because my past is over and done with."

"Not if you still carry the scars. And you do," she replied quietly.

"You're right," he answered slowly. "It's just difficult for me to talk about."

"If you really don't want to—"

He held up one hand, interrupting her. "No, you're right. It's time I told you," he said. "The Navajo way says that for there to be harmony, everything must be in balance. I know about you, so it's only right that you know about me." He paused, then continued. "Nicki was far more than just my partner. I cared a lot for her and she felt the same way about me, but nothing ever happened between us. Her little boy was her world, and she didn't want anything more. She'd tried being married, and it hadn't worked out so she didn't want to go that route again. I respected that. At the time I was pretty wrapped up in my work, and I really wasn't ready for any kind of relationship myself. It was enough to know that, while on the job, we could count on each other totally. Then one day, everything came crashing down on us. You know what happened."

"Do you still love her?"

He shook his head. "She's gone and there's nothing left of her in my life."

"Except memories."

"Those will always be a part of me, but it *is* my past. You're what matters to me now."

"Our lives both have shadows we can't seem to outrun," she said softly.

There was so much Daniel wanted to tell her. He wanted Hannah to know how after Nicki had died, he'd sworn never to care for anyone again. But from the day Hannah had come into his life, nothing had been the same. Through her, he'd found his heart again. "There's a lot I need to say to you, but this isn't the right time. You have to find your answers now and I need to help you do that. That's got to be our first priority until this case is closed."

She looked at him directly, her eyes wide and sad, and nodded. "I know."

It took over an hour to reach their destination. Northwest of Bloomfield and Blanco stood Navajo Dam, and beyond it for more than twenty miles lay Navajo Reservoir.

The road led across the enormous rock-lined dam, then into the forest that surrounded most of the lake. In the distance was a lighted marina where dozens of small boats were tied up for the evening.

Daniel found a small graded road and turned off to the right. After traveling another quarter of a mile, he stopped the SUV beside a steep slope that led down to the lake, a shimmering mirror now in the moonlight.

The gentle sound of water lapping against the shore was a comfort to them as they left the SUV and walked carefully down the slope to the water.

Wolf stayed at Daniel's side, relaxed but not totally off-duty. His expression was alert as he matched their pace.

Daniel led the way to a circle of tall piñon pines clustered on a shelf of the hillside thirty feet above the high-water mark, and sat down on the ground. "I used to come here as a kid even though, by then, the lake formed from the new dam had already covered the sacred junction between the two rivers. The stories about this place just drew me here and it became my favorite spot to visit when I needed to sort things out."

''You mean stories about the dam?''

Daniel smiled, and shook his head. ''Before these canyons were filled with the waters held back by Navajo Dam, this place was called Shining Sands. Our medicine men would come here during trying times to divine the future. The *hataaliis* would purify themselves, then move to the meeting place between the rivers. There was a sandbar there at a point where the waters met. Our Singers would leave offerings of corn pollen, white shell, turquoise and abalone, then come back the next day. They would then read the ripples in the sand and predict great events that would face the Navajo tribe.'' He glanced back at her with a sad smile. ''It's just another sacred spot that isn't there anymore, sacrificed to progress. But it's a place still worthy of respect.''

They sat beside each other silently for a long time. Wolf placed his head on her lap, and as she began to stroke his massive head, he closed his eyes.

''Let's place an offering in the waters like your people did before the dam, not for answers, just to pay respect to the past.''

He smiled his approval. ''Wait here.'' He climbed back up to the SUV, and returned with his medicine bundle. Together they walked down to the narrow strip of shoreline. Taking a pinch of the bundle's contents, he placed it in the palm of her hand, then took a similar amount for himself. Together, they scattered the mixture of pollen and shells onto the water. The offerings rose and sank with the rippling of the waves for a moment, then disappeared from view.

''That was beautiful,'' Hannah said. ''Thank you.''

''You're welcome. I was surprised that you asked, to be honest. I know you don't believe in our ways.''

''But I do believe in traditions and in honoring them. Your people were here first, so I'm your guest. A good guest respects the ways of her host.''

Hannah's words touched him deeply. This woman was meant to be his. He could feel it with every breath he took. It was like finding the only part of himself that mattered.

His eyes found hers, but no words came. Maybe it wasn't meant to be a time for words. He sat beside her and allowed the calmness of the waters to give them peace.

With a sigh, she closed her eyes, sitting with knees clasped against her chest. As the silver glow of the moon worked its way through the branches overhead, he studied the graceful lines of her face. She was perfectly formed and impossible to forget, even if he lived to be a hundred.

Almost as if sensing his gaze on her, she trembled. "You were right to choose this place. There's a certain magic here. It's as if the breeze itself is saying that it's okay for me to remember now, that I've got nothing to fear."

He hadn't intended to touch her, but some instincts were impossible for a man to deny. He shifted and moving behind her, placed her between his thighs, then pulled her back until she rested against his chest.

Daniel wrapped his arms around her waist, cursing himself for still wanting her even though he knew she was off-limits.

"You're safe with me," he said, his voice quiet and reassuring. "Reach into your thoughts and just let things come to you. And if something is frightening, feel me close to you, and know that you've never been safer."

He'd protect her, even from himself. He was on fire, and it was killing him by inches to hold her so close to the center of his body, and not be able to take it further. The pleasures he could give her, the pleasures she could give him, weren't theirs to take—not now, maybe not ever again.

"The memories are there. I can almost touch them."

"Listen to the sound of the waves touching the shore,

and let your thoughts flow as easily and naturally as the water,'' he murmured.

She shifted in his arms, turning toward him, and wrapping one hand around his neck, pulled up to kiss him.

He'd wanted to hold back, to brush her lips only enough to reassure her that this wasn't a journey she'd travel completely alone. But her mouth was impossibly soft. When her tongue darted inside his mouth, he groaned, his entire body aching to take her.

It was killing him, but he let her set the boundaries. When she pushed him back onto the soft sand, he allowed her to lead him and take what she wanted from him.

As her body seemed to melt into his, their kiss turned hot. He couldn't breathe, but he didn't want to. Just being with her was enough. It made him crazy to feel her pressing into him so intimately. She'd settled naturally between his thighs, her hips pushing into him instinctively.

With a groan ripped from his soul, he rolled over, pinning her beneath him, and kissed her again. It was a slow, hot, lingering kiss meant to last a lifetime. But he had to stop. And now.

As he pulled away from her, a shudder racked his body. ''We can't do this, Hannah. You're either mine or you're not. There's no halfway for us, not anymore.''

She held his gaze as if hoping he could see into her heart. ''I care about you Daniel, but love can only be given when the heart and the soul are whole. I can't offer anyone anything—not even myself. Until my past is settled, I have no future.''

He nodded. ''And that's the problem, Hannah, because I want more. If we ever make love again, it'll be because we both know we're meant to be together and because we're willing to do whatever it takes to see that it happens for us. There's no room in my heart, or in my life, for anything else—not when it comes to us.''

Stone-faced, Daniel returned to the SUV and began to

unpack some camping gear. Her words had ripped through him, reminding him that he'd promised to help her find the answers she needed, and that she deserved far more from him than responses fueled mostly by hormones, in spite of the fact that he cared for her too. But just being close to her made it difficult to hold a thought. A restless energy burned within him.

Moonlight bathed the area in a bright glow as they set up camp for the night under the stars and among the trees. "Will it be possible for us to stay here again tomorrow?" Hannah asked.

"No. Remember the weather report on the radio coming here? We'll want the heat inside the safe house then. At this altitude it'll reach freezing."

He watched her brush her hair, ready to settle for the night and realized that lack of heat wouldn't be a problem for him, not as long as they were together. At the moment, he wanted her more than he wanted to take his next breath, but watching her would have to be enough.

"Sometimes I wonder if I'll ever have a normal life," she mused, crawling into her warm sleeping bag. Wolf had found a spot to lie down by her feet.

"You will," he said with unwavering determination.

Hannah glanced over at him and smiled. "Sleep well."

"Good night, Hannah." There would be little sleep for him tonight. He'd need to come up with a solid plan. He'd promised her a victory and he would come through for her—no matter what it cost him.

SHORTLY AFTER DAWN, Hannah woke up. Daniel was already busy, packing up their gear and putting it back into the SUV.

Hannah got to her feet, and was helping him stow things away when her stomach suddenly growled loudly. She laughed. "I guess that tells you what my first question's going to be."

"When's breakfast?"

"I'm really starving. How about you?"

Daniel reached into his back pocket and retrieved his wallet, checking to see how much cash he had with him. Seeing it was almost empty, he pulled a padded envelope from his backpack and extracted a handful of bills. "There are fast-food joints in Blanco and Bloomfield, or we can wait until we reach Farmington. We can stop anywhere you want."

Hannah stared at the envelope, mesmerized. Concerned, Daniel studied her expression. He started to say something, but then stopped, obeying an instinct that told him not to interrupt her.

"The envelope I mailed... It was like that one—padded and brown. I'd stuffed it with the cash I found." She looked up at him, her eyes alive with an inner fire. "I remember, Daniel. I put the videotape in it, too."

"And the gun?"

"No, I kept that and showed it to my uncle, demanding he explain. We argued then. He wanted the money back, but I wouldn't tell him where it was. It was too late anyway, I'd put the package in the mailbox right before the mailman came, and it was gone."

"Who did you mail it to?"

She narrowed her eyes, thinking hard, but finally shook her head. "That, I don't remember. But Daniel, that wasn't the entire construction fund. There were a lot of bills, but mostly in small denominations. It was petty cash in comparison." She took a deep breath. "I know I've been right about another thing, too. My uncle is not a thief. That's not what this was about. There's something more—and less." She shook her head. "It's a gut instinct, not a memory, but I'm sure I'm right."

Daniel grasped her by the shoulders and forced her to turn around. "No, Hannah. Don't give up. Stay with it. You *can* remember."

She looked away. ''No, I...''

''Hannah, look at me,'' he ordered. The impact of those hazel eyes socked him squarely in the gut. ''Face it head-on, sweetheart. For both our sakes.''

For several moments she stood perfectly still, her gaze on his. Then, like ripples across a still pond, her expression slowly changed and recognition flashed in her eyes. ''I had a terrible fight with my uncle that day. He was furious with me. He demanded that I turn over the money and the videotape to him. He said that I was wrong about him and that I was about to ruin the only chance the church had of getting their construction money back.''

''From whom?''

''I don't know. Someone came in then. Men, at least two or three of them, I think, but I can't remember their faces.'' Her breathing became ragged and her hands began to tremble. ''I remember their guns clearly, then something happened—something really terrible. I can't visualize it but I can feel it in my heart. What I do remember is knowing with everything in me that if I didn't run, I'd die.''

Daniel tried to gather Hannah into his arms, but she pulled away. ''No. I've let down every person who has ever cared about me. Like my father before him, my uncle was in some kind of trouble and, instead of helping him, I just made things worse. I won't let that happen with you, too.''

He reached for her hand and brushed the center of her palm with his lips. ''You can't let me down. By giving me something to believe in again, you gave me back my soul.''

She stepped away from him though every feminine instinct inside her urged her to do exactly the opposite. ''I care for you, Daniel. You know that, but I can't pull you even deeper into my life—not until I know what's there. I have to finish what I've set out to do, and that means I've got to go talk to my uncle, the sooner the better.''

"He has a lot of security around him, Hannah. You're more likely to get arrested than anything else. Let me follow up on a hunch first. I'd be willing to bet that one of the men who came into your uncle's office that day was Pablo Jackson. We already suspect your uncle's been blackmailing him. I think Jackson may have countered by stealing passwords and making it look like you two were taking church money. The tape was probably the evidence your uncle was using against him, and may prove that Jackson is the real thief. Let me drop you off at the safe house with Wolf, then I'll go pay Jackson a little visit."

"No. I'm going with you. We can't split up now. I'll wear my wig, but I'm not staying in the background anymore."

"All right, but remember you're wanted for questioning. That means that whether you like it or not, you can't fight this battle in public."

"I know. But this isn't the time to stop taking risks. It's the time to go for it."

"All right."

They finished loading the SUV and then Daniel whistled for Wolf to get in the back.

Hannah watched the dog sit up straight instead of lying down as he normally did. "He's tense," she observed.

"I'm sure he's reacting to us. We're tense and he can sense it. We've got to be careful what signals we give him. If he's edgy, he's more likely to act on his own accord and take a bite out of anyone who gets too close to either of us."

Hannah called the dog and Wolf pushed his head between the seats to look at her. "Relax, boy. We need you focused, but not anxious." She scratched the special spot behind his ears, and he sighed contentedly and closed his eyes.

"You can wind any male around your little finger, you know that?" he observed with a gentle smile.

"It comes down to treating people and animals with understanding and kindness." She smiled ruefully. "Of course that works a little differently when dealing with a person who has little except anger and deceit in his head. When a person like that attacks others, as he's bound to do, he's more likely to expect a good offensive and respect nothing less."

"Being in tune with your opponent is the only way to stay ahead of his game." Daniel gazed admiringly at her. Hannah mixed gentleness with courage in a way that never ceased to draw him to her.

As they drove west, stopping only for a takeout breakfast at Blanco, a heavy silence fell between them. The sun was already over the horizon, and the day promised to be clear and cold.

"Why don't we go over to Jackson's office now and see if we can look around before anyone arrives?" she suggested. "It might really help to have a look at his files and computer," she said. "But it would mean breaking into the place. What do you think?"

"Lumberyards open really early for business, usually by seven. We're already too late for that kind of operation. Let's wait until later this morning. Jackson's bound to have several things on his mind by then, and having him distracted might work to our advantage."

"Okay."

They decided to travel to the safe house where they could wash up, change clothes and lose the sign and boxes that provided the delivery-vehicle disguise for the SUV.

After they arrived, Hannah helped Daniel remove the boxes and replace the rear seat. They both cleaned up then Hannah went into the bedroom, picked out a green wool sweater from her clothes bag and slipped it on. It fit smoothly and comfortably, accentuating the slimness of her body.

When she finally came out of the bedroom, Daniel glanced at her. "That was a good choice. It fits you well."

"Thanks," she answered, wishing that his compliments were more personal. Perhaps he was holding back now that she had voiced her own reasons for hesitation in their relationship.

Daniel now wore a long-sleeved, dark-blue flannel shirt and jeans. There was a simple, masculine ruggedness about him that made her body tingle with awareness. He gave her a wicked smile as if reading her thoughts, and suddenly a shiver touched her spine. Although she tried to suppress it, he was quick to notice her reaction and now she could see pure male satisfaction shining in his eyes.

For a moment Hannah wondered what it would be like to see that same expression on his face after making love to him. Realizing the direction her thoughts had taken without much prompting, she tried to concentrate on something else. Until the day came when she was no longer being hunted by her enemies, she couldn't allow her feelings for Daniel to come to the surface. It wouldn't be fair to either of them. Life had taught her many things, and at the top of the list was the knowledge that happily-ever-afters seldom happened to people like her.

Chapter Eighteen

As they drove back to Farmington, Hannah did her best to keep her thoughts centered on what they had to do, but fear and apprehension eroded her confidence. "What if we're wrong? What if whatever's between Pablo Jackson and my uncle has nothing to do with the missing money? If that's the case, we'll be back to square one."

"You don't believe that, no more than I do," he said.

"I'd like to think that we're nearing the end of the line, but I've had my hopes dashed too many times," she said quietly.

Daniel could hear the frustration in her voice. As an investigator he understood that feeling well, but he also knew the danger of indulging it. "Then look at it this way. We're pursuing a good lead. Good cases are built on them, and that's our goal. Detective work is never a straight line. What you have to do to get through it is stay focused on the objective."

"All right. I'll try," she said, her voice firmer now.

They arrived at Pablo Jackson's construction company a half hour later. A large and busy fenced-in lumberyard with covered storage bins for lumber and construction supplies surrounded an unpainted cinder-block building. The large sign along the top of the building read Big J Construction.

Daniel pulled into a customer parking slot beside the building, but remained in the SUV, watching employees load a flatbed truck with lumber and bags of premixed concrete.

"It looks like business as usual here," he said at last. "I doubt Jackson will give me any trouble with customers in the yard. I'll wear a mike so you can monitor the conversation, but remember to stay out of sight. If Jackson sees you, we'll be in a world of trouble. One last thing. Warn me if you see anyone you recognize drive up. I want to talk to Jackson alone, not with your uncle or anyone else from the church around."

"I'll keep a lookout, but be careful. If we're right, Pablo's got a lot to lose and that could make him dangerous—not to mention he has those goons working for him," she reminded him.

Everything was on the line now and he knew it. He placed the small mike in his shirt pocket, and tried to focus on the job ahead. "Keep your chin up. I'll be back as soon as I can," he said, handing her the vehicle keys. It was hard for him to leave her here in this place that held mostly unknown dangers. But he had no other choice. "Be very careful and keep a sharp eye out."

"Go," she said. "I'll be fine. For a second there I thought you were going to get all sentimental and mushy on me," she teased with a tiny smile.

"Evil woman," he growled, then, with one last look back at her, slipped out of the SUV, leaving Wolf to guard her.

Daniel walked inside the main door to the building, and saw the secretary's desk empty. A man wearing a hard hat and a blue shirt that had the company name on it came in and gave him a questioning look. "You have an order to fill?"

"No. I'm looking for Pablo Jackson," Daniel said.

"Grab yourself a hard hat," he said, gesturing to one

of several on wall hooks, ''and go out the back.'' The employee pointed to the door he'd just passed through. ''He's in the yard somewhere.''

The moment Daniel stepped through the door and walked outside, he realized that they would have problems with the listening device. A forklift passed by, and underneath a work area someone was using a radial saw to cut plywood. The noise would easily drown out voices unless all the machinery stopped at the right time.

Daniel tried to tell Hannah what was going on, but when he didn't get a reply, he realized that the device couldn't filter out the background noise. If he shouted, he'd only focus unwanted attention on himself so that wasn't an option either. Hoping she'd stay in the SUV and not worry, he continued what he'd set out to do.

Daniel walked down the rows of stored materials. Passing one of the loafing sheds containing bundles of shingles and roofing tar, he saw Pablo Jackson speaking to two men just under the roof, in the shade. Taking the next row, which backed up to the bin where Jackson was standing, Daniel got close enough to realize the men with Jackson were the same muscle boys who'd confronted Hannah and him before. Wanting to overhear their conversation, he moved in closer, pretending to examine a stack of plywood. Keeping his head bowed, he concentrated on their speech.

''All I've heard from you losers are excuses, and I'm tired of listening to them,'' Jackson said. ''Find the Jones woman and get rid of her. Don't try to take down the Indian again, just shoot him and get on with it. If Hannah Jones recovers the money and that videotape, then I'm finished, and so are you two. She'll hightail it to the police, explain what she knows, and they'll come looking for us all.''

''We've been concentrating on the uncle, hoping he'd lead us to her. He's the key,'' one of the goons protested.

"*Was* the key. Right now he's lying low because he knows he's helpless without the video. The real threat is Hannah, so stop wasting your time trying to get past Bob Jones's security people. Eventually, he'll run out of money to pay his guards, they'll walk, and that's when we'll strike. But everything depends on finding the woman and the tape."

As they walked away, their words were lost in the background noise, but Daniel had heard enough to know that Jackson didn't have any idea where the money or the tape were, and was determined to find them both.

As Jackson and his men reached the opposite end of the row, Daniel stood up and glanced across the yard. For a moment he couldn't do anything except stare. Hannah was walking down the same row with a bundle of surveyor stakes under one arm, and wearing sunglasses and a hard hat. She'd taken one of his shirts, which sagged freely over her, and was scarcely recognizable. But he would have known her no matter how good her disguise—even if Wolf hadn't been with her.

Daniel looked to see if anyone else had noticed her, then strode quickly over. "What the hell do you think you're doing?" he whispered harshly.

"I couldn't hear a thing with all the saws and vehicles going back and forth. I thought you might be in trouble, so I brought Wolf." The dog sat next to Hannah, at heel and keeping watch.

"Bad idea. The mutt stands out like a sore thumb here. Head back to the SUV. I'll follow. The three of us can't be seen together."

As he started to walk in the opposite direction to put some distance between them, a pickup drove past them. The driver did a double take and, for an instant, Daniel was eye-to-eye with Pablo Jackson. Recognizing Daniel, he glanced over at Hannah, and saw the dog. In a heartbeat, he slammed on the brakes, but there was no room for the truck to turn around and, as he tried, the front bumper jammed against a pallet loaded with bags of cement. He yelled to the pair in the truck with him. But Daniel, Hannah and Wolf were already rounding the corner and heading up the next row by the time the two men were out of the truck.

Daniel led her down the row, behind the bins of materials, trying to pick storage areas containing loaded pallets. That would slow down their pursuers since they'd have to search as they ran. Finally, reaching the last row which led back toward the main building, he stopped, keeping Wolf between them and their enemies.

"Go without me. I'll lead them back across the lumberyard while you sneak back to the SUV. We're cut off, and the only way you'll be able to get out of here is if I create a diversion."

"I won't leave you behind."

"We have no choice. Go with Wolf," he said, giving her a gentle push. "And don't look back, just run. If I'm not at the SUV three minutes after you get there, or if they get too close, take off. Go to the address in the glove compartment, and tell Silentman what happened. He'll send help."

"Are you crazy? You can't stay here alone! At least keep Wolf."

"No. You may need him more than I do." He held her by the shoulders. "Do you trust me?"

"Yes," she replied her voice shaking.

"Then, *go!* I can't protect both of us if they decide to use guns."

Hannah did as he asked, though it was the last thing she'd wanted to do.

Without waiting, Daniel ran back down the narrow passage, hearing the men. He was outnumbered, but he'd gone up against lousy odds before. All he had to do was get their attention and let them attack. That would buy Hannah enough time to get away.

Daniel flattened himself against one of the roof support posts and braced for a fight as the men approached. There were three of them. He saw the smallest of the trio pick up a section of pipe from the ground. They either didn't have guns, or they'd decided not to use them here.

Jumping out from his cover, Daniel kicked the pipe out of the man's hand. The other two jumped in almost instantly from both sides. One grabbed his left arm, but Daniel punched him in the solar plexus, then spun and kicked him hard enough to dislocate his knee. The man bounced off the stack of four-by-fours and dropped with a howl.

But there were reinforcements, and in seconds he was outflanked, with no direction to go. Unable to defend himself against so many in tight quarters, he had to attack. Picking the shortest distance to daylight, Daniel leaped forward with kicks and punches, blocking the blows from the surprised construction workers. He gained ground, but someone following him struck the back of his knee with a board and he fell.

Everyone grabbed him at once, and carried him hand and foot out into the yard. Realizing he was helpless at the moment anyway, Daniel made only feeble attempts to squirm free, saving his strength. He gave thanks that they were taking him where he'd have room to maneuver again—if he could only break free for a second.

They dropped him to the ground, and someone, maybe Jackson, kicked him in the side. Pain blinded him for a second, but he rolled with the blow and jumped to his feet.

"Give it up. I'll let you live," Jackson said. The man had stepped back after getting his blow in. "Or better yet, let's see how many punches you can take before you go down." He motioned for the others surrounding Daniel to move in. "Grab him, and we can take turns."

Daniel knew only his training now, and surrender wasn't

part of the deal. While he was still breathing, he could fight, and if he couldn't fight, he could endure until he could fight again.

Two men moved for his arms at the same time. Daniel kicked high to his right, and caught his attacker in the chest. The man flew back. Turning instantly ninety degrees and straightening his left arm, Daniel brushed past the man's outstretched arm and caught him in the jaw with a vicious uppercut.

The four other men paused, reconsidering their strategy.

''Gang-tackle him, you morons,'' Jackson yelled.

Daniel braced himself, but suddenly a car horn blared loudly right behind him. He looked over his shoulder and saw his SUV sliding to a stop, scattering Jackson and another man in the way. Wolf jumped out, racing like a bullet toward them. Teeth bared, the giant dog flew into Daniel's closest attacker, teeth anchoring onto the man's forearm.

The guy howled in pain as Wolf's momentum carried them both to the ground. Daniel was instantly forgotten as Wolf, like a wild animal gone berserk, attacked anyone who wasn't running away.

Daniel was already moving toward the SUV as Hannah threw open the door to the back seat. ''Get in,'' she yelled.

Daniel recalled Wolf, who whirled around and raced for the vehicle. The dog leaped onto the seat, and Daniel followed. ''Go!''

She slammed down on the accelerator, cutting a deep half doughnut into the ground and spewing gravel at the yard workers diving for cover. Fishtailing out the gate, she hopped the curb and flew out into the street with tires squealing.

''Are you okay?'' she managed, glancing back at Daniel and Wolf, who were still trying to recover from all the bouncing around.

''I took some damage, but it was worth it.'' He started to laugh, then coughed. ''If I live to be a hundred, I'll never forget the men's faces when they dove out of the way of the SUV and then saw Wolf barreling down on them like a hound from hell.'' He suddenly glared at her. ''But you could have been killed, coming in for me! Don't you *ever* listen?''

''You were outnumbered. I don't abandon people I care about. You should know that by now.''

''Yeah, I do,'' he admitted. ''You have your own system of priorities, no matter what anyone tells you. But, for the record, despite the odds, I would have made it.''

Her lips twitched, but she managed not to smile as she took another look at him in the rearview mirror. ''Is that macho pride I hear?''

''No, just the facts.''

''It didn't look like you were winning. They were all closing in on you.''

''I had a plan,'' Daniel replied unconvincingly. He tried to shift, but the pain in his side made him wince.

Noting it, she looked back at him once more. ''You're hurt. I'll bring Wolf up front, and you lie down on the seat.''

''It's nothing. I've just got some bruised ribs where Jackson took a cheap shot at me. I don't think they're broken or it would feel worse.''

''But you're still in pain.''

''Don't worry. I'll block it out. We've got work to do, and I can still fight.''

''Only if you're attacked by three-year-olds and elderly blind women. You've got bruises and cuts all over your face and hands, and maybe internal injuries. You need a doctor.''

He shook his head. ''I've been through worse and I know when something's broken. You're going to have to trust me on this. I'll be sore for a few days, but that's about it. Right now, we've got business to attend to. We need to go pay your uncle a visit.'' He told her what he'd overheard.

''Uncle Bob's not going anywhere, judging from what you just said. And they're not really after him—they're after me, so he's in no immediate danger. Let's go by the safe house first. That'll give you a chance to clean up and make sure you're as okay as you think.'' When he started to protest, she held up a hand. ''I've got the wheel now, so be quiet, lie back, and stop trying to give me orders.''

''Why, because you want to give them yourself?''

''Sounds like a plan to me.'' She glanced back at him in the rearview mirror and winked. ''For now you're entirely in my hands.''

He started to argue, then decided against it. All things considered, he couldn't think of a better place to be.

BY THE TIME they arrived at the safe house, Daniel looked like he'd recovered somewhat. The small cuts on his face had stopped bleeding, but it was his side that worried Hannah the most. Broken ribs were nothing to take lightly, and she wanted to see how badly bruised they were. If he couldn't get around, then she'd take him to the clinic for X-rays even if she had to trick him into going.

Daniel started toward the house, walking slowly. ''We shouldn't have come back here. We should be taking care of business.''

''You're my first priority right now,'' Hannah answered.

''It isn't supposed to work that way. I'm supposed to take care of *you,* not vice versa.''

''As of right now, I'm changing the rules,'' she replied flatly. Hannah walked into the small bathroom, turned on the water in the tub, then came back out. After getting a fire going in the stove, she placed a large kettle of water on to heat.

''You need to wash off all those cuts, Daniel, and try

to take it easy for a few minutes. A hot soak will probably do you a world of good."

Daniel gave her a slow, masculine grin. "Then you'll have to undress me. I'm suddenly *extremely* sore."

Hannah met his gaze. She knew what he was thinking. He expected her to back down, then once he had the upper hand, he'd insist they go to her uncle's right away. But Daniel wasn't in any condition for that.

"Sure I'll help you," she said. Her course set, and without any other options, she began to unbutton his shirt.

"Wait a minute."

"Are you suddenly feeling shy?" she teased.

He nearly choked. "I just don't think you're ready for this, sweetheart."

"I'm doing just fine." Seeing the uncertainty in his eyes made her even bolder. Hannah worked at his belt and pulled it free, then she slowly unbuttoned his jeans.

"You're playing with fire," he said, his voice a dark whisper.

"Lucky for me that you're too sore to do anything about it." She looked up at him with laughing eyes. "I mean that *is* what you said, and I know you'd never bend the truth."

"I heal fast." He grasped her wrists and held them, dark passion mirrored in his gaze. "Don't go any further. You're not ready."

"Are you trying to scare me?" she whispered. "It won't work, you know."

His eyes blazed with the wild fires that coursed through him. "Men twice your size are afraid of me."

"And maybe they should be," she answered, pulling back gently until he freed her hands. "But I know what you're like with me, and I'm not afraid."

She felt him shudder whenever her hands brushed his skin and saw the tension that gripped his muscled body. She undressed him slowly, taking care not to touch his cuts and bruises. At long last he stood before her, all aroused and powerfully male.

For several moments, she couldn't take her eyes off Daniel. He was beautifully masculine—all sculpted lines of hard muscle. Taking his hand, she led him to the bathtub. After adding hot water from the kettle, she waited until he sat down.

Working slowly, Hannah cupped her hands, and filling them with water, allowed the warm stream to trickle down his shoulders.

"Hannah," he managed, heat racing down to his groin. "Don't."

"You're not in control, Daniel. I am. Trust me."

Taking a bar of soap, she lathered her hands, then ran them over his chest, enjoying the hard feel of him. But it felt too good. Her pulse was pounding and her body began to tingle in places she didn't even want to think about. With effort, she tried to remember why she was doing this. She'd wanted to make sure he wasn't seriously injured, that was it. Struggling to stay focused, she ran her hands lightly down his left side. As she did, she saw him clench his jaw.

"Pain?"

His breathing was ragged. "That's the last thing I'm feeling right now, sweetheart," he said his voice low and raw.

"Your side has an enormous bruise. It's purple."

"That's impossible. All my blood is going elsewhere." He held her eyes.

Hannah smiled. "Tell me the truth, Daniel. Are you feeling better?"

"Oh yeah," he answered, his voice rough.

She dipped her hands into the water, then began to wash his legs, massaging them, moving upwards.

"You're killing me," he said, leaning back and closing

his eyes. It was sheer torture to feel her hands on him, touching him like that.

When her hands reached the swell of his manhood, he inhaled sharply. She drew back, but he grasped her hands and held her gaze.

"Don't stop. Touch me." He placed her hands on him.

She stroked him gently, feeling the shudders that traveled through him. It made her feel powerfully female to know that this man, tough enough to stand up to any challenge without so much as a groan, could fall apart under the tenderness of her touch.

When he couldn't bear it one more second, he lifted her hands and kissed them. "That's enough, my love."

He stood up and let her dry him off, knowing that it gave her pleasure, and loving the way he could affect her by doing nothing more than letting her have her way.

"Now do you see I wasn't so badly injured?" he murmured. "But I have to admit that your idea of a hot bath worked wonders. Any man who is a man can take a few punches, but only his woman's touch can send him over the edge."

Daniel saw the passion that darkened her hazel eyes and knew he could have taken her right then, without waiting, without preamble. Just fast and hard. But he wanted more—for her and for him. He had to know if her feelings for him went as deep as his did for her, and this was not the way to prove that.

There was another way. Love and fear were antagonistic emotions. Where one existed, the other couldn't survive. If she could trust him enough to lay her body and her heart bare for him, without holding back, even in uncertain circumstances, then he'd know that their love had a chance. Even undeclared, it would remain and become an unbroken link between them.

He took her hand and kissed it, then led her to the bedroom. "Take your clothes off for me," he said, taking a step back from her.

Sun streamed into the room, and there was no place to hide. She hesitated.

He devoured her with his gaze, waiting. "No barriers, Hannah. Let there be nothing our eyes can't see."

"My body isn't perfect...not like yours."

"You are perfect, and made for love."

She took off her blouse, then slid down her jeans.

"The rest," he commanded, his voice dark with the passion raging inside him.

It was so bright in the room she knew his eyes would miss nothing. Her hand trembled as she unfastened her bra.

As her breasts spilled free, he sucked in a ragged breath. She knew then that it would be all right. She pulled down her panties and felt his gaze smoldering over every inch of her exposed flesh.

Daniel wrenched her toward him and kissed her, their bodies pressed hotly together, fitting into one another. Blood seared through his veins when she shifted, instinctively easing her lower body between his hard thighs.

Holding onto her hand, he tossed the covers back, then guided her down to the bed.

She was beyond thoughts as he lay beside her, his copper skin gleaming with a thin layer of perspiration. She loved the feel of his hard chest and the way his muscles bunched and tightened as she smoothed her palm over him. Slowly, she ran her hands down his body, touching him intimately. He was impossibly big and so ready.

"Don't," he said, trying to maintain control.

"You've taken care of me. Now let me take care of you, Daniel," she whispered, her breath hot over his skin. "Surrender to me."

She straddled his body, holding his gaze. All the fires inside him, all the passion that held her, were mirrored plainly in the look that passed between them.

With a shaky breath, she lowered herself over his body, taking him inside her. She felt his body gliding through her tightness, past the pain and the heat. With every movement, he slipped deeper into her, touching her soul.

"All of me, Hannah," he said, guiding her hips down as he thrust up.

Passion met fire. Flames burned and danced over them. When she tired, he grasped her hips and moved for her, pulling her to him hard.

He felt her tremors, saw the darkness that turned her eyes hazy, then in a moment of brilliant awareness, she flowed into him, surrounding him with a sweet warmth.

He drove hard into her then, his breathing ragged as he took her to the edge again. She was wild, needing him, crying out his name. It was the way he wanted her. She was his.

A shudder ripped through him and seconds before he came, he captured her gaze and saw the woman he loved lost in passion, needing to be possessed by him as she'd possessed him. With a groan, he let go, his hot seed filling her.

Afterwards, exhausted, she lay over him. He held her tightly, their bodies still joined.

"You were right about me, you know," he murmured. "If there's one person who will never have to be afraid of me, it's you." He brushed a kiss on her forehead.

"No matter what happens, you'll always be a part of me," she whispered.

"May Sun record this day in our hearts."

Chapter Nineteen

It was dark outside by the time they entered the quiet residential neighborhood where Deacon Bob Jones lived. Daniel had decided to wait until now, afraid that their visit would be too public in the middle of the day, and hoping that the dark would increase their margin of safety.

Wolf sat up, his expression alert.

"He's tense," she commented quietly.

"He should be. What we're doing is risky." Before Daniel drew near the house, he slowed down and pulled off to one side of the road. "You better get in the back and stay down. I've got to get you past his guards, and if they see you, we'll never make it inside your uncle's house." He paused, gathering his thoughts. "This probably won't be the same team we saw the other day but, with luck, I'll know at least one of them. My plan will work a lot better if I'm dealing with someone who knows I can be trusted."

"What are you going to do?"

He drove up to the house slowly. "I have to try and talk the guards into taking a break. If they're friends of mine, that'll be easy. It's dark, and they probably could use a cup of coffee and a chance to shake off the cold. If I don't know them, I'll have to press it from the angle that we both work for the deacon."

As they pulled up, he saw a solitary man back in the shadows. "There's only one guy here tonight, at least from what I can see. The good news is that I think I recognize him." He opened the car door. "I'm not going to wear the mike, it's not that kind of operation. Keep an eye out. If the cop walks or drives away, then come on over. But stay in the shadows as much as possible when you approach, and don't make any noise that may alarm your uncle. We'll go in together."

"What about Wolf?"

"I'm going to take him. People expect him to be with me anyway, so it'll be okay, and it may help me convince the guy there to let me take over his watch for a few minutes."

Daniel left the car and, with Wolf by his side, approached the guard, giving him a friendly wave. The evening was chilly, and that made his plan even more likely to succeed.

Daniel glanced down at the dog. Wolf's level of excitement was going up as if he were anticipating trouble, and that was never a good sign. Wolf's instincts were seldom wrong. "Easy, Wolf," Daniel said softly.

"Hey, Daniel," the man greeted him, coming out of the shadows to meet him.

"I thought that was you, Paul. You never stood out in the light if there was a place to remain inconspicuous," Daniel said. "How long's it been? Five years?"

"Longer, I think." Paul answered, patting him on the back. "I hear you're working on your own now."

Daniel nodded absently, not wanting to elaborate. Most of the cops he knew thought he was freelancing, and that was fine with him. Only a handful suspected that he was with Gray Wolf Investigations.

Paul looked at the dog. "That animal looks like he'd be one heckuva partner. Maybe two partners."

"He is all that."

"So what brings you out into the cold? You need to talk to the deacon? I heard you're also working for him."

"Yeah, I have to touch base with him, but if you don't mind my saying so, you look beat. Need a break? Wolf and I can stick around here for a while if you'd like to go get some coffee and warm up a bit."

Paul considered it. "I worked a full shift, and I've logged in a lot of overtime on this job. I guess I'm starting to wind down a bit. A coffee break would really help."

"I thought he had two people working each shift," Daniel said. "Where's your partner? Around back?"

"No, he's out sick, so tonight I'm working solo."

"Go, then. We'll watch the house and make sure everything's secure."

"I suppose it's okay. We're on the same team," he said slowly.

"Right. Go on and take a half hour. I can handle this."

"I won't be that long," he said. "I'll just go to the coffee shop, refill my thermos and pick up a burger."

"Don't worry about it. Take your time. I'm not going anywhere."

"Thanks, man. I owe you."

Paul walked off toward his vehicle parked in the driveway beside Jones's sports car, got in, then drove away, never giving the SUV a glance. The moment the car disappeared around the corner, Hannah quietly hurried across the street. Daniel signaled Wolf to guard the rear of the house, then met her on the front porch.

Stepping up to the front door together, Hannah stood by his side as Daniel knocked firmly. A moment later, Bob Jones opened the door.

Jones stared at his niece, then pulled her inside the house quickly. Daniel followed, staying close beside her.

"Hannah, I'm so glad to see you! You look tired, but at least you're safe." He glanced at Daniel. "Thank you for bringing her back, Mr. uh, Lightning. I'll watch out for her now. Just have the agency send me the bill."

"Daniel's not going anywhere, Uncle Bob. You've been lying to everyone about me and what's going on, and I want to know why."

Daniel knew that confronting her uncle like this was probably one of the hardest things she'd ever done, but she appeared composed, and more in control than Bob Jones did at the moment.

"If I've lied, it's only been to protect you and the church. But now you have to tell me what you did with the money." Jones glanced at Daniel, then smiled sadly. "I don't know what she's told you, but believe me, Hannah is right at the heart of everything that's happened."

Daniel placed himself between the two of them. He knew Jones's bold statement had been meant to undermine Hannah's confidence. "I know about the money and the videotape that Jackson wants so badly he'll kill for it," Daniel challenged. "Stop playing games. I don't have time for this and neither do you. Your guard is taking a long break, at my suggestion, and I'm the only barrier between you and your enemies right now. The longer I'm here talking to you, the greater the risk now that your protection is gone."

"You sent the cop away?" He hurried to the window and, standing to one side, looked around outside. "You have no idea how stupid that was."

"Jackson's goons mean business. I've gone against them before and I don't relish doing it again. If you want my protection, then you better convince me you're worth it."

Jones looked at him, fear now etched clearly on his face. "If those men come here, we're all dead. If I'm right, and they caused those bruises on your face, then you know exactly how dangerous they are."

"Talk quickly then," Daniel answered.

''You never took the church's money, did you?'' Hannah asked.

''Of course not, Hannah. You know exactly what happened.'' He paused, looking directly at her, obviously puzzled. ''Jackson stole virtually all of the money in the church's construction fund account, and I was trying to get it back.''

''Convince me,'' Daniel snapped, taking a quick look out the window.

Jones ran a hand through his thinning hair. ''I first suspected what he was doing when I caught him at my computer at church one day, so I set a trap for him. I used a remote camera that showed the screen as he typed and videotaped him accessing the construction fund account and transferring the money to another account via modem. I had him nailed.''

''Why didn't you turn him over to the police then?'' Daniel asked.

''When I tracked down the bank account number he was using to deposit the money he took from us, I learned that it was going to a bank in Mexico. I found out that he'd opened the account in my name, and withdrawn all the deposits he made hours later. There was also another account opened in your name, Hannah, but I couldn't access that one.''

''I found out about that one recently,'' she said and explained what the police had found.

''I never thought he'd use your personal computer at home. I'm sorry now that I let the police have it.''

''It's okay. You didn't know,'' she answered.

''Although I didn't know the extent of what he'd done at the time, it was clear to me that he'd effectively framed both of us and, in the process, stolen a considerable amount of money. Since I had no way of knowing where he'd transferred the cash, I came up with a plan to blackmail him into giving the money back to the church. Everyone would win then. We'd be off the hook, and the church would still get its funds back.''

''You still should have talked to the police, Uncle Bob,'' she said, shaking her head.

''I didn't want to risk it. What I had on Pablo might not have stood up in court, and we were both implicated heavily. But I knew my plan would still accomplish the right goals. Then you found one of the cash payments Jackson had made to me along with the original videotape and the gun I kept for protection. You were extremely upset and I just couldn't reason with you. Don't you remember?''

Hannah tried to speak, but the words didn't come.

''Unless you tell me what you did with the money and the video, we're both going to end up in jail. I've deleted most of the entries made through the church's computers, but I'm sure Jackson's left other trails of phony evidence that will be tracked back to you and me.'' He paused, then sighed. ''Of course none of that really matters—we won't live long enough. Without that tape to bargain with, Jackson won't hesitate to kill us. Hannah, you've got to give me that tape or we're dead. *Where* did you hide it?''

''Before I answer you, tell us the rest. What happened when Jackson and his men came into your office?'' Hannah pressed.

Jones looked at Hannah curiously for a long moment. ''You don't remember, do you? You were so upset... It makes sense.'' He was about to say more when Wolf barked once.

Holding up one hand, Daniel signaled them to be quiet and went to the window, peering out from the side of the curtains. ''I'm going outside—''

He never had time to finish. Suddenly something hit the door hard. Daniel yanked Hannah down to the floor, then came back up in a fighting stance, but he was a split second too late.

Two men were standing in the doorway, their pistols trained directly on him. Moving inside a few steps, Pablo Jackson motioned for his muscle-bound companion to lock the door behind them.

"You're fast, but not that fast," Jackson said, "so be a good boy and do as you're told."

By now Wolf was barking angrily and pacing just outside, searching for a way in.

"You can start by telling that damn dog to shut up. Otherwise I'm going to shoot him."

"Fine. Go outside and try it. Or better yet, get near the window and point the gun at him. You'll get one round off before he tears your throat out—or I do."

"Brave words, but my man will make sure you're both dead before I ever hit the ground," he said, gesturing to the beefy goon with him. "So what'll it be?"

Daniel whistled once and Wolf grew quiet, but continued to pace back and forth on the porch. Daniel knew Wolf would be silent now, but no less of a threat to the men holding the guns. They were trapped inside too, only they didn't know it.

As Jackson looked at Jones, Daniel dove across the room in a lightning-fast move reminiscent of his nickname, and hit the wall switch. Moving in the pitch black, he hurled himself at Jackson's henchman, though the man's outline was barely a memory, and wrenched the pistol out of his hand.

Suddenly the lights came on again, and he saw Jackson by the switch, his gun pressed against Hannah's temple.

Her face was pale, her eyes wide. He could see her trembling as Jackson pressed his forearm against her throat.

"He needs you, Hannah," Jones called out to her from the floor, where he'd sought safety. "He won't hurt you."

"I wouldn't count on that, Deacon," Jackson snapped.

There was a sudden flicker in Hannah's eyes and understanding slowly dawned over her features. "My uncle's wrong, Daniel. Jackson's plan has always been to kill me, and I know why."

Jackson's man reached over and took back the weapon Daniel had forced from his hand. Suddenly Wolf flew through the picture window, shattering the glass in a thunderous explosion. As shards rained over them, the gray fury sank his teeth into the man's arm at the elbow.

While Jackson was trying to decide where to shoot, Daniel kicked him in the shoulder, breaking his hold on Hannah. Jackson crashed into the wall, then slumped down as a large painting fell from above, knocking him on the head with a glancing blow. Daniel removed the gun from the dazed man's hand.

As the smell of blood filled the small room, Hannah shrank back into the corner, her hands pressed against the sides of her head. There were too many memories crowding in and it was too much to handle all at once. A red haze descended over her eyes and, for a moment, she felt herself slipping down a dark tunnel of confusion and terror. Then she heard Daniel's voice calling to her.

"You're a fighter, Hannah. Don't let them beat you. I'm here with you, and you're safe now."

She hung on to his words and the sound of his voice like a lifeline. Slowly, her vision cleared and the red haze disappeared like fog under the sun. Memories she'd thought she'd lost forever were now hers once again and with those came a new understanding—of herself and of the events.

With renewed courage, she stood tall, came away from the wall and walked to where her uncle stood. "I saw you get shot in the church that day, Uncle Bob. I thought you were dead. That's why I ran, and why I was so terrified that I blocked everything out. It was just too much like the day I saw my dad die. And I know now that was the day all your lies began."

Robert Jones looked away, but didn't answer.

Hannah shook her head. "You're my father's brother, but I don't think I ever really knew you."

Daniel quickly used the curtain pulls to tie up Jackson and his partner, then moved to where Wolf sat, checking him for injuries, especially around his eyes.

"Is Wolf okay?" Hannah asked quickly, noting the blood on his chest and front legs.

"Yes, thanks to his thick, rough coat. He has some scratches, but he'll be fine. He's a pro," Daniel said proudly, then dialed the police.

Hannah stared at Jackson in disgust. "You wanted me dead because I saw you shoot my uncle. You couldn't afford to let me go to the police."

"I'm not saying anything—not without my attorney. But I'm not the only one going to jail. I'll testify that I heard you accuse your uncle of murder just before you disappeared. That will cause another investigation. Just who did *you* murder, Deacon?"

Hannah looked at her uncle. "It's time for you to stop hiding from the truth."

"It was an accident," Jones said quietly.

There were tears in Hannah's eyes, but she refused to let them spill down her cheeks. "I think it was seeing that gun among your things at the church that day that brought it all back to me," Hannah said.

"Did your uncle kill your father?" Daniel asked.

"Yes. My uncle and my dad were business partners but the hardware store had been losing money steadily and we were nearly bankrupt. One afternoon I overheard Uncle Bob arguing with my dad. He wanted to burn the store down and collect the insurance, but my dad refused to go along with that."

No one moved as Hannah continued. "My dad and I returned to the store unexpectedly that night because I'd left one of my school books by the cash register. When we got there, we found Uncle Bob tampering with the fuse box, trying to overload the circuits so the place would catch on fire."

Hannah looked at her uncle, who refused to meet her gaze. "You pulled a gun on Dad and ordered us to leave so you could finish the job. Daddy didn't believe you'd ever shoot us, so he tried to take the gun away."

"It *was* an accident, Hannah. The gun just went off. The truth is that I didn't even know it was loaded. That pistol belonged to your father. He kept it at the store because the area had experienced so many burglaries."

"My father died right in front of me, and there was nothing I could do to stop it." Tears now ran freely down her face.

"Nor could I," Jones answered. "But you can't really believe that I purposely murdered my own brother."

Crossing the room, Daniel drew Hannah into his arms. "But you knew exactly what she was suppressing and you used her guilt and confusion against her all these years," Daniel spat out. "You let her believe a lie to save your own butt."

"I didn't mean for you to suffer, Hannah," Jones insisted. "I loved my brother, and I love you. I gave you the best care I could afford."

"But you used and manipulated my feelings all this time..."

"I admit I didn't want you to remember what really happened. But I raised you as if you were my own daughter. And I *have* paid for what happened to your dad. I've spent my entire life atoning for that. I'm an active member of the church and I've always done more than my fair share."

"And you did risk your life for mine," she added quietly.

"So you remember the rest," he said wearily.

"What I want to know is what you did with the videotape,'' Jackson interrupted. ''We searched everywhere for it. Was it in your car? I had that compressed into scrap metal.''

''You don't deserve an answer,'' Hannah said. ''You were willing to kill me *and* my uncle unless we gave you that video.'' Hannah looked back at her uncle. ''You've spent your entire life running away from my father's death, just like I have. But at least, in the end, you came through for me. Jackson would have taken me apart piece by piece until I told him where the video was if you hadn't tried to stop him. You got shot trying to save me.''

''I have always protected you, Hannah. But you played right into Jackson's hands by taking that tape. Luckily, you somehow escaped from his goons but, without that video, I couldn't prove that neither of us had taken the construction fund. And, with you on the run, I knew that once the police got involved, our luck would run out.''

''Wait a minute. I'm missing something here. You were shot at close range, but Jackson missed?'' Daniel asked Jones.

''You know what they say—God protects fools and children. I had my metal card holder in my shirt pocket filled with a stack of business cards. Had he been using a higher caliber weapon, I would have been a goner, but as it was, the bullet barely penetrated my skin. It knocked the wind out of me, but the actual wound was superficial. The cut on the head that I got when I hit a shelf and fell to the floor was far worse.''

''So you played dead until Jackson and his goons were gone?'' Daniel asked.

''Yes, and as soon as possible after that, I made sure he couldn't get at me.''

As Daniel walked over to the broken window to check for the police, Jackson suddenly jumped to his feet and grabbed the pistol Daniel had placed on the table. ''Next time you tie someone up, loser, check to make sure there are no sharp objects around—like glass.''

Daniel stepped in front of Hannah. ''You've already lost, Jackson. The police are on the way. There's no place in the country you can hide now and, by pulling this, you're only working for longer jail time.''

Wolf came up to stand beside Daniel. The dog's lips were peeled back, exposing his teeth, and his growl came from deep in his throat.

''Hold that dog, or he dies,'' Jackson warned, shifting his aim.

Daniel grasped Wolf's collar loosely.

Jackson looked at Hannah. ''Tell me where I can find the video, and I'll be on my way. Nobody has to die.''

Hannah was shaking, but she met his gaze squarely. ''No.''

Making sure to stay out of Daniel's reach, Jackson shifted the barrel of the gun toward her uncle. ''He saved your life once. Will you do the same for him?''

Hannah knew that it was no bluff. ''I mailed the video and the money to someone I know in another state. I don't have them anymore.''

''Then let's go get them. Just the two of us.''

''Don't do it, Hannah,'' Daniel said.

When she hesitated, Jackson smiled coldly. ''Maybe there's someone you care about more than your uncle.'' He brought the gun up in line with Daniel's head. ''You've got three seconds. One—''

In a heartbeat, chaos erupted. Wolf lunged at Jackson, and a gunshot exploded in the confines of the small room, deafening everyone inside.

Wolf sank his teeth deep into Jackson's arm and shook as hard as he could. Screaming, Jackson dropped the gun and hammered at Wolf with his free hand, but the dog refused to let go.

Daniel scooped up Jackson's gun, then tried to get Wolf

to release him. It took several tries before he got Wolf to obey the command.

When he did, Wolf staggered back, then lay down, panting heavily, his side covered with blood.

Hannah crouched next to the dog. "He's hurt, Daniel."

Daniel shoved Jackson against the wall, his arm just beneath his neck in a choke hold and held him there. "Don't even breathe," he said menacingly.

Just then, three armed cops, including Daniel's friend Paul, came crashing through the door. Immediately, as the cops brought out their handcuffs, Jackson tried to plead innocence. "This is a big mistake. I'm not guilty of what these people are accusing me of doing. All I wanted was to get back the videotape Jones was using to blackmail me. Hannah Jones stole that tape from her uncle. It's *them* you should arrest."

"You're forgetting about attempted murder." Daniel glanced at one of the cops, who had already handcuffed Jackson. "Get him out of here."

Daniel joined Hannah, who was crouched at Wolf's side, and began to check him over gently. He spoke to the dog softly as he ran his hands over the blood-soaked mat of hair. An eternity later he looked up at Hannah and smiled. "It looks much worse than it is. The bullet just grazed him, carving a groove in his side and causing a lot of bleeding. It's a deep cut, I'm not minimizing it, but he didn't take the hit. I think the round's probably imbedded in the wall. Wolf reached him before Jackson could pull the trigger, and the collision deflected his aim. But I've still got to get him to the vet's." Daniel started to lift Wolf up into his arms, but the dog shook him away and stood up on shaky feet.

Hannah smiled. "Just like a guy—he doesn't want to let anyone know he's hurt."

"He's a tough cookie," Daniel said, petting the dog gently.

"Like you?"

He gave her a slow, masculine grin. "That all depends who you ask."

They walked slowly to the SUV with Wolf, but before Hannah could get in, one of the police officers came over.

"Sorry, ma'am. You'll have to stay and make a statement." He looked at Daniel. "You can go take care of the dog, but get down to the station as soon as you can."

"I'll be okay, Daniel. Go. Take care of Wolf. I'll handle things from here."

Daniel looked at Hannah. Now that there weren't any more shadows for her to fear, she no longer needed him. Would tonight be the time for their final goodbyes? He ignored the pain in his gut. There'd be time to face that later. Right now his partner needed him. Wordlessly, he lifted Wolf into the SUV, and with a nod to Hannah, drove off quickly, racing for the animal clinic.

HANNAH SPENT THE HOUR at the police station answering questions about everything that had happened, beginning with the day she'd disappeared.

She also learned that a citizen had come forward, admitting having struck Calvin Beck by accident when he'd stepped out onto the highway.

"Exactly what did you do with the videotape?" the detective finally asked. "If it clearly shows Jackson making those money transfers on screen it's crucial evidence."

"I mailed it to a friend in California along with a note asking her to hang on to the inner, unopened package until the end of the month, and not try to contact me. If she didn't hear from me by then, she was to call the Farmington District Attorney, tell him about the package and where it came from."

"We'll need to get her name, telephone number and address."

She wrote it down quickly, then stood. "I've signed my

statement and told you all I know. If I'm free to go, then there's a friend I need to go see.''

''Please don't leave town without notifying us until we have everything sorted out.''

''I won't be far if you need me. You have my telephone number.'' As she started out of the office, she saw her uncle being fingerprinted at the booking desk after confessing to his involvement in her father's death. An infinite sense of sadness and loss filled her.

Jones exchanged some quick words with the arresting officer, then came over, the officer accompanying him closely. ''Hannah, I want you to know I never meant you any harm. You're my only family and I love you.''

''No matter what else you did, I won't forget that you risked your life for mine, Uncle Bob. I'll stand by you and help with whatever lies ahead. But it's time I started building a life of my own, one that's not connected to the past, or haunted by it.''

He gave her a long look. ''Will Daniel Eagle be part of your future?''

''I wish I knew.'' Seeing the officer tug at his arm, she said goodbye. ''Take care of yourself, Uncle Bob.''

Hannah stopped by a pay phone in the lobby and called the emergency veterinary clinic where Daniel had taken Wolf. Only one in town offered services this time of night, so it was easy to track down. The vet on duty wouldn't give her much information, only that Daniel was no longer there, and that Wolf would be spending the night, but was expected to recover fully.

Hannah stood by the main entrance for a moment, lost in thought. She had no way of getting home and no money with which to pay a cab.

''Excuse me.'' Daniel's friend Paul approached her. ''Now that you're finished giving your statement, do you need a ride home?''

She smiled gratefully. ''Yes, as a matter of fact I do.''

"Then I'll go get my car and come around for you."

Hannah stepped through the door and stood outside, letting the darkness and the winds of an approaching thunderstorm enfold her. She was finally free to do as she pleased, but she'd never felt more lonely. She wondered if Daniel would disappear from her life now just as mysteriously as he'd appeared. He'd told her once that he loved his freedom, and that his job didn't leave room for relationships.

As lightning flashed across the sky, she saw Daniel walking toward her across the parking lot. She watched him approach, her heart beating at a furious pace.

"Hannah," Daniel whispered, joining her.

That one quiet word contained a world of tenderness. He held her gaze and reached for her hand. "I came back because I wanted you to know..." his words trailed off and he looked away, shaking his head. "I'm no good at this. I just don't know how to say what I need to tell you."

"I'm not going to try and hold you, Daniel," Hannah said with a heavy heart, mistaking his frustration and hesitation for an attempt to say goodbye. "I know that lightning never stays long in one place."

With a groan, he cupped her face in his hands. "I wanted to give you your freedom. You've fought hard for it," he said, his voice a ragged whisper. "But I can't just let you walk away from me. I want you with me. But don't you see? It's far more dangerous when lightning lingers." He pulled her tightly against him and lowered his mouth over hers.

His kiss was like the man he was—all hardness and velvet, tenderness and strength.

"Tell me plainly how you feel," she asked, her voice a soft plea against his lips. "You've spent too many years not letting anyone know what you're thinking, or what you really want. I need to hear you say the words, Daniel," she said.

He looked at her in surprise. ''I love you, Hannah. How can you *not* know that?'' He pulled her against him and kissed her again, his mouth hot and possessive.

She sighed and snuggled against his chest. ''I needed to hear you say it.'' She looked up at him and smiled. ''But, just so you know, showing's good, too. And if you should happen to run out of ways, I have a few suggestions.''

''Anything that gives you pleasure is yours for the asking—and for the taking. Nothing's off-limits between a husband and his wife.''

Her breath caught in her throat. ''Did you just propose?''

He nodded. ''So what do you say?''

Her soft ''yes,'' gentle yet strong, rose above the thunder, issuing a loving challenge to Lightning, the man who had won her heart.

* * * * *

It's the silent ones you have to watch....

Don't miss Burke Silentman's story
next month in the exciting
final installment of the
SIGN OF THE GRAY WOLF *series:*

#681 NAVAJO JUSTICE

by Aimée Thurlo

Turn the page for a sneak peak!

Chapter One

It was a beautiful morning in late March. The sky was a clear, almost brilliant, blue, the air clean and crisp—the kind of day where the breeze whispered of dreams that were still in the making, and the songbirds celebrated the coming of spring.

Laura Santos drove back home from the post office slowly, taking the backstreets off the main highway that, although graveled and bumpy, gave a great glimpse into the true character of their small New Mexico town. One-story houses stood like sentinels between fields of sandy soil dotted with tall clumps of blue-green sage and eager green and yellow native grasses. Horses wandered lazily, seeking the fresh green fare. Their slowly shedding, thick winter coats were now the only reminder of the long, cold winter behind them.

Today, she could afford to take her time and enjoy the day. She'd finally finished her latest novel, *Dawn of Desire.*

As she entered the more densely populated neighborhood where she lived, the pavement began and the dust level dropped noticeably. Turning onto the street that led to her home, Laura looked down the block and caught a glimpse of her new neighbor, Burke, sitting astride his motorcycle, adjusting something by the engine. The tall, black-haired Navajo man had the palest brown eyes she'd ever seen and a smile that, although rare, could undoubtedly coax a pulse out of a stone.

As she slowed to make the turn into her driveway, her gaze strayed over him. Catching her eye, Burke waved. She smiled back at him, feeling her heart start to beat a little faster.

Burke had moved in about a week ago, and had already doubled the machismo level on their street, as every woman on their block would have happily attested. There was something powerfully and wonderfully masculine about the man. She had no doubt that it was partly due to the arrogant confidence with which he did virtually everything. His long-legged stride, so filled with purpose and a hint of aggression, gave something as mundane as "walking" an entirely new meaning.

She'd have to make it a point to talk to Burke and find out more about him next time he came up to the cedar fence that bordered their properties. So far only her *madrina,* Elena, had actually spoken to him. With luck, her fantasies would come to a screeching halt once she met him and found out he was a salesman with a high-pitched voice and the tendency to try and sell life insurance policies to everyone he met.

Laura switched off the ignition, grabbed her purse and climbed out of her sporty but sensible Chevrolet sedan. Flipping through her Scooby-Doo key chain on the way up the sidewalk, she found the right key and unlocked the front door.

The second that she stepped across the threshold, an invisible cloud of foul-smelling gas slammed into her like a massive wave. She staggered back, coughing and fighting to catch her breath. All the oxygen inside had been replaced by natural gas, making her light-headed.

She turned her head away from the house, trying to get one deep breath so she could go back inside.

"Elena!" Laura called out frantically, waiting and striving to hear, but there was no response.

"Elena, where are you?" She yelled again, fighting the feeling of nausea from the noxious gas. Laura stepped back away from the door, looking around for Burke, hoping she could ask him to call 911, but she couldn't see him now. Knowing there was no time to lose, she took two deep breaths of fresh air, then rushed into the house.

For a moment, her blood turned to ice and she couldn't move. The interior of her home was in shambles. Everything that had been on the bookshelves was now on the floor, having been swept off into random piles. Cushions from the sofa and chairs had been slashed, then torn open and gutted. Stuffing lay scattered around the room like the aftermath of a bizarre snowstorm.

She tried to focus her thoughts quickly, feeling dizzy from lack of oxygen. Her godmother was here someplace and she had to locate her and get her outside, fast.

Laura's lungs felt as if they'd burst any second. Knowing that she had to take a breath, she rushed to the living-room windows and threw open the first one she reached. She took a deep lungful of air, then plunged back into the nightmare her home had become.

Laura quickly searched the bedrooms and the kitchen, resisting the urge to turn on the lights and risk a spark-initiated explosion, but Doña Elena wasn't there. Halfway back to the living room Laura was forced to take a breath. She tried to make it a shallow one, but the smell was overpowering. She ran into the bathroom, slid back the small window, then taking a breath, dove back into the poisoned atmosphere.

The hall seemed endless as she ran through it, heading directly for the closest window. But when she tried to lift the window sash, it was stuck tight. Out of air now, she was forced to take a short breath, but that proved to be a mistake.

Suddenly very dizzy, she leaned against the wall. Elena was in here somewhere and she had to find her but her eyes had lost the ability to focus. Vaguely, she remembered the garage and turned to head in that directly. As if someone were playing with a dimmer switch, the room grew darker and she slipped slowly to the floor.

Laura fought to stay conscious, but oddly shaped patterns exploded before her eyes. Asphyxiation—she didn't want to die this way. Yet even as the thought formed, it slipped away and darkness greeted her.

Laura wasn't sure when her thoughts began again, but she awoke to the feeling of being carried. A man's arms, strong and warm, were wrapped around her, pressing her securely against a rock-hard chest. His strength was comforting, but also deeply stirring on a primitive level.

Still groggy, she wondered if this was what happened to romance authors when they died—perhaps God had created a special heaven for them. She didn't struggle. If she'd gone to romance writers' heaven, she'd enjoy every single moment of it.

As a strong light hit her eyes, she buried her head against his chest. The Light. It was harsh. She'd expected more—or maybe less. And where was that tunnel she'd heard about, and those departed loved ones stepping up to offer encouragement?

Slowly, she realized that she was able to breathe now. Did the dead breathe?

"You're going to be okay," a deep, sure voice said.

She turned her head up to look at her rescuer, but his face was covered in an iridescent haze. The soft glimmer in his eyes seemed to pierce that somewhat and she found herself captivated by the light brown eyes that held hers. "Am I dead?"

"No, not hardly, though you'll probably have a killer headache later on."

The haze that clouded her vision began to give way and,

like a slowly developing photograph, his face grew clearer. She knew this man. It was her next-door neighbor, Burke, and his pale, brown eyes were shining with a vibrant inner fire. She allowed herself to bask in the warmth of his gaze, the knowledge that she was alive and safe sufficient for now.

Then suddenly another thought made a bolt of panic shoot through her. "Elena!"

"She's not at home. Relax," he said, his voice utterly compelling and reassuring.

Burke set her down gently on the grass of her front lawn. "I heard you calling for her and coughing, then saw you rush inside the house with your hand over your mouth. I tried to stop you but I couldn't reach you in time."

Relief flooded all through her, easing her fear. "I thought—" her voice broke and she buried her face against his shoulder again.

Burke held her tightly. "What you did was very brave, but completely unnecessary. Miss Elena left a half hour ago in the Senior Center's van."

It felt wonderful to be held by him. He was all hard muscle and lean strength. "I don't know how to thank you."

"Let me show you." He leaned down and captured her mouth in a tender kiss.

He tasted of cinnamon and strong, dark coffee. Seconds stretched out as a sweet, slow fire coursed in her veins.

But it was over too soon, and he drew back.

"Now we're more than even. In fact—I may owe you, lovely lady."

FALL IN LOVE THIS WINTER

WITH

HARLEQUIN BOOKS!

In October 2002 look for these special volumes led by *USA TODAY* bestselling authors, and receive a MOULIN ROUGE VHS video*!

*Retail value of $14.99 U.S.

See inside books for details.

This exciting promotion is available at your favorite retail outlet.

Only from

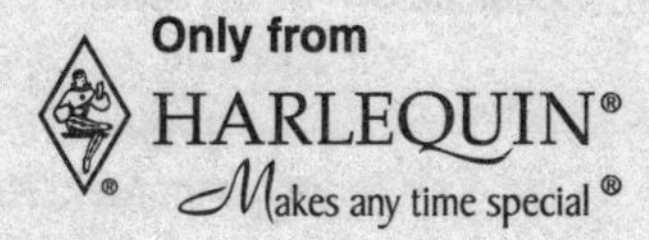

Visit Harlequin at www.eHarlequin.com PHNCP02